To my Bonnie Lass, the love of my life, my best friend, and my partner through all the seasons of our lives. They said we'd never do it, but we showed them. Happy 25th Anniversary, Sweetheart!

Love's Second Chance

By
William Speir

Published 2023 by Progressive Rising Phoenix Press, LLC
www.progressiverisingphoenix.com

ISBN: 978-1-958640-39-5

Printed in the U.S.A.
1st Printing

Cover Photograph: "Happy Passionate Couple In Love Touching, Kissing And Huging" by Lipik Stock Media, ShutterStock Photo ID: 1768987862, used under license from ShutterStock.com.

Book and Cover design by William Speir
Visit: http://www.williamspeir.com

CHAPTER 1

The storm raged outside. Lightning flashed through the windows, and the lights flickered off and on. Katherine Delaney, a lithe, five-foot-four-inch-tall woman with a lean dancer's body and wavy auburn hair cut above the shoulder, looked around the main room of the upstairs apartment over her garage. The lights continued to flicker. She walked toward the side table next to the couch, where there was a hurricane lantern and a box of matches. She lit the lantern; then she glanced over at the papers strewn across the nearby table. She walked over to the table, curious about what her tenant, Carl, was up to. Her eyes opened wide when she saw what was on the papers.

A loud crash of thunder and a brilliant flash of lightning just outside caused the lights to go out altogether. She didn't see the shadowy figure of her tenant rush toward her from the bedroom. He slammed into her, knocking her down. The lantern landed next to her but didn't break.

Katherine cried out in pain as her shoulder hit one of the table legs. Then Carl was on top of her. She saw the glint of the knife blade reflecting the light from the hurricane lantern. Carl tried to plunge the knife into her chest, but she grabbed his wrists, keeping the knife away from her. Carl shifted his weight, and the knife inched closer and closer to her chest. When it seemed that nothing could stop the knife from ending her life, she heard a voice shouting…

"Cut!"

As the soundstage lights came on, the director, C.J. Walsh, leapt from his chair in frustration. "It's still not working," he muttered to one of his production assistants.

Derek Perkins—the actor portraying Carl—pulled the prop knife away from his co-star, rolled off Katherine, stood, and offered her his hand to help her up. "Sorry about that, Kathy. I think I pushed you down too hard that time."

Katherine brushed herself off and smiled. "It wasn't the way you hit me, it's how I fell. I hit the table leg. I hope that's not why C.J. is unhappy with the take. I honestly don't know how many more times we can do this scene before I end up getting really hurt."

Katherine glanced around the sound stage. There was no real storm raging outside. In fact, it was a beautiful August day at Eagle Rock Studios in Norcross, Georgia—just outside Atlanta. The storm had been movie magic created by the production crew of "The Spy Upstairs," the film that C.J. was directing.

Katherine and Derek carefully stepped around the gas lines that crisscrossed the floor of the set as they waited to hear what C.J. would say. The script called for Derek to smash the lantern after plunging the knife into Katherine, destroying the evidence as he made his escape.

Even though the scene they had been working on all day was Katherine's death scene, it was not the last scene she'd be filming. But this was the last scene using the set she was standing on, and they needed to get the scene finished so the set could be demolished and another one built in its place, allowing production to continue without delays.

C.J. prided himself on keeping his movies on schedule, and

Katherine knew that he was just as frustrated as the actors were that, after twenty-five takes, he still wasn't satisfied.

As Katherine took a bottle of water offered to her by one of the assistant directors, she glanced across the sound stage at the writer, Marcus Buchanan. She knew he was an award-winning screenwriter and bestselling novelist, and while they had spoken a few times during filming on-location around Savannah and Charleston, they had never really had the chance to get to know each other.

And as handsome as Marcus was talented, Katherine very much wanted to get to know him.

She watched C.J. storm over to Marcus, who was busy writing in his notebook. "It's not working, Buchanan," C.J. roared. Marcus never looked up; he just kept writing. "Are you listening to me?" C.J. shouted.

Marcus looked up and handed C.J. several sheets of paper. Katherine couldn't hear what Marcus was saying, but C.J. ran his fingers through his close-cropped, graying hair and began pacing in a circle, reading the papers.

Katherine noticed that Derek and most of the crew were watching C.J. and Marcus. Every few minutes, C.J. would stop pacing and point to a passage on the paper. Marcus would respond, and C.J. would resume his pacing and reading.

After about ten minutes, C.J. stopped and faced Marcus. Even from that distance, Katherine could tell that C.J. was smiling. "Yes, yes, YES! This works! Good job!"

C.J. turned to face the cast and crew. "Huddle up! We're going to try something different."

Katherine, Derek, and the crew walked over to C.J. and Marcus.

"I know you're all tired and frustrated. We've been at this all day, and it's well into the evening outside. But our writer, here, has re-written the scene, and I think it'll work much better. It'll require a few changes to several subsequent scenes, but fortunately we haven't shot any of them yet, so no re-shoots are necessary. Let me walk you through the changes. If you can find the strength for one more take, I'd like to try this."

C.J. read the revised scene to the cast and crew. Katherine was confused about what this change would do to her character, but she immediately saw that it was better than the original scene.

"I'm willing to give it a go," Katherine said when C.J. looked at her.

"Me, too," Derek agreed.

"All right," C.J. began with a huge smile on his tanned, lined face. He handed the pages to Katherine and Derek. "Study this and practice your lines with each other for the next ten minutes."

Looking at the crew, C.J. added, "I want to see the camera, lighting, sound, and special effects people over on the set." As he led the crew away from Marcus and the two actors, Katherine heard him say, "I want four cameras for this take. One wide, two close up, and one above looking down on the scene. The entire scene will be lit by the lantern, lightning, and fire…"

Katherine looked up from the pages at Derek. "I guess you don't kill me after all."

"At least not in this scene," Derek said. "Shall we give it a go?"

Katherine nodded, and the two actors began rehearsing.

Ten minutes later, C.J. shouted from across the soundstage. "Are the two of you ready?"

"Ready, C.J.," Katherine shouted back.

She and Derek returned to the set. C.J. spoke to them for a few minutes, telling them how he wanted the action to flow. Derek nodded in agreement. Katherine nodded, too, but was still confused about what these changes meant to her character. She glanced over at Marcus, who was watching everything that was going on. *I need to talk to Mr. Buchanan after we wrap for the day and find out just what he has planned for me.*

"From the top, people," C.J. yelled.

Derek took his place behind the bedroom door. Katherine took her place on the landing outside the upstairs apartment. One of the production assistants stepped onto the set with the clapperboard. He held it up to all four cameras. "Scene twenty-three, take twenty-six."

Once the production assistant was safely behind the cameras, C.J.—sitting in his chair surrounded by the monitors showing what each of the four cameras was capturing—yelled, "Action!"

Thunder crashed and lightning flashed outside the upstairs apartment over the garage. The lights flickered and then went out. A lit hurricane lantern could be seen approaching the door leading to the landing. There was a knock on the door, but no one answered. The door opened, and Katherine entered.

She held up the lantern and called out, "Carl, are you here? It's Mary. I'm checking to see if the lightning struck the house and fried any of the wiring. May I come in?"

There was no answer.

Mary began searching for storm damage, checking the electrical outlets and sniffing the appliances in the tiny corner kitchen. As she passed the table, the lantern illuminated the papers strewn across the surface. As she examined the papers, Derek entered the set from the bedroom.

"You shouldn't be here, Mary," he said softly.

"What is all this, Carl?" Katherine asked.

"None of your business." Carl advanced menacingly, pulling out a knife from a sheath tucked in his waistband.

Katherine saw the knife and reacted quickly. She swung the lantern, and it hit Derek across the side of his face. He fell, the lantern shattered, and the spilled fuel from the reservoir caught fire. The room, with its wooden floors, was soon ablaze. Katherine looked around—terrified—at the fire spreading, and then she fled from the room.

The cameras didn't catch the stagehand draping a fireproof blanket over Derek. Even though the fire was coming from carefully hidden gas lines along the floor, so the sound stage wouldn't catch fire, C.J. didn't want to take any chances with the safety of the cast and crew.

"Cut!" C.J. shouted as he jumped up and punched the air with his fist. "That's perfect! Print."

The special effects team turned off the gas, and stagehands rush out with fire extinguishers to prevent any remaining flames from setting the floor and furniture around the set on fire. They also checked on Derek, who was safe and unsinged underneath the blanket. The crew applauded, and C.J. motioned for everyone to gather around. He put his arms over Katherine and Derek's shoulders.

"That was absolutely perfect. Great job, everyone. We had planned to start tearing down the set tonight, but the second unit needs to use the set tomorrow morning to show the fire spreading and how Derek's stunt double escapes from the inferno, and I need to be there. So, we won't be ready to start on the next scene until tomorrow afternoon. Katherine, you and Derek don't need to be in Hair & Make-up until noon, and we'll start rehearsing the next scene at one o'clock sharp."

Looking at the crew, C.J. added, "Okay, everyone, that's a wrap for today. See you all tomorrow."

C.J. and one of his production assistants, a perky blonde named Trish Crawford, walked toward C.J.'s office. As C.J. passed Marcus, he said, "You're free until tomorrow afternoon as well. Great job on the scene rewrite and your suggestions for the other changes. Top notch work. See you tomorrow." Then C.J. and Trish left the set.

Derek held out his hand to Katherine. "Great job, Kathy."

"You, too, Derek."

Derek headed for Hair & Make-up to get cleaned up before

catching the shuttle heading back to the hotel. Most of the crew, who weren't locals, were heading for the shuttles to take them back to the all-suites hotel that the producers had booked for the cast and crew. In fact, the entire hotel had been reserved for the movie production. It made transportation easier, but there was little privacy.

Katherine was about to follow Derek when she saw Marcus stand and start putting his notebook and script away in a canvas briefcase that had a stitched logo on it she didn't recognize. She estimated that he was a little over six feet tall, with short brown hair that had streaks of gray in it. He was tanned, had a close-cropped beard and mustache that also had streaks of gray in them, and was incredibly handsome. *No one's around. Now's my chance to talk to him alone.*

She walked over to Marcus. "Marcus? I loved how you changed the scene. Thank you. I was worried we'd never get it the way C.J. wanted."

Marcus smiled. "My pleasure, Miss Delaney. And please, call me Marc."

"Kathy," she replied. She brushed a strand of her auburn hair from her face. "But I'm confused about what happens to my character now. This was supposed to be my death scene."

Marcus looked around. "Where are you heading right now?"

"Hair & Make-Up. I have to get cleaned up and change out of these clothes."

Marcus nodded. "Let's head over there, and I'll explain what's going to happen now."

They started walking to the far side of the massive soundstage, where the Hair & Make-Up trailers were located. The soundstage was filled with several sets that the production company had built. C.J. liked to film all of the scenes that called for a particular set before moving on to the next set. Once production was finished with a set, it was torn down to make room for another set needed later. Each scene would be edited into the correct sequence in post-production

As they walked, Marcus said, "You know that the Brenda Winslow character, played by Sierra Blake, is an FBI agent who has been chasing the wrong man. The way she finally discovers that the Carl character is the spy had some problems, too. Right now, your character is the only one who knows. Instead of dying, you're going to be the one who convinces the Brenda character that Carl is still alive and is the spy. Instead of them killing each other in the climax of the film, he'll kill her, and you'll kill him!"

"So, I'm going to be in the climax?" Katherine asked.

"And the sole survivor," Marcus confirmed.

Katherine looked at the ceiling, trying to remember something. "So, that means I'll have more scenes, and I won't wrap until… what, two weeks later than planned?"

Marcus nodded. "Is that a problem?"

Katherine wagged her head. "Not a problem… *per se*. My sons are at summer camp, and their father is supposed to take them for a week, so I can decompress when I get home before getting thrown back into family life and the new school year. If I can convince him to keep the boys longer, then sticking around to film the additional scenes is no problem at all." She reached for her phone. "Might as well find out now."

Marcus nodded. "C.J. said he's going to talk to you about it while you're in Hair & Make-Up tomorrow, so it'll be good to have all the arrangements made on your end before then."

Katherine stepped aside and placed a call to her ex-husband, Greg Murphy. They talked for several minutes, and then she hung up and walked back to Marcus. "Well, that was unexpected."

"What?" Marcus asks.

"My ex is actually going to be in L.A. until January, and he asked if he can keep the boys for a month, rather than a week, to make up for all the time he's missed with them this past year. He even wants to get them ready for the new school year."

"Perfect!" Marcus said.

They continued walking toward the Hair & Make-Up trailers. "Why didn't C.J. tell me this himself before he left the set?" Katherine asked.

Marcus snorted. "You saw who he left with?"

"Yes… isn't her name Trish?"

Marcus nodded.

"What about it?" Katherine asked.

"They're dating," Marcus replied, "if that's the right word for it. They're together every night, and evidently the late hour was encroaching into her time with him."

As they approached the trailers, they saw the hotel shuttle leaving. Katherine's stomach rumbled, and she blushed as she looked at Marcus. "I don't know about you, but I'm starving."

"Me, too," Marcus agreed. "I know it's late, but we don't have to be back here until noon tomorrow, and I know this little steakhouse on Peachtree, just off Buford Highway, that has great food. I was going to head over there, since the restaurants around the hotel will be packed by the time we get there. If you're interested in grabbing bite with me…"

Katherine smiled. "I'd love to. Do you mind waiting while I get cleaned up and changed?"

"Not at all. Where do you want me to meet you?"

Katherine gestured toward the trailers. "You can wait in the Hair & Make-Up trailer. It's not like it's a big secret what goes on in there." She glanced at the taillights of the hotel shuttle disappearing in the distance. "How do we get to the restaurant?"

"I have my car here," Marcus replied.

"Perfect!"

An hour later, they were sitting in a booth at The Peachtree Depot Steakhouse. There were several steakhouses in the Norcross area, but Marcus explained that he liked this one because it was smaller, more intimate, and the staff and guests minded their own business. It was a great place to eat without being disturbed. As Katherine placed her napkin in her lap, Marcus couldn't help but stare at her slim figure, big eyes, and full lips. He had to remind himself that this was just dinner and to keep things casual.

"What's good here?" Katherine asked as she picked up the menu.

"I'm partial to the crab cakes and either the filet or the prime rib, but if you're feeling really hungry, they have a tomahawk for two that's amazing," Marcus replied.

"How do you take your steak?" Katherine asked.

"Medium."

Katherine smiled. "Then let's go for the Tomahawk."

When the server came back to the table to take their order, it was clear from the expression on her face that she recognized Katherine. Marcus and Katherine ordered their food, and Katherine ordered a glass of wine. Marcus ordered tea.

"No wine?" she asked.

"Not when I'm driving," Marcus replied. "I never take chances with a passenger's safety. I prefer to drink at home."

Katherine nodded, impressed with his answer. While they waited for the food, Marcus noticed that she appeared nervous. She took a deep breath, let it out slowly through her mouth, and asked, "So, why wasn't the scene working? And why did you need to make such a dramatic change to my character?"

Marcus flashed a guilty smile. "My original vision for Mary was that she would be just an incidental character, with the Brenda character being the sole female lead. But when you were cast, that just didn't work anymore. You're a much better actress than what the role called for, and I think C.J. didn't want you killed off so early in the film. Once I realized what his issue was, and I saw the advantage of having an actress with your talent at the climax, the scene changes just came to me in a flash. I'm glad he liked them."

"I appreciate the vote of confidence," Katherine said. "No one has ever re-written a scene just to retain my character before."

"Had I known that you would be cast in the role, I would have written the scene differently from the beginning," Marcus admitted.

Katherine smiled and took a sip of her wine.

Marcus then asked, "Do you mind if I ask a personal question?"

"Go ahead."

"I've noticed that your appearance has changed quite a bit from your earlier roles and that you've started taking very different parts than you did in your early career. But it wasn't a gradual change, it was quite sudden. Why is that?"

Katherine nodded. "It's simple. I became a mother. When I first started out, my agent and everyone else told me that I needed to show skin if I wanted to get parts, so I did. I did nude scenes, I did sex scenes, and I developed a reputation for being a… a…"

"A sex kitten?" Marcus interjected.

Katherine blushed—her face turning from pink to red and back to pink. "Exactly. Even after I started dating Greg, my ex, he encouraged me to continue taking sexy roles, and that's most of what my agent sent me. Greg was an actor, too, and he wanted me to get parts and be successful. By then it was just… normal. I didn't even think about it. It was embarrassing, though. You've been on set before and seen them filming one of those scenes, right? There's twenty to thirty people behind the camera… all just watching. There's no privacy, no intimacy, no emotion, no pleasure, just… acting."

"I've never understood why they don't close the set when filming a nude or a love scene," Marcus remarked. "All you need is the director, the photographer, the sound guy, the lighting guy, and maybe a wardrobe person to help you cover up between takes. Nobody else needs to be there. It's perverted."

Katherine nodded. "And the camera shows every flaw, every blemish on your body. I started out as a bikini model before acting, and it was a lot of work to keep my body in shape for that. As the years passed, it became harder and harder to stay in shape for love scenes, and it started to bother me. When I got pregnant with Jack, I thought, 'When my child is old enough to go out on the internet and look up my career, what will he or she find out about me?' I knew I could explain the bikini modeling, and being a 'sex kitten' in my early films could be explained in the context of what it takes to start a career in a business this competitive, but if I continued taking roles like that after I had children, how would I explain that? What would it say about me? That I'm just whoring for parts? If I'm supposed to be a role model for my kids, what kind of example am I setting if I keep taking my clothes off on camera? It just didn't feel right. That's the same time that my hair straightened. I hear it's normal once you have children. When I was young, my hair was more blonde and curly. After I had Jack, my hair went more red and straight. Being a mom, and my new appearance, led me to take on more mature roles. I accepted parts that allowed me to grow as an actress, I negotiated shooting schedules around school or when my ex could take the kids, and I made balancing my life a priority, rather than letting my career *be* my life. Greg wasn't thrilled with my decision, and neither was my agent. So, eventually, I fired my agent, and a year after Ben was born, I divorced Greg."

Marcus nodded. "My late wife said the same thing happened with her hair when she had the kids. In the photos of her before children, she had thick, poofy, curly blonde hair. The photos after children showed her hair darken and get much straighter. The waves came back, but the curls never did."

Katherine reached up and fluffed the bottom of her hair with her palm. "My waves have come back, but not the curls. How close in age were your late wife's kids?"

"Eighteen months and one day apart," Marcus replied. "They were nine and ten when we met, and they were nine and eleven when we married."

"My boys are nine and eleven," Katherine remarked.

"Fun ages," Marcus noted. "Everything is still new and interesting, they haven't let their peers make them cynical or jaded, and they still love being with their parents. It's quite a blow when that changes. The environment where you raise your kids is vital to help soften how outrageous they become when they reach their teens."

"Did you have your late wife's kids in the right environment?"

Marcus shook his head. "No. My daughter was strong enough to keep her friends from influencing her negatively. She didn't turn snarky until college, and it only got worse from there. My son… well, let's just say that his friends easily influenced him to do everything the opposite of the way we raised him." Marcus went on to explain his relationship with his stepchildren and what had happened between them after the death of their mother.

"I'm sorry things worked out that way for you," Katherine said. "When did she pass on?"

Marcus had a distant look in his eyes, as if haunted by painful memories. Katherine instantly regretted asking the question, but Marcus answered before she could say anything. "Five years ago. One day she was fine, the next day she was feeling poorly, the day after that I took her to the hospital to be checked out, and the following day she was gone. They never did help me understand what killed her. All I know is it was the worst 72 hours of my life. I threw myself into work, and I've been there ever since. It didn't heal the grief, but it made it harder to feel… anything."

Changing the subject, Marcus asked, "Is Greg still an actor?"

"No, he's a producer now."

Marcus cocked his head. "Really? What's his last name?"

"Murphy."

Marcus stared at her open mouthed. "Wait, I know him. He was one of the producers on my film, 'The Poison Gardener.' I had no idea he was your ex. Do the two of you get along?"

"Oh, yes," Katherine confirmed. "We're still good friends, and we try to be good parents for the boys. We just weren't good spouses. Our schedules kept us apart more than we were together, and when I wanted to stay home with the boys after they were born, he wasn't happy that I wasn't keeping my career first in my life, like he was. When I asked him why we were married and had kids if we both wanted our careers to come first, he couldn't answer. That's when I knew the marriage was over. But he's a good person, and he's someone who tells me what I need to hear—things that no one else will tell you, you know?"

Marcus nodded.

The server arrived with their salads and appetizers. Both of them starving by this time, they attacked their food with more gusto than intended. When they realized what someone watching them might think, they started laughing.

"My table manners are usually better than this," Katherine confessed. "But it's all so good."

"Wait 'till the tomahawk arrives," Marcus said. "And I normally don't eat like a man who hasn't seen food in a week."

They finished the food on the table, and after the plates had been cleared, the server brought fresh plates and two razor sharp steak knives. A few minutes later, the tomahawk arrived, still sizzling on the platter.

Katherine's eyes bulged. "How do you eat something that big?"

"You cut it into very small bites and then chew the bites carefully."

Katherine looked at Marcus like he was insane, but when she saw him trying not to smirk, she laughed. "Okay, okay, Mr. Writer. I may have deserved that, but you didn't have to take the bait."

Marcus held up his hands. "Fair enough." Grabbing his knife and fork, he said, "Let me cut you a piece to start with. Do you prefer ends or the center?"

"Both."

Marcus nodded. He cut the steak in half, carefully cut the bone away, placed one half on Katherine's plate, and put the other half on his own. Then he divided the vegetables and roasted potatoes between their plates, leaving only the bone behind on the platter. "Dig in," he said.

Katherine needed no encouragement. She ate until she was stuffed, and she still had enough food on her plate for more than one meal. "If that's a tomahawk for two, I'd hate to see what a tomahawk for four looks like."

Marcus chuckled as he finished his last bite. "If you're anything like my late wife, this *was* a tomahawk for four. Whenever we went out, I'd finish my meal, but she'd take most of hers home and make one or two more meals out of it. Judging by what you ate and what you have left, I'd say you could easily make two more meals out of your half."

Katherine slid her plate over to Marcus. "Help me finish it? There's a fridge in the hotel room, but no good way to re-heat the meat there. I don't want it to go to waste."

Marcus stared at her, and then he nodded. He cut off a third of her remaining steak, but before he could move it to his plate, she stuck her fork into it. She cocked her head slightly to one side, smiled, and jiggled her head in a quick, side-to-side motion, which Marcus would later discover was her gesture for triumph or victory. "That's mine. You take the rest."

Marcus hesitated, but he could see that she was serious. Finally, he nodded. "This will be my dessert, then." He forked the larger piece of steak and moved it to his plate.

They both managed to finish their pieces, and when the server came over to offer them the dessert menu, but both declined. "Just the check, please," Marcus said.

After Marcus paid for dinner, and Katherine signed autographs for the server and the hostess, Katherine thanked him. "You didn't need to do that," she said. "You've already done enough for me today."

"You mean keeping your character alive? I just wish I had done it sooner."

Katherine beamed.

As they left the restaurant and walked toward Marcus' SUV, she asked, "So, how is it you have your car here in Georgia? Did you drive it all the way from L.A.?"

Marcus chuckled. "No, I have a place in L.A., but I actually live and do my writing in Chattanooga. It's only about two hours from here."

"Is it as beautiful as I've heard?" Katherine asked.

"I don't know what you've heard, but it's probably more beautiful than you could possibly imagine. The Appalachian Mountains, the Tennessee River, Lookout Mountain, the trees… it's heaven. I live southwest of town near the Georgia border. The house is set on a ridge along Raccoon Mountain, facing east toward Lookout Mountain."

Katherine had a dreamy look on her face. "Nice neighborhood?"

They reached the car, and Marcus held the door open for her. "It's not really a neighborhood. I live on about two hundred and fifty acres of forest with a house near one end."

He closed her door before she could react to what he just

told her. He walked around, opened his door, and slid behind the wheel.

Katherine stared at him. “Two hundred and fifty *acres*?”

“And it was the most incredible deal you ever heard of. The original owner died with no heirs, so the property was auctioned off. I bought it for a third of its true value, and the house came with it. It wasn’t finished, but what was there, I loved. The original owner wanted an English manor house look and feel, and the architect and builders had done a great job delivering just that. But it was going to be too big for just my wife and me, even though we liked visitors, and we liked to entertain. We cut half the guest rooms off the second floor, axed the guesthouse, which was supposed to have another four to eight bedrooms, scaled back the Olympic pool to something more normal, and cut the pool house down to something manageable. The owner also wanted a 12-car garage for his vintage car collection, and we shrunk that down to a 4-car garage. The architect changed the plans for us and updated all of the blueprints, and the builder felt he could finish the house with the materials he had on hand.”

“I’m afraid to ask what it cost you,” Katherine said, wanting to know anyway.

“Nearly everything I had at the time,” Marcus admitted. “This was six years ago, when I was still living in Texas, and Leigh, my late wife, encouraged me to buy it anyway. I guess she knew my books and screenplays would keep doing well, and she was right. I’m able to live quite comfortably there. The Tennessee cost of living is so great that I got a house and all that land for less than what a third of the house alone would cost out in L.A.”

“Are you originally from Texas?”

Marcus shook his head. “Alabama, but I left after college. It’s a big, exciting world out there, and I wanted to be part of it. Alabama is beautiful, but there’s not much to do.” As they drove back to the hotel, Marcus asked, “What about you? Where do you call home?"

"I'm a southern California girl, born and raised. I have a two-story cottage in the hills overlooking the Valley. It's quiet, the neighborhood is great for walking and hiking, and I can keep the boys away from most of the craziness of L.A. They're in a private school, so that also helps keep them away from so much of the nonsense that defines southern California today."

Marcus nodded. "I didn't know you were a hiker. I have hiking trails all over the property, along with streams and a waterfall that's next to the master bedroom, and there's a state park nearby with miles of trails that go all over the mountain. The views are spectacular from the top of the ridges."

"It does sound like heaven," Katherine remarked.

"You'd have to see it to believe it."

Katherine glanced over at Marcus. *If only that were an invitation.*

They arrived at the hotel a few minutes later, and Marcus grabbed his briefcase and came around an opened Katherine's door.

"I was meaning to ask you… what's that logo on your briefcase?" Katherine asked.

Marcus held the briefcase so she could see the logo more closely. "It's my publisher. They give these to all of their authors who do book tours. I take it every time I travel."

Marcus walked Katherine to her hotel room, which was just down the hall from his own.

"Dinner was wonderful. Thanks again," Katherine said.

"You're welcome," Marcus replied. "Do you want to grab breakfast before we have to head over to the studio in the morning?"

Katherine wanted to say yes, but she was so stuffed that she couldn't imagine eating again that soon. "How about brunch?"

"Ten o'clock?" Marcus suggested.

Katherine nodded. "I'll meet you in the lobby at ten."

Marcus hesitated for a moment, but then he stepped back so Katherine could unlock her door without feeling any pressure. As she entered her room, he said, “Goodnight, Kathy.”

“Goodnight, Marc.”

Marcus turned and headed for his room.

As Katherine closed her door, she leaned her back against it and fanned herself with her hand. *Wow! That’s a real man.*

CHAPTER 2

After a long night of not being able to get Marcus out of her mind, Katherine finally got up, showered, dressed, and went downstairs to the hotel lobby to meet Marcus for brunch. She arrived five minutes early, but Marcus was already there, sitting on one of the overstuffed couches and scribbling in his notebook.

"Changing my character to die in the next scene?" she asked as she sat next to him.

Marcus looked over at her and grinned. "No, but I am working on something else for your character."

As he closed his notebook, she asked, "What?"

"Can't tell you. C.J. has to approve it first. Ready to eat?"

She nodded. He stood and held out his hand. She took it, and he gently pulled her up off the couch.

"I don't know how hungry you are. There's a diner across the highway that's good, or there's a Cuban place near the steakhouse we ate at last night that has great food. Do either of those interest you?"

"Let's do the diner today and save the Cuban place for another time, okay?"

"Okay." Marcus led her to his car.

When they were seated at the diner, Katherine decided to act bolder than usual. She inhaled deeply and then let it out through her mouth. “So, how do you normally get to know someone who interests you?”

“To be honest,” Marcus admitted, “the last time I really got to know someone new was with my late wife, and that was twenty years ago. I’m… kind of out of practice. What about you?”

“It’s hard to find someone who interests me enough to *want* to get to know them,” Katherine replied. “That’s the curse of this business. But I’ve tried games before.”

“Like what?” Marcus asked, leaning forward.

“Oh… Pictionary is a great way to see if someone has a sense of humor, Truth or Dare can help push someone to the next level who’s stuck in the same place for too long, Never Have I Ever is a great icebreaker…” She named a few others.

The waitress came over and took their order.

“I always thought of Truth or Dare as a foreplay game, and Never Have I Ever as a drinking game,” Marcus commented after the waitress left.

“Never Have I Ever is usually a drinking game, but there are ways to play it that don’t involve alcohol. You can play for money, you can play for points, you can play for favors… there are a whole host of things you can play for that don’t involve drinking. Do you want to give it a try?”

Marcus grinned. “Why not? What have I got to lose?”

“Exactly,” Katherine said confidently.

“No, I mean what am I going to lose? What are we playing for?”

With a mischievous twinkle in her eye, Katherine said, “Let’s just play for points this time. Low score wins. We can up the stakes another time.”

Marcus had a shrewd look on his face as he responded, “Fine. But one stipulation. Details are required. You can’t just admit to something without explaining the circumstances."

Katherine's shoulders slumped slightly. "I was hoping you wouldn't say that. Oh, well. I'll go first."

Marcus nodded and took a sip of his water.

"Never have I ever… cheated on a lover."

Marcus nearly spewed his water across the table. "I didn't know you planned to get that personal."

"Wanna forfeit?" Katherine asked innocently.

"No," Marcus said, "but make certain you can finish what you start. And I don't get a point for that question."

"You've never cheated on a lover?" Katherine asked. *I've met very few men who haven't cheated at least once… especially in this business.*

"Not once. You?"

"No… I was dating two people at the same time once, but I don't classify either of them as a lover."

The waitress returned with their order. They started eating as the game continued.

Marcus nodded. "Okay. It's zero to zero. Never have I ever… slept with an ex."

Katherine laughed. "Subtle, but the answer is no. I never slept with Greg after the divorce."

"Even though you're such good friends?"

Katherine leaned forward, and with a low voice, said, "It's because we don't sleep together that we remain good friends. Oh, he tried once, about a year after the divorce, but his cheek was red and bruised when he left."

"You smacked him?" Marcus sounded surprised.

"I'm not afraid to defend myself, even from a friend."

Marcus nodded. "Good for you. The score is still zero to zero. Your turn."

Katherine put a finger to her lips, thinking about what to ask. "Never have I ever… slept with someone to get a job."

"Get a job or advance your career?" Marcus asked.

"Either or," Katherine replied.

"Then put me down for a point," Marcus said.

Katherine feigned looking shocked. "Do tell."

"I was in college, and I was working as a dishwasher in a restaurant. I wanted to work up front with the customers, not back in the kitchen. The assistant manager who ran that part of the restaurant was a couple of years older and very cute. She told me that she'd move me up to her section if I slept with her. I did. She didn't. And I quit the next week."

Katherine snickered, and then she added a point to her score. Marcus stared at her wide-eyed.

Katherine explained. "When I was nineteen and had just started bikini modeling, I really wanted this gig being held at a local surf competition. A friend told me that all I had to do was sleep with the owner of the surf shop sponsoring the event, and I'd be in. He was cute, so I did, and it's where I got discovered. He expected me to show him gratitude for letting me participate and getting discovered, but I reminded him that he'd been paid in advance. I never spoke to him again."

"Is that the only time?" Marcus asked.

"Yes," Katherine replied. "Oh, I knew all about the 'casting couch' creeps from my agent… and about the agency creeps from friends in the business, but I refused to allow any of them seduce me just to advance my career. It's one thing to *act* like you're having sex on film, but it's something else altogether to whore yourself for real to get a part. I swore that's a line I'd never cross again after the surf shop owner, and I never have."

"I'm impressed," Marcus said. "Okay. The score's one to one. My turn… Never have I ever been attracted to a co-worker enough to act on it. And I don't mean a casual attraction. I mean attracted enough to actually pursue a relationship."

Katherine immediately put a point next to her name. Marcus indicated for her to put a point next to his name. "Spill," he said.

"It has happened to me twice," Katherine said. "Greg was the first. We met on set, and… well, you know what happened."

"And the second time?" Marcus asked.

Katherine finished the last bite of her food and looked at her watch. "My, look at the time, we'd better hurry up and pay the check so we can get to the studio on time."

"Nice try, Kathy," Marcus said. "Finish it."

Katherine locked eyes with Marcus. "You're the second one."

Marcus held her gaze, then he smiled, and Katherine felt like she was being bathed in sunlight. "You're my point, too," he admitted.

The waitress stopped at the table and asked if they needed anything else. After Marcus declined, the waitress handed him the check, and he paid her. "Keep the change."

"Thank you," the waitress said.

As Marcus and Katherine walked to the car, he said, "The game's tied and two to two. How do we break the tie?"

"Sudden death," Katherine replied.

"How's that played?" Marcus asked warily.

"Like this." Katherine put her arms around Marcus' neck and kissed him. She felt his arms encircle her, and she held him even tighter. The kiss was electric, sending shivers from her ears to her toes, but the longer they held their embrace, the more that tingling changed into a warmth that radiated out from her core to every part of her body. Even if she had wanted to, she couldn't pull away.

It was several minutes before she finally released Marcus and pulled back to look at his face. She could tell in an instant that he had enjoyed the kiss as much as she had. She smiled, and he returned the expression.

Katherine jiggled her head triumphantly. "And I win the game."

"How do you figure that?" Marcus asked, releasing her

from his embrace. "As far as I can tell, it's still a tie."

"I kissed you first."

"And that gives you the win?" Marcus asked.

Katherine smirked. "Didn't you enjoy it?"

"Of course, I did."

"Then I win," Katherine stated. She got into Marcus' car with a grin on her face, jiggling her head again.

Marcus shook his head as he closed her door. One they were heading toward the studio, Marcus asked, "So, what happens now?"

"We go to work," Katherine laughed.

"That's not what I meant, and you know it," he countered.

"Ah… what do you want to happen?"

"Oh, no. You confessed first, you kissed first, you finish this first."

Katherine shifted in her seat to face Marcus. She inhaled deeply and then let it out through her mouth. "We see where this leads. We're here for another month or so, and there's no reason why we can't see each other every day if we want. When our work on the film is done, we look at where things are and decide what happens after that. How does that sound?"

Marcus glanced at her and smiled. "It sounds wonderful." He pulled into the studio complex and parked near the soundstage where their movie was shooting. When he turned off the car, he asked, "Dinner tonight?"

Katherine nodded. "Early or late?"

"I have a conference call at six with my agents, so—"

"Agents?" Katherine interrupted. "You have more than one?"

Marcus nodded. "One for my books, and one for my screenplays. They're with two different agencies, and neither likes that I have the other, so they make my life hell trying to schedule my time. Apart from that, they're both great. They want to look at the calendar for the rest of the year and see what we can fit in. I wanted them to meet without me, but they insist that I have to be there. If I let them, they'll have me on the phone for three hours, and we'll get nowhere. But if I were to tell them that I have a dinner meeting at six-thirty, I can keep them focused, and we might actually accomplish something together. Can you wait that late to eat?"

"Absolutely," Katherine confirmed. "Depending on how today goes, I might not even be ready until seven."

"Don't say that," Marcus had a scared look on his face. "They need to hear your voice at six-thirty so they know I didn't make up the part about having a meeting tonight."

Katherine laughed. "Then my voice will be ready for you at six-thirty. The rest of me though… well, we'll just have to see what happens."

Marcus laughed as they got out of the car. He walked her to the Hair & Make-Up trailer, looked around quickly to make sure no one was watching, and kissed her passionately on her lips. "See you on set."

"See ya," she said.

Marcus dialed into the conference call a minute before six that evening. Filming had wrapped for the day, and Katherine and the rest of the actors from the day's shoot were in Hair & Make-Up, getting cleaned up and changed before leaving the studio.

Marcus hated cell phones. The reception was always lousy, and the more sophisticated the device, the worse the phone features worked. He preferred landlines so he could hear what was being said. As far as he was concerned, cell phones were for taking pictures and sending text messages. He usually kept his phone in his briefcase, so he always knew where it was, but he frequently went days without checking it, which drove his agents crazy when they needed to get a hold of him.

When his agents joined the call, Marcus started the meeting. "I have another engagement at six-thirty my time, so we need to wrap this up in thirty minutes."

"What?" Julia Freeman demanded. Julia was his book agent in New York, and she was a no-nonsense firecracker who earned her fees and acted more like a mom to most of her authors. She had a special place in her heart for Marcus, since he was one of her best earners, and she was very protective of him. "There's no way we can wrap this up in thirty minutes, Marc."

"Then you and Frankie should have worked it out between you and presented your recommendations for my approval. If you'll remember, I don't work for you two. You two work for me, and if you can't work together, then I may be forced to find two people who can. You both know the reason why I need to separate agents. Frankie knows her way around the TV and movie business; you don't. You know your way around the publishing business; she doesn't. As long as I write novels *and* screenplays, I'll have two agents representing me, and those two will have to learn how to work together, if they want to continue representing me. Don't force me to make a change. I love both of you, and the work you do for me, too much to toss one or both of you aside lightly."

There was stunned silence on the line. Then Frankie Talcott spoke. "Okay, Marc. Let's see how much we can get through now, and if we don't finish, I'll call Julia tomorrow and work out the rest with her."

"Thanks, Frankie. That's all I ask. Now, what do you two ladies have for me tonight?"

"We need to finalize your autumn book tour for the first book in your new espionage series," Julia said quickly. "Possibly two tours. The US tour for your new book will start in New York and end in Los Angeles. I'd like to schedule it to start in early-October and end in early-November so we can capitalize on the Christmas sales season."

"And I need to schedule you for some meetings with a couple of directors who want you to write their next blockbusters," Frankie said. "If I can schedule those for when you get to L.A. in November, we can get that all wrapped up before Thanksgiving. Are you okay staying in L.A. for a couple of weeks at the end of your tour?"

"It sounds perfect," said Marc, thinking about spending time with Katherine—and possibly her sons—while still in California. "I want the week of Thanksgiving left free."

"I also want to schedule a book tour for Britain and Canada in December," Julie continued. "We should be able to wrap it all up before the week of Christmas, if I can get the scheduling worked out."

"Strange time to do a book tour in Canada, but I can make it work. Any objections to that, Frankie?" Marcus asked.

"No, but I'll need you here in January for some meetings. There's a film franchise that's getting re-launched, and there's talk of you taking the writing helm for the entire series."

"And I get the novelization rights, too?"

"Of course, Marc. That's standard in all of your contracts. I'll make sure they understand that there's no negotiating on that point."

"Then we're good there. Julia, what else do you have for me between now and Valentines?"

"Nothing definite, but it depends on when the publisher decides to release your new stand-alone novel. We may have to react quickly if they keep dragging their feet on setting a date."

"Push them to set a date, but don't piss them off," Marcus suggested. "And let's send a few pre-release copies to our contacts in Hollywood. Who knows? We might be able to time the book's release with an announcement of the film rights sales. The two of you should work together on that."

"Right-o," Julie promised.

"I'll do whatever you two need me to do," Frankie stated.

They talked about a few tentative items that might end up on the schedule over the following months. Toward the end of the thirty minutes, Frankie asked, "So, who is this meeting with tonight?"

"Do you know Katherine Delaney?" Marcus asked.

"The actress?" asked Frankie.

"That's the one," Marcus confirmed.

"She's a cutie," Frankie commented. "Why are you taking a meeting with her? Getting into memoir writing?"

"No, we're just having dinner."

There was a long pause on the call, and Marcus envisioned both women punching the air and doing a happy-dance in their office chairs. They had both been trying to fix him up and encouraging him to date ever since Leigh had died.

"Well, that sounds wonderful," Frankie said calmly after a moment.

"Wonderful, hell," Julie practically shouted. "Are you sleeping with her?"

Before Marcus could answer, Katherine walked up. "Are you ready to go, Marc?" she asked loud enough for the ladies on the call to hear.

Marcus waved to her and smiled. He gave her a thumbs up, and then said, "I'll be right with you, Kathy. Ladies, my next meeting has arrived. Let's reconvene once the tentative items are less tentative and once we have the tour and meeting schedules confirmed."

"You didn't answer my question," Julia accused him.

Marcus ended the call. "Your timing was perfect, Kathy. What sounds good tonight?"

"Any good Mexican places around here?"

Marcus grinned. "I think we can find something you'll like."

Over the next week, they had dinner together every night and met for a couple of breakfasts. They spent the time getting to know each other better, and the more they were together, the more they wanted to be together.

As they left the studio one evening, after a particularly difficult day of shooting, Marcus asked Katherine where she wanted to go for dinner.

"How about that Cuban place? I've had it on my mind ever since you first mentioned it."

"Cuban it is."

Once they had placed their order at the counter, Katherine and Marcus sat at a table in the corner.

Marcus reached out and took Katherine's hand. "So, tell me... you reinvented yourself as an actress after you had the boys, you reinvented yourself again by becoming a single-mom, and now your life revolves around being a mother first. What do you see happening with your career, or do you even see it as a career anymore? I don't mean to sound judgmental—far from it. I've just never met anyone in this business who was willing to make such a drastic change."

Katherine sat quietly for a moment, then she replied, "I still see acting as my career, but I no longer see it as my life. I'm a mother and an actress, rather than an actress who has children. Do you see the difference? It's a matter of perspective and balance. I act because I love the craft. Did you know that I participate in local theatre in L.A.? I try to do three or four productions a year—mostly musicals. I don't get to sing in the movies, so I sing on stage. Acting live is such a rush, and Greg watches the kids while I'm at rehearsals and performances. So I continue to hone my craft, but I use a different criteria now for which parts I choose to play. It can't just be about the money or the fame. It has to be what's best for my family first, and what's best for my career second. I've even thought about leaving L.A., settling somewhere that's best for the boys. My agent has a number of clients who don't live in L.A., or in California for that matter, and yet still have fulfilling careers. The problem is finding someone who can watch the boys while I'm away making movies. But… I'm about to have that problem anyway."

"What do you mean?" Marcus asked.

"Greg's talking about leaving L.A. Now that he's a producer, his production company is thinking about relocating near one of the other studio complexes. Atlanta is one of the places they're looking at. So is Dallas, and so is Chicago, although I can't see Greg willingly move to snow country. He's a warm weather boy, through and through."

An elderly Cuban man arrived at their table with their food. "Here you go, Miss Delaney. My wife and I are honored to have you in our restaurant. We're both big fans of your work. Please enjoy your meal, and let us know if there's anything you need."

Katherine beamed at the man. "Thank you so much. And tell your wife that I'm thrilled the both of you enjoy my films."

The man nodded with a wide smile and then shuffled back to the kitchen.

"That was sweet," she commented as she tasted her food. "And this is excellent!"

"I thought you'd like the place. I make a point to eat here whenever I'm in town."

"I can understand why." Katherine ate another mouthful. "Where was I?"

"Explaining that Greg is potentially leaving L.A., and that will be a crimp in your ability to work in local theatre and movies because you won't have anyone who can watch the boys for you."

"Wow, you really got to the heart of the problem," Katherine said.

"What happens if you end up having to stop acting?"

Katherine shook her head. "I hope it never comes to that,

but if it does, I'll do what I have to do to support the boys."

"That'll be tough in L.A., wont' it?"

"Tough, yes, but not impossible," Katherine stated. "And I suppose I could always head up the drama department of a high school or college. I have directed before, and I've produced two movies that I starred in, so it wouldn't be that much of a stretch. Besides, the hours and the commute would be better than jetting around the country all the time."

They continued eating. After a few minutes, Katherine asked, "Would you ever give up writing?"

Marcus shook his head. "Even if I never published another book, I'd keep writing. It's who I am. Ideas come to me so they can be released from my head and live a life of their own on paper. The ideas don't come *from* me, they come out *through* me. As long as the ideas come, I'll write them down. Now if the ideas stop coming… well, that's another matter altogether."

"It sounds like you don't have a lot of ego about your work," Katherine remarked.

"Have you ever been in an acting workshop where everyone critiques your performance?"

"Of course," she replied.

"How did it make you feel?"

"Angry, embarrassed, irritated, infuriated… about how you'd expect."

"The editing process for a novel is the writer's equivalent of that," Marcus said. "People get paid good money to shred what you've written. If you can look at your work dispassionately, and view the critiques as ways to improve the work—as opposed to an attack on your work—you'll do well. Otherwise, you have no business writing. If your purpose is to create the best work possible, you'll seek out every critique you can get to help refine what you've written. Otherwise, the reviewers and readers will shred the work far worse than the editors ever would. But if your purpose is to be the center of attention with people fawning over every golden word that drips from your pen, then you've already failed. I don't like to fail, so I strive to produce the best work possible, and that takes an editorial team who can be merciless and ruthless. In the end, they help create a superior product. That's all I want. So yes, I have little ego about my work, because I know that perfection is not and cannot be defined by me. It's defined by the reader. And in the case of my screenplays, well, you already know how many people are involved in taking a script and bringing it to life on the screen for the audience. There's no room for a writer with an ego in this business, because the writer is just the beginning of the process, not the end of the process."

Katherine just shook her head. "You are a most unusual man, Marc, and you're definitely not like any other writer I've met."

"Is that a good thing or a bad thing?" Marc asked as he finished his sandwich.

"A good thing," she replied. "It's a very good thing."

After dinner, they walked around for a while, letting their food settle before heading back to the hotel.

Katherine was unusually quiet as they walked. She was wrestling with feelings that she hadn't felt in years. When faced with a dilemma, she listed out the pros and cons in her mind and weighed them against each other. That's what she was doing as they walked. She was faced with a serious dilemma, and it involved the man walking next to her. In spite of how little time they had known each other and spent time together, she felt herself falling for Marcus, and the thought terrified her. *It's too soon to have feelings like this. It's not natural. We've only been seeing each other for a week. I dated Greg for over a year before I started feeling this way... and look at how that turned out. This is the first time I've felt this way since, and I don't understand why it's hitting me so hard and so fast. Are these real feelings, or is this just another Hollywood Romance that starts and ends during a film shoot? It feels real, but can I trust my feeling after what happened with Greg? And how does Marcus feel about me? If we're not feeling the same way for each other, what happens then? And how do I find out how he feels if I don't say something? And if I do, will that ruin what we have, or will it open us to the possibility of something closer? A girl could go crazy trying to figure this all out. And then there's the boys. How will they react to me dating someone who lives on the other side of the country? What I do impacts them, not just me. This is making me bonkers!*

"Penny for your thoughts," Marcus said gently as he led her to a park bench across from a statue shrouded in shadows from the setting sun.

Katherine sat next to Marcus. She took a deep breath, let it out slowly, and said, "Whenever I'm faced with a decision, I list out and weigh all the pros and cons to help me figure out what to do."

Marcus nodded. "Do you give each pro and con the same value?"

"What do you mean?"

"Well, without going into details, I'll share something I had to face a while back. I was with one of the largest consulting companies in the world. I was on the partnership track, my career was going well, I was a newlywed with two children the same age as your boys, and I woke up one day and wanted to be a writer. I tried to find a way to do it all, but I couldn't. So I sat down with Leigh and asked her what I should do. She had me list out all the pros and cons. There were dozens of reasons not to become a writer—career, income, prestige, the usual stuff—but there were only three reasons in favor of becoming a writer: setting free the ideas in my head, spending more time with Leigh and the kids, and making me happy. After looking at the list, I told her, 'Well, it's obvious that I should remain in consulting.' She said, 'Is that what you take away from your list?' I said,

'Sure. It's twenty-five to three.' And then she said something that has stuck with me ever since. She said, 'They're not all equal weight, you know. One—the right one—can outweigh a hundred reasons against doing something, just as one—the right one—can outweigh a hundred reasons *for* doing something. It's not a numbers game, it's an understanding game. Once you understand the pros and cons, then you can decide how important each pro and con is. And remember this: never underestimate the importance of being happy. Sometimes it can be the most precious gift we're ever given.'"

Marcus put his arm around Katherine's shoulder. "And then she told me that I should be a full-time writer, even though it would mean a major reduction in our income. She said that doing something that would make me happy was far more important than the money earned by travelling all over the world and never seeing my family. So I took the biggest risk of my life, quit my job, and started writing fulltime. Since then, twelve of my first twenty novels have been made into films, and I got to write the screenplays, too. Most of all, I got to spend more time with Leigh; time that I would have missed out on and regretted terribly when I lost her. I still make lists of pros and cons to help me understand situations, but thanks to her, I now know to determine which pros and cons are important and which are just points of fact to be considered but not allowed to sway the decision one way or another."

"I never thought about it that way. Thanks."

Marcus pulled her closer. "Anytime."

After a few minutes, Katherine suggested, "Let's walk some more."

Marcus stood and held out his hand. Katherine took it, and they walked hand-in-hand around the park.

"Do you believe in second chances?" Katherine asked after a while.

"Depends on the context," Marcus replied. "Some things

are so terrible that no second chance is possible. Other things… well, it depends on fate, or God, or the universe, or whatever force you believe is in control of our lives." He looked at her. "Did you have something specific in mind?"

She took a deep breath and exhaled slowly. "Would you ever remarry?"

Ah," Marcus said. "That. My agents ask me that about every three months, and I'll tell you what I tell them. Am I opposed to marriage? No. Do I believe I'll meet someone that I'll want to marry? I have no idea, but I'm certainly open to the possibility. If you consider *that* a second chance, then I'd say yes, I believe in second chances. I don't believe that loneliness is the natural state of men and women, but some are destined to live a solitary life, due to circumstances either of their own making or beyond their control."

"If you did marry again, do you think you'd want kids?"

"Biological children? At my age? I don't think that would be in a child's best interest. I'd be in my late sixties by the time they finished college. Now, if the person I married had children already, and you're asking how I feel about stepchildren, I'll tell you that I'm perfectly fine with that. I've been a step-father for 20 years, so I know what it's like. And maybe marrying someone with children of their own would give me a second chance at being a dad. Maybe I'd do better the second time around. You know… not make so many stupid mistakes."

"How come you and Leigh never had children of your own?"

"It's simple. She couldn't have any more children after her youngest was born. It was never an option for us, and since she already had two children who considered me their dad, I never felt like anything was missing from my life. They could already talk, clean themselves, and dress themselves by the time I entered the picture, which made life *much* easier for me."

Katherine laughed. She believed things were better the

second time around, since most of the mistakes, and how to prevent them, had already been learned the first time around. She was contemplating where a relationship with Marcus might go, but it was not something she could decide on her own. Her life didn't exist in a vacuum. She had the boys to consider, and they had their biological father in their lives. He had a say in what happened with his sons. As much as she liked and was attracted to Marcus, pursuing a relationship with him was not something she could just do. There were other factors to consider, and it was those factors that made any decision so hard to reach.

Marcus interrupted her thoughts. "You're going somewhere with all this. What's eating at you?"

"I like you," Katherine blurted out. "I'm attracted to you. I enjoy being with you. You make me feel special, and that's something I haven't felt in a very long time. But… it's complicated."

Marcus smiled. "Well, in answer to the questions you've been trying to ask, yes, I like you; yes, I'm attracted to you; and yes, I'm open to exploring a relationship with you. It doesn't seem all that complicated to me."

"It is for me," Katherine stated.

"Let me guess," Marcus said gently, gazing intently into her eyes. "There are the boys to consider, their father is still active in their lives, your life is in L.A., and mine's in Tennessee. Does that about cover it?"

"Um… yes, that covers it."

Marcus chuckled. "Don't worry about it."

"What?" Katherine demanded.

"Don't worry about it. You can't *think* your way into or away from a relationship, if that's what you're fretting about. You have to *feel* your way. The heart wants what the heart wants, and it'll find a way to get what it wants no matter what mountains have to be moved. Just follow your heart, and let the rest sort itself out. In the end, that's what's going to happen, so you might as well let it happen from the start. It'll save you a lot of time and angst."

"I don't know how to do that."

"Then let me help you," Marcus said. "There's nothing you've told me that can't be overcome, if you're willing to try, in spite of the obstacles that you already seem to have thrown up in our way."

Katherine stared with her mouth open, unable to say anything. Part of her was elated that he felt the same way toward her that she felt toward him, but part of her was indignant that he saw to the root of her problem so easily and could put it into words better than she could.

"Here, let me help you with that." Marcus cupped her face in his hands and kissed her. It was a long, passionate kiss that gave Katherine that warm feeling she had with their first kiss, but this one had twice the intensity, and she felt weak in her knees. Had he not been holding her, she was certain that she'd collapse.

When their lips finally parted, Katherine opened her eyes and gazed into his. "You're not making this any easier."

Marcus smiled. "I'm sorry; I didn't know that was my job."

She hit him playfully on his shoulder, and then she placed her head in the same place, wrapping her arms around him. "I think this would be easier if we'd known each other longer, don't you?"

"Don't ask me about timing and relationships," Marcus said. "I met Leigh at a wedding, our first date was a month later, the next week we were dating exclusively, and the next weekend we got engaged and had all of the wedding planning finished. We were married less than two months after that. What I've found is that time doesn't play a factor in whether something is right or not. If it's right, less time doesn't change the outcome, and if it's not right, no amount of time will make it work. Again, you can't think your way through this. Just follow your heart.

Yes, we've only been going out for a little over a week, and we haven't really known each other longer than that, but I already feel like I've known you for years. Did time play a factor in that? I don't think so."

"So… what do we do?"

"Like you said last week, we spend as much time together as possible while we're both here. That way you'll have more time to add to your pro and con list until you reach a decision you're comfortable with, even though I'm fairly certain you already know what you *want* the decision to be."

"And how do you know that?" Katherine asked.

"Because you're still holding on to me," Marcus replied.

Marcus drove back to the hotel and walked Katherine to her room. She kissed him when they reached her door, and she didn't want to let him go. But they both had early calls on set in the morning, so they knew that this wasn't the right time to test any other aspects of a relationship. She respected him when he pulled away, but she hated it more than anything in that moment. They made arrangements to grab a quick breakfast in the morning, then she said goodnight and entered her room quickly, so she wouldn't be tempted to pull him inside with her.

Marcus walked back to his room, grabbed his ice bucket, and headed for the ice machine. He wanted something to munch on as he reviewed his notes for the final rewrite of the script.

When he arrived at the ice machine, next to the vending machines, Trish was there getting ice. She was wearing an oversized T-shirt, and Marcus could tell that there was nothing on underneath.

When she heard him approach, she spun around and stared him. She blushed as she pulled her T-shirt down as far as it would go. Then she held the ice bucket in front of her as if she were trying to hide behind it.

"Good evening, Trish."

"Good evening, Marc. How go the script rewrites?"

"Almost finished. How was C.J. this evening?"

"Awesome as alwa…" She blushed again and fled with her ice bucket back to C.J.'s room.

Marcus chuckled as he got his ice and headed back to his room. He looked forward to finishing the re-writes, giving him something to distract him from Katherine… and how close he had come to asking her to spend the night.

CHAPTER 3

A week later, Marcus received a call from Frankie, his agent in L.A., just before six in the morning.

"What are you still doing up at this time?" Marcus asked. "It must be nearly three in the morning out there."

"I was waiting until I knew you'd be awake. I don't know if you're aware of it or not, but you were mentioned in the tabloids this past weekend… along with Katherine Delaney."

"What?!"

"Someone got a picture of you two kissing, and the tabloids out here picked it up. They're referring to you as 'Delaney's New Man'." Frankie proceeded to read part of the article to him.

Marcus laughed. "Whoever wrote that should be ashamed."

"I agree," Frankie said. "How do you want me to deal with this? I assume you'll want to get out ahead of it, right?"

Marcus thought about it. "It's not like we're doing anything wrong or embarrassing. I'll talk to Kathy about it this morning. But unless she wants to deny the story or clarify what's going on, I wouldn't do anything if I were you. If someone asks for a comment, just say we're working on a movie together and that's all you know at the moment."

"That's likely to stoke the fires at the tabloids," Frankie

pointed out.

"So? It's free publicity for the film, and it certainly won't hurt my reputation. Like I said, I'll talk to Kathy. But for me, it's a non-issue."

"Okay, I'll wait to hear from you before saying anything to anyone."

"Thanks for the call, Frankie, and get some sleep."

"Will do, Marc."

Marcus ended the call and grabbed his tablet. After a few minutes of searching, he found the photo and the article, which turned out to be only a paragraph. He read it and, finding nothing inaccurate with it, downloaded the photo to his personal directory. *It's a great photo of the two of us. Might be nice to have a photo of us kissing for times when we're apart.*

He finished getting dressed, and then he packed his notebook and electronics in his briefcase and walked down to Katherine's room.

He knocked on her door, and he heard her say, "Just a minute."

A moment later, she opened the door. The security latch allowed the door to open only a couple of inches, but Marcus could see that she was wrapped in a bath towel.

"Marc, what are you doing here so early?"

"I'm sorry about the time, but we need to talk. Can I come in?"

Katherine looked confused. "Uh… sure… give me a minute."

The door closed, and Marcus waited. A minute later, the door opened. Katherine was wearing a thick terrycloth robe over the towel. She stepped aside so Marcus could enter. When she closed the door, she asked, "What's up?"

"We made the tabloids," Marcus said, pulling the tablet from his briefcase and setting the briefcase on the floor next to the wall.

"What do you mean we made the tabloids?" Katherine demanded.

Marcus showed her the photo and the article.

She looked at the photo and smiled. The she read the article. "It doesn't really say much, does it? I like the part about you being my 'new toy,' but since I don't have any old toys lying around, it seems a bit silly. How did you find out?"

"Frankie, my agent in L.A., called me a few minutes ago. She wanted to give me a heads-up and find out how I want her to handle it."

"What's there to handle?" Katherine asked. "It's not like we're doing anything scandalous. We're not cheating on anyone, we didn't really meet until after you rewrote my part, so it's not like I seduced you for more time on-screen…"

"That's what I said," Marcus responded. "It certainly won't hurt *my* reputation. But I thought you might want to make sure your agent knows what to do… and you might want to tell Greg and the boys. You probably don't want them finding out some other way."

Katherine sat down on the edge of her bed. "I hadn't thought about that." She glanced at the clock on the nightstand. "It's way too early to call now. I'll try to call them at the lunch break."

Marcus took the tablet from her and started to turn it off. Before he did, he commented, "It is a good picture of the two of us, don't you think?"

Katherine smiled again, and her head jiggled slightly. "It is. Do you think you can send it to me?"

Marcus pulled up the photo in his personal directory and emailed it to Katherine. "Done," he said with a grin. "I saved a copy for myself, too."

Katherine looked at the clock again. "There's something I wanted to talk to you about, and as long as you're here, do you mind if we chat while I finish getting dressed?"

Marcus looked around, trying to find somewhere he could sit so she could dress in private. Finding nothing that worked, he sat down in one of the chairs facing the window. "Okay. What did you want to talk about?"

"What are you doing?" Katherine asked.

"Trying to give you your privacy while you dress," he replied.

"Do you mind turning around so I can see your face? Looking at the back of your head isn't going to work for what I need to say."

Marcus stood and turned the chair around. "Better?"

"Scoot the chair closer," she insisted.

Marcus stood and moved the chair right in front of her.

"Perfect," she said. She leaned forward and took his hands in her own. "I don't want to seem forward, but I need to say something, and I don't want to wait for a better or more perfect time."

She hesitated. Marcus sat quietly, waiting for her to find the words.

Katherine took a deep breath and let it out. "I love you, Marcus. I know we've only been together for a couple of weeks, but I'm certain of it. I haven't worked out all the… what did you call it? Obstacles? I haven't worked them all out yet, but I don't want to think about it anymore. I want to do something about it…" Katherine shrugged. "And I believe that we both deserve a second chance at love. I've been alone since Greg and I divorced, you've been alone since Leigh passed, and it's not right. I think we both have a lot of love to give left in us, and… I want to give mine to you."

Her words failed her again, and she continued holding his hands while she searched for words and wondered what he would say. After a minute, she couldn't stand the silence any longer. "I really need you to say something right now."

Marcus turned his hands so he was now holding hers. As he

gently stroked her soft skin, he said, “I love you, too. I’ve known it for a while, but I didn’t want to say anything, because I knew you were wrestling with a lot of conflicting thoughts. I’m glad you finally decided to just let go and follow your heart.” He lifted her hands and kissed them. “So, what does this mean to you?”

“It means I want to move forward with this… this… I want a relationship with you. A real one, not just a Hollywood one.”

Marcus knew what she meant by a Hollywood Romance. He had seen it too many times working on other films, and he knew that the close working environment of a film shoot often blurred the lines between physical attraction and true feelings. The last thing he wanted was a relationship that started during filming and ended before the movie’s premier.

Marcus smiled. “I want the same.”

Katherine looked relieved as she gazed into his eyes. “Which brings me to the second thing I wanted to ask you about. As you know, my last scene was supposed to be shot on Thursday. Thanks to you and your script rewrites, I’m now in several more scenes, but none of them begin shooting until Tuesday of next week. I was thinking about getting away for the weekend… and I want you to come with me.”

“Where do you want to go?” Marcus asked with a twinkle in his eyes.

“C.J. would go ballistic if we went too far away. I was thinking about getting a suite at one of the nicer hotels downtown and ordering room service for a couple of days. If you come with me, perhaps there’s more than room service we could enjoy together…”

“Are you ready to take things to *that* level?” Marcus asked. “If you’re exploring a serious relationship between the two of us, casual physical pleasure is not the way. If you’re serious about what you want, then we’re talking passion, emotion, and a connection of souls, not just the connection of bodies. Is that what you're asking for?"

Katherine nodded, her eyes never leaving his. "Yes."

Marcus nodded slowly. "I imagine we're both a little out of practice."

"Then who better to learn it all over again with?" Katherine remarked. "We're both probably in the same place. It's better that way, don't you think?"

Marcus chuckled. "It's a great sales pitch, that's for sure. Just out of curiosity, do you have a particular hotel in mind?"

"The Four Seasons."

"*That's* a nice hotel. I imagine we'll be quite comfortable there."

"And this is my treat," Katherine said. "After all, you've been buying dinner every night. I want to do something for you."

Marcus leaned back and grinned widely. "Hey, you don't have to do this just to say 'thanks for the dinners'."

Katherine swatted his shoulder. "I'm not doing this to thank you for the dinners, Marc. I'm doing it because I want to be with you more than I've ever wanted to be with anyone before, and I feel like I'll burst if we wait much longer." She looked around the hotel room. "But I don't want to do it here. This is a comfortable hotel room, but we don't need funny looks and tongues wagging about us because the rest of the cast and crew knows what we're doing. It's a distraction I… *we* don't need. It's not keeping it secret, it's just keeping it private. You know what I mean?"

Marcus nodded. "I think that's a good idea. We'll need to plan our exit so no one knows we left together."

"I'll take care of everything," Katherine assured him. "And we won't take your car. That'll give the appearance that you're still here."

"You're a conniving little minx, aren't you?" Marcus was impressed with the way she was thinking.

Katherine stood. "Hey, you might not have to worry about

your reputation, but I do. I don't need anything getting back… anything *more* getting back to my ex and the boys."

She leaned down and kissed Marcus. He pulled her close, and soon she was sitting on his lap as they embraced. When she finally pulled away, she said, "Oh, no! I need to finish getting ready!"

"Do you want me to go?" Marcus asked.

"No, I won't be a minute." She took off the robe, revealing that she was still wearing the towel underneath, and put it on the closet door hook. Then she stepped into the bathroom.

A minute later, Katherine reappeared, wearing jeans, a T-shirt, and deck-shoes. She ran a brush through her hair and grabbed her purse. "Ready?"

Marcus stood and followed her out the door… and right into C.J. and Trish.

"What were you two doing in there?" C.J. asked in his blustery manner as he gave Katherine and Marcus an appraising look.

"I was showing Kathy an article about her," Marcus said smoothly. "The writing is terrible, and I thought she might want to have her agent provide a better written account. I offered to write it for her, but she's still deciding if she even wants to respond. You know how these posts are. 'Much ado about nothing'."

C.J. chuckled. "If I responded to half the crap printed about me, I'd be writing rebuttals full time. My advice? Don't do a thing. It'll go away faster if you ignore it. Commenting just gives them a reason to write more and worse about you."

Trish nodded in agreement.

"You're probably right, C.J.," Katherine said. "If they cared what they printed, they'd make sure to get it right the first time."

"Exactly," C.J. said. He and Trish turned to take the stairs down to the first floor. "See you on set."

Once C.J. and Trish were out of earshot, Katherine

whispered, "Nicely handled. Now you see why I don't want to do anything here."

Marcus nodded. "Perfectly. Let's grab something and eat in the car on the way to the soundstage."

When C.J. called for a lunch break, Katherine grabbed her cell phone, walked over to a corner of the soundstage, and placed a call to her ex-husband, Greg. She knew the boys would be with him, having been back in L.A. from summer camp for two days.

"Hello, Kate," Greg said when he answered the phone. He was the only person who called her that.

"Hi, Greg. Do you have a minute?"

"Sure. What's up?"

"Did you see the tabloids over the weekend?"

"No, I was with the boys all weekend," Greg replied. "Why? What don't you want me to see?"

Katherine rolled her eyes and shook her head. "There's a photo of me in one of them."

"Doing what?"

"Kissing someone."

There was a pause on the line, and Katherine could imagine what Greg must be thinking. "After all this time? Good for you! Who was it?"

That was not the response Katherine was anticipating. "Marcus Buchanan."

"The writer? I know him. I co-produced one of his screenplays. He's a great guy. How long have you two been together?"

"Not long," Katherine admitted. "Only a couple of weeks."

"Is it serious?" Greg asked.

"I think it is."

"Wow, Kate! I'm happy for you. Were you worried I'd see

the photo and overreact?"

"Honestly, I didn't know what I thought. I just wanted you to hear it from me. And I think I need to tell the boys, in case one of their friends sees the photo and shares it with them."

"That's a good idea. You want to tell them now?"

"Yes, please."

"You want me on the line, too?"

"Do you mind? They may have questions that they'd be more comfortable asking you than me."

"Sure thing. Hang on a minute."

Katherine heard him call for the boys, and soon she heard the thumping of them racing down the stairs.

"Hi, Mom!" they said when Greg told them who was on the phone.

"How was summer camp?" Katherine asked.

"It was great," the boys said. They started telling her everything that they had done. After a couple of minutes, Greg interrupted them and told them that their mother had something she needed to say to them.

"Go ahead, Kate," Greg said.

Katherine took a deep breath and let it out. "Thanks, Greg. Boys, I wanted to tell you that I've started seeing… dating someone. His name is Marcus Buchanan… Marc, and he's a screenwriter and a novelist. He wrote the script for the movie I'm filming now. We met on set, and we became… friends. Your father knows him and has worked with him before. And… anyway, I wanted you to know, in case you hear about it from anyone else."

"Are you getting married, Mom?" Jack, the oldest, asked.

"Oh, it's too soon to be thinking about that, Jack," she replied. "And I couldn't marry anyone that you and Ben didn't like. You two always come first. You know that."

"We know. Thanks for telling us. Are we going to get to meet him?"

"We're working that out, but I imagine so. I'll let you know."

Greg came back on the line, "Boys, why don't you finish getting ready?"

"Okay, Dad," Jack said. "Bye, Mom!"

"I love you, Mom," Ben added.

"I love you both," Katherine said.

"I'm taking them to finish buying their school supplies and new school clothes," Greg said. "The school has a new uniform code, so nothing they had before will work this year."

"Typical," Katherine muttered. "Thanks for taking care of that for me, Greg."

"No worries, Kate. How much longer are you going to be out there?"

"Two more weeks of shooting, thanks to a rewrite that's keeping my character alive, but I don't know if I'm going to come straight home or not. I'll let you know, but for now the plans are a little up in the air."

"I understand. Let me know when you know, and break a leg."

Katherine laughed. "Thanks, Greg. You're the best."

"Remember that when you get the bill," he joked.

"Oh, you can count on that. Bye."

"Bye."

After making a quick call to her agent, who had already seen the photo and agreed that the less said the better, Katherine made her way over to the catering tables where Craft Services provided lunch each day. Marcus handed her a bottle of juice when she got there. She selected a sandwich, and they walked over to a cluster of chairs to sit and eat.

"You didn't have to wait for me," Katherine said, taking a bite of her chicken salad croissant.

"I wanted to make sure you got something. You know this crew and leftovers. In another ten minutes, everything would be gone." Marcus let her take another bite, and then he asked, "How was the call?"

"Good," Katherine replied. "Greg remembered you and was very happy for me. The boys seemed okay. They want to meet you, obviously. Oh, and my agent agrees that it's best to say nothing to the tabloids."

"You know I'm going to be in L.A. this November, don't you?"

"I think you mentioned it once. Do you know for how long?"

"A couple of weeks at least," Marcus replied. "Plenty of time to get together with you and the boys—give them a chance to know me and give you their opinion of me and us."

Katherine nodded. "That seems like such a long way off, though. I know there's no way you can meet them in person before then, but maybe we can have them meet you on a video call before the movie wraps?"

Marcus agreed. "Had Greg seen the photo when you called?"

"No, but I'm sure he's found it by now. Whether or not he'll show the boys is anyone's guess."

They finished their lunch and then headed back to the set to start rehearsing the next scene.

The limo pulled up to the soundstage Thursday evening after most of the cast and crew had left. Katherine, with a single bag, hopped into the back and told the driver where to take her. The driver nodded, closed her door, and drove out of the studio.

The driver pulled into the parking lot of an auto body repair shop about three blocks from the hotel where the cast and crew were staying. Marcus was there waiting for them. Kathy opened the door, and Marcus got inside with his bag. He kissed her as the limo pulled back into traffic and headed for I-85 toward downtown Atlanta.

Marcus felt Katherine trembling slightly as she snuggled close to him. "Nervous?" he asked.

"A little," she confided, taking a deep breath and letting it out.

"It's not too late for a change of plans," he noted.

Katherine shook her head. "Not a chance. The nerves are… well, they'll go away. Besides, I want to be with you more than I'm afraid of being with someone again."

He put his arm around her. "Just breathe and relax. I'm here with you, and we'll take the weekend at whatever pace you want. No pressure, no expectations, no performance critiques. And don't be afraid to tell me what you want. I don't read minds, so feel free to give directions, and I'll do the same. That way we'll know if we're doing it right or if we need to… adjust the approach, so to speak. We're in this together. You don't need to worry about how you're doing. We'll both make sure we're doing right by the other. We're a couple, now, right? That means we're a team, and this weekend is about the both of us. Just sit back and enjoy the fun of it all."

Katherine nodded, and then she chuckled. "It did used to be fun, didn't it? Why am I having performance anxiety?"

"Because you're letting yourself think about how long it's been, rather than how great it feels and how fun it is. Get out of your head, and just let it happen. You won't do it wrong, believe me. And even if you think you *are* doing it wrong, I'll be there to help, just like you'll be there to help if I think I'm doing it wrong. And since we're going to be there until Sunday, we have three nights and two days to practice, practice, practice. Trust me, by the time this weekend is over, we'll have it right for both of us."

Katherine turned and stared at him. "Just how many times are you planning for us to do… it?"

Marcus smiled. "As many times as you want, as many times as we can manage, and as many times as it takes to get it just right."

Katherine kissed him. Then she pressed the intercom and said to the driver, "Any chance of going faster? I'm suddenly in a hurry to get to the hotel and check in."

Katherine's stomach was rumbling as they checked into the hotel, but she couldn't tell if it were nerves, hunger, or both. Either way, she decided that she needed to eat before doing anything else.

They ordered a light supper from room service once they got to the suite—which was amazing and had a fantastic view of the city—and as they waited for the food to arrive, Marcus noticed that Katherine was still trembling slightly.

He sat next to her on the couch and put his arm around her. "I have an idea," he said. "It's obvious you're still nervous, and that's no good for either of us. So, here's my thought. How long has it been since you've slept with another person? I don't mean slept as in sex, I mean actually had your head on the pillow, eyes closed, and slept with someone lying next to you in the same bed, who's doing the same."

Katherine looked at him. "Since the divorce. Greg was my last. You?"

Marcus nodded. "Not since Leigh passed away. So, it's been years for both of us. How about this? Let's take sex off the table for tonight. We have plenty of time this weekend for that. Right now, I think what we both need is to just feel comfortable with each other. If we're going to be sharing a bed for the next three nights, shouldn't we make certain that we're compatible sleeping so close together? Let's figure that out first and then worry about the other… stuff. I don't want you nervous, and I don't want you trying to calm your nerves with alcohol, because that'll dull your senses, and you'll miss out on how wonderful I plan on being with you."

Katherine laughed. "I love your sense of humor, and that's the sweetest suggestion anyone has ever made. Thank you. And you're right. Being nervous is no good for sharing something that's supposed to be pleasurable. But are you sure you're willing to wait?"

Marcus pulled her close. "Absolutely. I'd wait an eternity for you. Besides, we're in love, not in heat. Let explore being in love for now. The rest will come in time—when you're ready."

She looked into his eyes. "I do love you, you know."

"I love you, too."

CHAPTER 4

It was close to midnight when they finally decided to go to bed. Marcus changed into his sleep shorts in the living room, while Katherine changed in the bathroom. Marcus walked into the bedroom and noted that the night tables each had a panel that controlled the bedroom and bathroom lights.

"Do you prefer the left side or the right side?" he asked her.

"Right side, please," she answered from the bathroom.

Marcus walked over to the left side of the bed, opposite the bathroom. As he was turning down the covers, Katherine walked into the bedroom. She was wearing a dusty pink outfit consisting of a loose-fitting crop T-shirt and an equally loose pair of drawstring shorts that were cut high on the leg. It was the first time Marcus had really seen her legs up to her thighs, and they were toned like a dancer's. For a single mom, she was in amazing physical shape.

"Like what you see?" She asked, spinning around slowly.

"Very much," Marcus replied. "You must spend a lot of time at the gym."

"Not really," she said as she sat on the bed and rolled onto her knees to face Marcus. "I mostly hike in the hills around my house, I do yoga a couple of times a week, and I try to stay active—easy enough to do with two boys."

Marcus started to join her on the bed, but she held up a hand to stop him. "Not so fast, mister. It's your turn." She gestured for him to turn around so she could get a better look at him. Marcus grinned, stepped back, and slowly turned in a circle.

"Any comments or critiques?" he asked.

"Ah… no… I mean… um… wow! How do *you* stay in such good shape?"

"I live in the mountains, remember? I hike around my property all the time, when I'm home, and there are always things that need doing on that much land. I have people who help, but I like doing much of it myself. It's therapeutic, more than anything else, but I guess it does keep me in shape."

He joined her on the bed, propping himself up with his left elbow. She uncurled herself off her knees, stretched out, and snuggled up close to him as he pulled up the covers and turned off the lights. The blueish ambient lighting from underneath the bathroom cabinets provided a dim glow, but not enough to be distracting. Marcus slid his left arm underneath Katherine's shoulder, and she draped her left arm across his chest.

"Goodnight, Gorgeous," Marcus whispered.

Katherine gave Marcus a kiss. "Goodnight, Handsome."

Marcus was asleep in less than ten minutes.

Katherine wasn't.

She lay awake, listening to Marcus breathing. The problem wasn't that she was sharing a bed with a man for the first time in years. The problem was that he was asleep. She had been touched when he suggested just sleeping together on the first night. It was such a thoughtful gesture, and it made her feel like he truly cared about her comfort. But as the evening progressed, her nervousness had faded. Now, she was lying next to an amazing man, and instead of joining him in sleep, she was awake wishing that he were awake, too.

For the next hour, she tried to sleep, but she couldn't. She couldn't stop thinking about what they could be doing together.

After another thirty minutes, she carefully sat up, trying not to disturb him. She pulled her knees up and wrapped her arms around them, trying to figure out what to do. Now that her eyes had adjusted to the low light from the bathroom, she could see him more clearly. Unable to help herself, she lifted the covers so she could see the rest of him.

She stared at his shorts, trying to figure out what he looked like underneath. *How can I peek without waking him?* Curiosity got the best of her, and she reached over and carefully lifted the waistband. *Oh, my holy God!* What she saw left her breathless. She wanted to touch it, but she knew it would wake him.

She rolled onto her knees and moved the covers aside, exposing most of Marcus' body. She noticed that his sleep shorts were loose fitting, so she started gently tugging at the bottoms, hoping Marcus wouldn't discover what she was doing.

Marcus shifted, and as he turned slightly, Katherine pulled harder. Soon his shorts were below his knees. A minute later, they were on the floor at the foot of the bed.

She looked at him, and then she looked down at what she was wearing. Her top joined his shorts on the floor, and soon her shorts were there, too. She carefully pulled the covers over and snuggled next to him again. She placed her left hand on his chest, but it didn't stay there long. She gradually moved her hand down, reaching for the object of her curiosity.

When she finally held it in her hand, it responded immediately to her touch, stiffening and growing in length and girth. She was flush with excitement, and she felt her own body responding to his arousal. She changed hands so she could stimulate herself at the same time.

Unable to stand it any longer, she straddled him, using her body to continue stroking him. She heard him gasp, and his eyes flew open. She put a finger on his lips so he wouldn't say a word. Then she shifted, allowing him to penetrate her.

The sudden sensations caused by that physical connection were mind-blowing for Katherine. She raised and lowered herself—slowly at first, but faster with each passing minute. Marcus breathed deeply, letting out the occasional low moan of pleasure. Katherine cried out several times as she climaxed—each one stronger than the last. One hit her so hard that her right leg began trembling uncontrollably. She stopped moving, allowing Marcus' hands to begin exploring the parts of her in easy reach.

When the trembling subsided, she began moving again. She had to stop several more times when the trembling returned, leaving her breathless. Her low moans became louder and higher as she approached each climax, and at least two times she felt she would lose consciousness.

Katherine could tell that Marcus was approaching his own climax. She increased the pace of her motion, determined not to stop until he'd had his release. Faster and faster she raised and lowered herself until she heard him cry out and felt a sudden warmth deep inside her. All of a sudden, both of her legs started trembling from the sensation he shared with her.

She leaned forward and kissed him once her legs stopped shaking. He looked up at Katherine with a questioning look on his face.

She smiled innocently. "I stopped being nervous."

They made love two more times that night, trying different positions and techniques until they found what the other liked the most. After the last time, Marcus got up and placed the Do Not Disturb sign on the door, and then he grabbed a couple of bottles of water from the mini-bar on the way back to the bedroom. They both made sure that they were hydrated before pulling up the covers and snuggling close to each other—their clothes still on the floor where Katherine had tossed them earlier. She was finally able to drift off to sleep just after four o'clock that morning.

Katherine woke up and looked over at the clock. It was ten-thirty. She looked over to Marcus' side of the bed, but it was empty. She saw one of the hotel's thick terry robes lying across the corner of her side of the bed, and she heard Marcus' voice coming from the living room.

She got up, put the robe on, and walked into the living room. Marcus, who was wearing a robe like hers, had just hung up the phone when she came up behind him and put her arms around his neck.

"I looked for you, but you were gone. Who were you talking to?"

"Room service. I ordered brunch for us."

"Thanks. I'm starving!" She came around at sat on his lap. "Good morning, Lover," she purred as she kissed him. "No one has ever done what you did for me, with me, to me last night. I feel like I ran a marathon or hiked the side of a mountain, but I feel more alive right now that I have… ever!"

Marcus kissed her and grinned. "You never told me that you could be so… oh, what's the right word… insatiable! For a moment, I thought you were going to keep going all morning and into the afternoon before calling a break."

"Hey, a girl needs her sleep. A few rest breaks are necessary now and then. And I like your idea of making love into the afternoon. But first things first. Food now, lovemaking after the food settles. Don't need a cramp from getting too vigorous on a full stomach."

"Agreed," Marcus said. "But there's one thing I need to know."

"What's that?"

"Do you have any freckles? It was too dark last night to see. Oh, I could see your outline and your facial expressions, but the finer details were in the shadows most of the time."

Katherine laughed. "You really want to know?" She stood and removed the robe. "See for yourself." She turned around slowly so he could see the light dusting of freckles across her shoulders. He took the opportunity to look at the rest of her as she turned.

"Thank you," he said when she pulled her robe back on. "Are there any parts of me that you missed last night when you undressed me?" he asked playfully.

Katherine blushed furiously. "I couldn't help myself. You were asleep, and I was awake, and I got curious, and then I… well, like I said, I couldn't help myself."

"I take it you enjoyed yourself?" Marcus asked.

Katherine shook her head. "I don't have the words to tell you how much I enjoyed myself and how much that meant to me. You're the most amazing lover I've ever known. I'm… I'm in awe."

"You were great yourself," Marcus responded.

"Not too aggressive?" Katherine asked.

"Maybe a little at first. I've never had someone start without me like that. I'm usually awake and participating from the beginning."

Katherine laughed. "What went through your mind when you woke up and found what I was doing?"

"That I died and went to heaven."

Katherine's eyes opened wide. "Really?"

"Really. Seeing you on top of me like that was like looking at an angel taking me home."

Katherine beamed at the compliment.

Ten minutes later, there was a knock at the door. "That should be brunch." Marcus stood and walked to the door as

Katherine adjusted her robe and sat at the table in the corner.

The room service waiter rolled the serving cart into the suite and quickly transferred the trays and serving pieces onto the table, along with carafes of coffee, tea, and orange juice.

“Will there be anything else you need?” the waiter asked.

“That should be everything,” Katherine said. Marcus signed the check, and the waiter rolled the empty cart out of the suite.

Marcus closed the door and joined Katherine at the table. She lifted the lids off the food plates, looking at all of her favorite foods that Marcus had ordered. “This’ll help build our strength back up,” she commented as she started piling her plate with food.

An hour later, the food was gone, and Marcus and Katherine were sitting on the couch, just enjoying being next to each other. They didn’t say much. They didn’t have to. What they felt was far more profound than words could express.

After thirty minutes or so, Marcus wondered if Katherine was taking a nap, but she suddenly stood. “Stand up,” she commanded. He obliged.

She opened his robe and pulled it off his shoulders. It fell onto the floor at his feet. Katherine pushed him back onto the couch, let her own robe slide off, and straddled him. As she kissed him, she said, “I can’t wait any longer.”

“Okay,” Marcus gave in enthusiastically.

It was nearly six in the evening before they finally decided that they need to stop, shower, and get dinner. The shower in the suite’s bathroom was large enough for two people to shower at the same time, which cut down on the time it took to get clean… in spite of the extra time they spent helping each other with those hard-to-reach places.

Katherine wanted to keep it casual, so she wore jeans, a

button-up shirt that tied at the waist, and tan deck shoes. Marcus wore jeans, a golf shirt, and brown deck shoes. They both wanted to stretch their legs, so they decided to walk to one of the local restaurants near the hotel. Marcus forgot his phone and left it in the hotel room.

Being a Friday night, most places were already crowded, but Katherine and Marcus found an Italian place near the hotel that had a table available. The restaurant was a converted house, and the ambiance was perfect, as was the food.

Katherine was recognized by one of the servers, and once it was known that there was a celebrity present, the staff seemed extra attentive to their needs. Oddly enough, Marcus was recognized by the wife of the owner, who was a fan of his novels. The staff kept a respectful distance during the meal, and they kept the other patrons from bothering Katherine and Marcus while they ate, but after they had paid the check and were heading for the door, they both had to stop to sign autographs. They finally managed to slip away before any news crews showed up and plastered their pictures all over local television.

They strolled hand-in-hand back to the hotel, laughing about the scene they caused at the restaurant.

"I've lived in L.A. too long," Katherine said. "If you're not an A-Lister, you get used to being ignored. It's funny getting recognized all the way on the other side of the country."

Marcus chuckled. "I get recognized in bookstores, or at Comic Con, or at premiers, but I almost never get recognized when I'm just out and about. I forget what it's like. But they were all nice to us back there, and I guess we did give them something to tell all their friends about. I mean, how often does a Hollywood actress show up in the middle of downtown Atlanta on a Friday night?"

"What about a best-selling author showing up?" Katherine asked. "Don't forget that you're a celebrity, too."

"It's not the same, though," Marcus pointed out. "You're

the face in front of the camera. I'm just the guy behind the words. I'm not complaining. I love what I do. I'm a storyteller. I create the story. You bring it to life. But at the end of the day, you're the one they remember, and I prefer it that way."

"Why?" Katherine asked.

"Because I can't act. I don't know how to hide my feelings. I am what you see. That's fine for a writer, but I imagine it's not fine for an actor."

"Not really. But I'll tell you this. If it weren't for writers like you, I'd be out of a job."

"And if it weren't for actors like you, no one would ever get to see my stories brought to life. It takes both of us to delight an audience."

Katherine nodded. "I like that. It's nice knowing that our careers don't conflict with each other. We don't compete, we complement."

"Well said," Marcus approved.

They arrived at the hotel and got into the elevator heading for the top floor, where their suite was located.

"Sooooo, what do you want to do when we get upstairs?" Katherine asked.

"I'm sure I'll want to do whatever you want to do."

"That's not an answer," Katherine pouted.

Marcus turned and faced her. "Okay, what do *you* want to do when we get upstairs?"

"I have few things in mind. We haven't tried everything I want to try before we leave on Sunday. Are you up for it?"

"With you? Always."

Sunday morning came too soon for Katherine and Marcus. They had spent almost all day Saturday in bed, only getting up when it was necessary. Late Saturday night, Marcus actually brought her to tears—not from pain or sadness, but from exhilaration and the intensity of their emotional connection, which transcended the physical connections they had shared that weekend.

Marcus just held her as she wept uncontrollably for several minutes after her biggest climax of the weekend. But once she stopped crying, she didn't want to stop making love. If anything, she wanted the physical and emotional connection with Marcus more than ever.

When the sun rose Sunday morning, they showered, dressed, and went downstairs to eat in one of the hotel restaurants. Then they went back upstairs to finish packing. Katherine checked out of the hotel before they left the suite, and they took the elevator to the lobby, where they were to meet their limo driver in five minutes.

As the elevator headed down for the ground level of the hotel, Katherine asked, "So, did you have a good time this weekend?"

Marcus laughed and kissed her. "The best time ever. You?"

"I'm actually a little mad at you," Katherine answered.

Marcus looked confused. "Why?" He couldn't think of anything he'd done to anger her.

"You're addictive. The more I'm with you, the more I want and need to be with you." Katherine smiled at him, wide-eyed.

"I'm afraid there's not much I can do about that," Marcus said. "But if you're asking me to keep away so you can wean yourself off of me, I respectfully have to decline."

"Good! I intend to overdose on you, dying with a happy happy smile on my face."

"I'm fine with all of that except dying. That's not allowed."

Katherine realized that mentioning death might have been the wrong thing to say, so she quickly tried to cover up her remark. "Okay, fine. I'll just go into orgasmic shock instead."

"I can accommodate you there," Marcus said as the elevator doors opened. He knew what she had meant and let the death comment pass.

As the limo drove them back to Norcross, Katherine said, “It’s going to be strange being back on the soundstage after this weekend. I’m glad my next scene isn’t until Tuesday. If I had to go back to work tomorrow, I think I’d be a total wreck.”

“And you’d drive your make-up artist batty. You’re glowing, and I don’t think there’s enough make-up in the southeast to cover that up. You need a day to tone it down. Plus, you don’t want everyone getting jealous. One look at you and the women on set will be seething at how happy you are.”

The limo driver let Marcus out a couple of blocks away from the hotel. Then he drove Katherine to the hotel. Katherine felt that would divert any suspicion that they had spent the weekend together.

They had dinner again that night, but afterwards, Marcus walked her to her room and said goodnight. They wanted to kiss. They wanted to stay together. But they had agreed to keep their relationship private, and that meant what they had shared over the weekend could not continue while they were in Norcross. It took all of their strength to part ways at Katherine’s door.

Once she got inside her room, she called the boys to find out how the new school year was going. After an hour of catching up on their classes, their teachers, and their friends, the boys had to get ready for dinner. Greg came on the line.

“So, how have you been?” he asked.

“Good. I had a few days free, so I got away for a long weekend.”

“By yourself?”

“No,” Katherine replied.

“With Marc?”

“Yes.”

“So, it *is* serious.”

“It is now,” Katherine confirmed.

“I am truly happy for you, Kate. You deserve love again.”

"Thanks, Greg."

"Are you going back to his place once shooting wraps?"

"I don't know. His agents are trying to schedule meetings and book tours, and until they finalize those plans, his schedule is up in the air."

"Has he told you about his house?"

"A little," Katherine replied. "Why?"

"When he and I were working together on 'The Poison Gardner," one of those architecture magazines did a spread on the place. I've talked to people who have actually been there, and even though the photos in that magazine were amazing, they say that pictures barely scratch the surface of how terrific the place is. Did you know he has two cannons in his front yard?"

"What?"

"He has a circular drive in front of the house. There's a flagpole in the center, and two cannons—one on either side."

"What kind of cannons?"

"Do you remember when we want to Orlando right before we got married?"

"Of course. That was a great trip."

"Do you remember the pirate ride that you wanted to go on over and over again?"

"Sure. It was so different from the California version. I couldn't get enough of it."

"Do you remember—as you're walking in the line before you get to the boats—there are cannons that look like they're protecting the fortress?"

"Yes."

"That's the kind of cannons he has. They're the same cannons used in fortresses in the 1700s and early 1800s. But unlike the cannons at the ride in Orlando, these are real—not original antiques, but real, firing, cannons. The magazine showed him shooting them in one of the photos."

"I want to see those photos!" Katherine was intrigued.

"They're probably online somewhere. Do a search, and you'll find them out there."

"Thanks, Greg. I will."

"Call me when you get your plans worked out, okay?"

"I will. Good night."

"'Night, Kate."

CHAPTER 5

The next morning, after the cast and crew had left for the soundstage, Katherine sat in her hotel room alone… and frustrated.

Being with Marcus over the weekend helped her block out all the obstacles her mind kept throwing at her, but being back in Norcross without him next to her allowed all those anxiety-inducing thoughts to come crashing back upon her. Chief of these thoughts were these: *What if Jack and Ben don't like Marc*, and *what if they do like Marc and we want to be together or get married, but we can't agree on whether to live in California or Tennessee?*

To distract her, she looked up the architectural magazine article on Marcus' house. After ten minutes of searching, she finally found it… and was blown away. The house looked amazing, and when she saw the cannons, she was stunned. *It looks like a house for a retired British admiral, not an American novelist. If Greg's right, and the photos don't do the house justice, then I hope I get to see it for myself.*

Not being able to clear the thoughts that were invading her peace and happiness from the weekend, she began studying the updated pages from the script rewrites, so she'd be prepared to shoot her new scenes in the morning. She spent the rest of the day rehearsing her lines to make certain that, when she arrived on set the next day, she'd be prepared for whatever C.J. needed from her.

A chime on her phone notified her that she had a text. It was from Marcus, asking her to dinner that night. She texted him back that she was looking forward to it, and he texted that he was heading back to the hotel and to meet him at his room in thirty minutes dressed in casual attire. She confirmed and began getting ready.

Thirty minutes later, wearing a loose tank top and jean shorts, she knocked on his hotel room door. He opened it and motioned for her to come inside. He was holding his cell phone with the speaker on, so she could hear the conversation. He gestured for her to sit at the table, and he sat across from her and put the phone down so he could write down what the two women on the phone call were telling him.

Katherine quickly realized that he was talking to his agents, who were confirming the upcoming book tour dates and meeting dates. Evidently, he was going to be spending a few weeks in California, and even though he would have meetings during the day, Frankie had managed to schedule all of them for mornings, leaving his afternoons and evenings free. As Katherine read Marcus' notes upside down, a trick she had learned years earlier, her mind began working out how they'd be able to spend time together over the next couple of months.

When the call ended, Marcus said, "Sorry about that. I didn't think we'd be on the phone that long." He leaned over and kissed her. "How was your day?"

Katherine's smile faded a bit.

"Ah," Marcus said. "You got inside your head again."

Katherine took a deep breath and let it out slowly. "I couldn't help it," she confirmed. "I was all alone, missing you, and all those obstacles I thought I had pushed past came back to haunt me."

"Which ones?"

"Mostly about the boys and whether or not they'll like you, but also about how we'd deal with me in L.A. and you in Tennessee, if you and I keep moving forward."

Marcus nodded. "Well, it looks like there will be opportunities for me to spend time with you and the boys. That's why I wanted you to come to my room, so I can walk you through what Julia and Frankie have lined up for me, and see where you and I can use their schedules to our advantage."

Katherine perked up. "I'd like that."

"Good. Dinner should be here in about fifteen minutes, so relax, and let's see what we can come up with."

"What did you order for dinner?" she asked, kicking off her shoes.

"Just what you told me you wanted… surf and turf from that seafood place you love."

Katherine beamed. Marcus handed her a notebook and a pen, and then he started sharing the results of his conference call. Katherine created a calendar to help visualize what he told her.

At the end of presenting the information, he said, "So that leaves us several windows of time that we can put to use. First of all, the film shoot will be done in two weeks, and from what I learned from C.J. this morning, we're slightly ahead of schedule, so I think we can assume that two weeks is a firm date. You don't have to be back in California for almost two weeks after that, if I remember how long you said Greg was keeping the boys. I don't have to leave on my book tour until three days later. So I was thinking… why don't you come back to Tennessee with me for ten days? It'll give you a chance to see where and how I live, in case you decide that you like it more than L.A. The leaves will be just starting to turn, so even if you don't get the full autumn effect, you'll get to experience a little of why I love the mountains."

"I love that idea," Katherine said excitedly. "I saw pictures of your place from that architectural magazine article, but I hear that it's even more impressive in person. I can't wait to see it."

Marcus smiled and nodded. "Good." He wrote in his notes that Katherine would be staying with him for those ten days, and Katherine marked it on her calendar.

"Okay," Marcus continued. "The book tour will meander across the States from New York to L.A. I'll arrive in L.A. the first of November. I have meetings the first week that I'm there, but I'm keeping most of the next two weeks free, so I can spend time with you and the boys. I'm staying in Marina Del Ray, at the apartment that Frankie's firm reserves for me. How far is that from your house?"

"Not far," Katherine remarked, "by L.A. standards. It's about an hour drive in light traffic."

"That's not too bad. I'd like to come see you, and I'd like for you and boys to come see me. We can finalize those details later. There may be one or two other meetings during those two weeks, but nothing that will keep us from spending time together."

Marcus paused. Then he asked, "Do the boys get the week of Thanksgiving off, or just Thursday and Friday?"

"The whole week," replied Katherine.

"Good. What about this? Assuming everything goes well with the boys, why don't y'all fly back to Tennessee with me the weekend before Thanksgiving and spend that week with me at my home. It'll give the boys a chance to see my world and decide if they like it. By the end of that week, your concerns about whether the boys will like me or like Tennessee will be satisfied, and we'll both know how we're going to move forward with this relationship."

Katherine nodded. "I'm all for that!"

Marcus wrote that down, and Katherine added it to her calendar.

"Do you have anything scheduled between now and Thanksgiving that I need to know about?" Marcus asked.

"No," Katherine replied. "I was going to be part of a holiday musical that was to start rehearsals in October, but the theatre has a foundation and electrical problem that won't be fixed in time, so my schedule is wide open, apart from any auditions that my agent can arrange. I plan to spend as much time with the boys as possible."

Marcus nodded. "Let me know if anything comes along, okay?"

Katherine agreed.

"So, after Thanksgiving, I have the second book tour, which starts in London and ends in Vancouver right before Christmas. If things go well with the boys, why don't I come down to L.A. and spend Christmas with you? We should know what we both want by then, and we can finalize, or formalize, our relationship and where we're going to live. Plus, I have some meetings in L.A. in early January, so I can be with you through the New Year, deal with those meetings, and then come back to Tennessee to start working on a new potential project that I can't tell you about yet."

Katherine nodded, curious about his mysterious project. "Will we have opportunities to talk while you're on your tour?"

"Of course. We can video chat every day. It's not the same as being next to each other, but we'll have to do the same thing when you and I are on film shoots, so it'll be good to see how we like it before we go much farther. It's going to end up being a normal part of our relationship, as long as we're both in this business, right?"

"Right, as long as you remember to have your phone with you and don't leave it somewhere. Okay. I'll need to let Greg know that I'm not coming home at the end of next week."

"How much does he know about us?" Marcus asked.

"He knows we went away together this past weekend, but

none of the details. I think he's genuinely happy for me. Oh, and get this. He texted me this afternoon and said that it looks like his production company *is* moving to Atlanta. That means he'll only be two hours away from the boys, if we end up in Tennessee. That's not much longer of a drive than he has now when he comes to see them."

"That'll work out nicely," Marcus noted. "One more reason Tennessee could be a wonderful home for you and the boys."

"You mean besides being with you every day?"

"Of course." Marcus grinned.

There was a knock at the door, and Marcus got up to see who it was. "Dinner's here," he announced.

Katherine moved the papers off the table and onto the bed while Marcus tipped the delivery girl and brought the insulated box to the table.

"That smells *so* good," Katherine said, inhaling the aroma of the food. She helped him take the individual containers out of the box and place them on the table. Marcus procured a couple of beverages from the mini-bar, and then he sat down and they began eating.

After dinner was done, and the empty containers put back in the box for easy disposal, Marcus asked, "Does it sound like we have a good plan for the next four months?"

"I think so. I can't wait to see your place, and I can't wait for the boys to meet you. I've got a good feeling about… well, everything."

"Me, too."

"How about we call the boys and let them meet you?" Katherine suggested.

Marcus nodded. "I'd like that. Are we going to tell them our plans?"

"Not yet," Katherine said. "I don't what to overload them on the first meeting. Let's just make this the introduction, and then we let them in on the plans later."

"Okay."

Katherine placed a video call on her phone to Greg and asked him to put the boys on. When their faces appeared, she said, "Boys, I want you to meet a friend of mine. His name is Marcus Buchanan—Marc—and he's the writer for my movie. He's the guy I told you two about. I've been talking about you two so much that he wanted to meet you."

Katherine angled the phone so the boys could see Marcus. "Marc, this is Jack and Ben."

"Hi, Jack. Hi, Ben."

"Hi, Mr. Buchanan," the boys said.

They chatted for a while, and then Katherine said, "Boy's, I know it's almost dinner time for you. I'll say goodnight. I love you both!"

"Love you, Mom," the boys said.

Katherine ended the call.

"They're great kids," Marcus said.

"Yes, they are. And now that they've met you, it'll be easier to talk to them about you."

As it grew later into the evening, Katherine didn't want to go back to her room, but she knew she had to.

"Don't worry," Marcus told her as he walked her to his door. "In less than two weeks, we'll be away from here in Tennessee, and we'll have ten days to do… *anything* that you want to do. Just be patient. You're going to be so busy for the next several days that time will fly."

They kissed, and Katherine held him tight for several minutes. When she finally pulled away, she said, "I love you, Marc."

"I love you, Kathy."

She left his room and walked back to her own room down the hall… and the large empty bed that she knew was going to feel even emptier that night.

When Marcus arrived on set the next morning, C.J. was meeting with Katherine, Derek Perkins, Sierra Blake, several extras, the lighting supervisor, the cinematographer, and the camera operators. Katherine had taken the shuttle from the hotel to the studio so she could be there early to rehearse the first of her new scenes with the other actors. She saw Marcus and winked at him as C.J. was explaining how he wanted the action to build in the scene.

Marcus found his chair, pulled a notebook and his copy of the script from his briefcase, and sat down so he could watch and listen. As he turned the pages of his script to the scene that C.J. was about to start shooting, he glanced at Katherine, and a thought started gnawing at him.

I love this girl, but something is holding her back. One minute we're having the time of our lives, and the next she's worried that her sons won't approve of me or want to live with me. And rather than identify ways to make things work in spite of the boys' disapproval or unwillingness to move, she's as much as said that what we have will come to an abrupt end, unless her sons are totally onboard with every aspect of our relationship. They seem to be great boys, and I know she puts her sons first and that their happiness is important to her—hell, EVERYTHING to her—and I get why that's so important. But I don't understanding being willing to sacrifice her... our happiness just to please her sons. Life is about compromises, life is about finding a way, it's not about absolutes... I want to convince her that I'm the right guy for her, but how can I when she's seems to be leaving the decisions about our future together in the hands of a nine-year-old and an eleven-year-old? I have nothing against her sons, but they don't have the same stake in this that she does, and yet they have the final say in what happens? Oh, well... I knew this from the beginning, so it's not like she just sprung it on me. But now that we've grown closer, and now that the film shoot is nearly over, there's not as much time left before we know what's going to happen with us. I just hope this doesn't turn out to be another Hollywood Romance and that I've been duped. I don't think she'd do that to me, or to herself, but I have too much emotion invested in this relationship to willingly walk away because of two children. She should be guiding them to make the right choice, not allowing them to make life-altering choices for someone else when they have no idea what's at stake for all concerned.

Marcus heard the snap of the clapperboard and heard C.J. call "Action!" Marcus shook his head and returned his focus to the script in his hand and the action taking place on the set in front of him.

A couple of hours later, during a break between takes, C.J. walked up to Marcus. "Those rewrites are perfect, Marc. The scenes flow better, and the story makes more sense. I think it'll have more audience appeal keeping Kathy's character alive until the end."

Marcus noticed that C.J. called him "Marc" when he was happy, and "Buchanan" when he was angry or frustrated. "I'm glad you like it, C.J. I just wish I'd written it this way from the beginning."

C.J. smiled broadly. "What's that old expression? It's not what you start with, it's what you end with. All that matters to me is the finished product. You did right by me and this production, and I'm pleased."

Marcus bowed his head at the compliment. "Thanks, C.J."

C.J. slapped Marcus' arm, then turned and yelled, "Let's rehearse the next scene and see if we can shoot at least one take before lunch!"

Katherine came to find him at the lunch break. He was sitting at one of the picnic tables outside, making notes in the margins of his script. She sat across from him, trying not to disturb his train of thought.

Even though September was normally a warm month in Atlanta, chilly winds were blowing in from the north, making it feel more like late October. Katherine was wearing a sweater to keep her arms warm as she ate.

She was nearly finished with her soup when Marcus finally put his pen down and looked up. "Hi, Kathy! How long have you been sitting there?"

"Long enough to eat half a sandwich and almost a whole cup of soup."

Marcus looked embarrassed. "I'm sorry. I was so involved in what I was doing that I tuned out everything else."

"What are you working on?" she asked, pointing to the script.

"Oh, well, I don't know if I mentioned it, but whenever I write an original script that gets made into a film, I have the exclusive rights to create and publish the novel of that script. I try to keep the book and what's on the screen as close as possible, although scenes that end up on the cutting room floor are often still in the book because the book has to be finished before the film edit is, if the production company wants to use the book as part of the marketing campaign. There was some great acting this morning, and I wanted to jot down what I remembered so I'll know how to novelize the scenes later."

"When is the novel due?" asked Katherine.

"I have to have it to my editors in early December."

"That soon?"

Marcus smiled. "I'll let you in on a little secret. I stay up late every night writing out the scenes that were shot that day. I'll have the first draft finished while I'm on my book tour in October, but I always like to review it a few times before I send it in. That way I can make sure that I've assembled all the pieces of the book the same way they'll be assembled in the film. The transition between scenes is just as critical in the book as it is on the screen. I use shortcuts to make the writing process go faster, but it can be nerve-wracking trying to sync the script with the director's vision and the actors' performances."

"Will I get a copy of *The Spy Upstairs* when it comes out?" Katherine asked.

"Autographed first edition," promised Marcus.

Katherine finished her lunch. Then she looked at Marcus with her head cocked to one side. "Are you mad at me?"

"Heavens, no! Why would you ask that?"

Katherine took a deep breath. "You seem a little distant," she said. "You hardly looked at me this morning, and usually you never take your eyes off of me."

Marcus hesitated. He didn't want to accidently trigger a fight, but he didn't want to be anything but completely honest. "It's not that I'm mad, it's just that… your recurring angst has started causing *me* some angst, and I'm wrestling with it. That's all."

Katherine's smile faded. "I'm sorry. I knew I was dumping a lot on you, but you never said anything. I guess I should have kept it to myself."

Marcus reached across the table and took her hand. "No, I'm glad you feel comfortable enough to share your feelings with me. I don't want you to feel like you're going through any of this all by yourself. I'll always want you to let me share your burdens. It's just that, every now and then, it may stir up doubts or uncertainty in me, and it takes a while for me to process it. That doesn't mean I want you to ever hold back from telling me things, but it may mean that I need time to understand it's impact on me and come up with a plan to overcome it."

"A plan to overcome it?" Katherine said, surprised.

"As I've said before, obstacles aren't absolutes. They're

just roadblocks to be overcome. All obstacles or setbacks are just a test of our resolve and our ingenuity. They're not to be feared, they're to be conquered. I like to plan my attack so I can overcome them quickly and completely before moving on to more important things."

Katherine's shoulders slumped. "I've never learned how to do that."

"And that may be the biggest difference between us," Marcus noted. "You seem to look at obstacles as the answer, and you use them as a hard stop to end whatever they're interfering with. I look at obstacles as something to go around, go over, go through, or… some other way of overcoming them and moving past them. They're not an answer, they're an inconvenience. That's why I think of them as a test, and I hate failing tests."

Katherine nodded. "So, what angst are you wresting with because of me?"

Marcus was silent for a moment. Then he said, "I understand your desire to put the needs of your sons first. I do. But do you think that letting them have the final say in what happens with us is the right way to decide the fate of our relationship? They're too young to understand what's at stake, and any decision they make not only affects your life, it affects mine, and that makes me a little uneasy."

"Do you know how many kids in our neighborhood are left alone or in the company of strangers all day because their parents are too busy with their own lives and careers? I don't want my sons to grow up like that. I want them to know that they come first so they feel like they're important and are part of a loving family, not a household of strangers."

"I get that," Marcus stated. "But isn't there a… a happy medium between showing them that they come first and allowing them to dictate the rest of *your* life… *and* mine?"

"I'm sure there is," Katherine acknowledged, "but I haven't found it yet; and until I do, I need to err on the side of my kids."

Marcus held up his hands in surrender. "Okay, okay. All I ask is that you remember there are more people involved than just the three of you when it comes time to make your final decision. And keep this in mind. I know what I want, and it's you, and no obstacle is going to keep me from being with you, making you happy, and letting myself be happy. You may feel like you need to walk away because of the boys, but don't expect me to willingly do the same. I'm willing to fight for you… for us. I'm not going to let you go easily."

A tear appeared in the corner of Katherine's eye as she squeezed his hand. "I want to kiss you so badly right now. I guess that's a bad idea, though."

"Not a bad idea at all, just the wrong timing. Come to my room tonight, and I'll order dinner in. I promise you can kiss me all you want once we're alone."

"But eventually I'll have to leave," Katherine lamented.

"I have some thoughts about that, too. I'll share them with you tonight."

Katherine faked being indignant. "What? You're going to make we wait until tonight?"

"Why not?" Marcus responded with a twinkle in his eye. "You were going to make we wait until after filming the movie is over in two weeks. I'm only asking you to wait for six hours. I think you're getting off easy, don't you?"

Katherine pouted playfully. "Fine."

Marcus was about to say something when the bell rang, summoning the cast and crew back to the set to resume filming.

Katherine arrived at Marcus' room a few minutes after he texted her that he was there. She was wearing her jean shorts, a halter-top, and a long-sleeve shirt tied in the front with the sleeves rolled up.

"Come in," he said when he opened the door.

"What's for dinner?" she asked once she was inside.

"I haven't ordered dinner yet," Marcus replied. "I will, but I wanted to share an idea with you first."

Katherine sat on the edge of the bed. "Okay, shoot."

Marcus turned off all the lights except for the small light above the door. "Take off your clothes."

"Marc, we can't do that. We've talked about this. Someone will hear us and know what we're doing, and we don't need the gossip!"

"Let me put your mind at ease about that," Marcus said, kneeling in front of her and removing her shoes. "First, this is a corner room. The stairs are across the hall, and the two rooms next to the stairs are vacant as of this morning. The people in those rooms wrapped just before noon, and I saw the limo pick them up to take them to the airport."

He untied the long-sleeve shirt and slid it off her shoulder. "Second, the assistant director in the room next to me is out for the evening and won't return until after midnight. She's having a girl's night somewhere downtown."

He removed his shirt and tugged at the snap and zipper of her shorts. "Third, this is the hotel's top floor, so there's no one above us."

He pulled her shorts off and tossed them onto a chair with her shirt. "Fourth, the room downstairs is also vacant, and will be for the next two weeks. You see, I booked it when I found out the occupant had also wrapped and had left for the airport."

He stood and removed his pants. Next, he removed her halter, exposing her bare breasts. "So you see, no one will hear a thing. No one will know what we're doing. And even if the person next door comes back early, her bathroom and closet, and my bathroom and closet, are both along the adjoining wall, creating a sound break between her bed and this bed. She won't hear a thing, no matter what sounds we're making."

He removed his shorts, and then knelt down again and removed her panties, kissing her inner thighs and letting his tongue teased her for a minute. He stopped and looked up at her. "Any questions?"

She put her hands around his head and pushed it back down so he could continue what he had been doing. "What are you waiting for?"

Marcus needed no encouragement. He soon had Katherine trembling. Lying prostrate, she arched her back and clutched the edge of the bed with both hands to keep herself in place as the first climax hit. She let out a high-pitched squeal of delight as her stomach muscles spasmed. When she was certain that she couldn't take much more, Marcus stood, turned her over until she was on her hands and knees at the edge of the bed, and penetrated her deeply while still standing. He climaxed soon after, but he never stopped.

Marcus grabbed the bed covers and yanked them out of the way. After pushing her gently toward the center of the bed, so he could join her on the bed without losing the connection, he reached around her waist, lifted her up, and turned over so she was on top, facing away from him. She spun around to face him, keeping the connection intact, and she began raising up and lowering back down at a frenzied pace as she climaxed again and again.

They made love for the next two hours without stopping once, even though both had climaxed multiple times by then. When they finally broke the connection, they were exhausted, but deeply satisfied.

"My God, I'm still shaking," Katherine's voice quivered. "How are you able to keep doing that for so long?"

"Let's just say I was highly motivated," Marcus said softly. "And I think we both needed this tonight, don't you?"

"Yes! But I don't think I can walk."

Marcus chuckled. "Then I'll carry you to the tub and let you soak for a while. While you're bathing, I'll order dinner and take a quick shower. By the time the food arrives, there won't be any evidence of what we've done… except for the sheets." He sat up. "How do you like the water? Warm, medium, or hot?"

"Medium-hot, please."

"And what do you want to eat?"

"Surprise me," Katherine answered.

Marcus went into the bathroom and started the water running in the tub. He added some of the bubble bath provided by the hotel, and then returned to the bed. He put his arms underneath Katherine, picked her up, and carried her into the bathroom. He gently deposited her into the tub and gave her a kiss. Then he returned to the bedroom, made the bed, and brought Katherine's and his clothes into the bathroom.

After he ordered dinner, he turned on the shower faucet, grateful that his room had a shower separate from the freestanding tub.

Katherine was still in the tub when he exited the shower and started drying himself. "Do you need help getting out?" he asked.

"I think so," she replied. "Do you mind?"

"Of course not. Can you open the drain?"

Katherine opened the drain, and the water level in the tub began dropping. Marcus grabbed two towels from the shelf next to the shower. He handed one to Katherine so she could wipe the suds off her front. He took the second towel and slid it underneath her. He reached down and picked her up, taking her over to the vanity counter where there was a stool. When she was seated, he helped her finish toweling off, and then he helped her get dressed. Once her clothes were back on, he carried her to the other room and placed her into a chair at the table. He quickly dressed and joined her.

"I don't remember you being unable to walk this past weekend," he said with amusement.

"That's because I didn't have to get up right after we finished," she remarked. "Believe me, I was in the same boat then as I am now. It'll be a while before the legs start working normally again. You have no idea what all that trembling and spasming does to a girl. It's like being at the gym, using every piece of equipment non-stop for most of the day."

Marcus grinned. "So… you're saying that I'm a great workout routine?"

"The best!"

There was a knock at the door. Marcus got up to see who it was. He returned a minute later with the food. "I wasn't sure if you wanted something heavy or not, so I got us something light for tonight. I hope that's okay."

Katherine nodded, looking inside the insulated container at what he'd ordered. "Fried chicken and mashed potatoes is light? What do you call heavy?"

"Hey, I also have roast chicken if you don't want good southern fried chicken," he pointed out. "And don't forget… you said you wanted me to surprise you."

"I did say that, didn't I? What's in these containers?" She asked, holding up two large cups.

"Green beans and coleslaw."

Katherine looked inside one of the containers and laughed. "These aren't green beans. They're flat."

"So?"

"Green beans are round. These are called these Italian-Style Beans."

Marcus chuckled. "Growing up down here, the flat beans were called Green Beans, and the round ones were called Pole Beans. I never knew that the rest of the world didn't call them that until I moved up north and got laughed at."

After all the food was on the table, Katherine sighed happily and said, "Thanks for tonight, Marc, and thanks for suggesting and helping me with the bath. I feel clean and tingly all at the same time."

Marcus caressed the back of her hand. "Happy to."

After they had eaten and cleaned away the serving containers and plates, they sat together on the couch. "I want to stay here tonight," Katherine said.

"I was hoping you'd say that," Marcus said. "But if you're worried that someone will see you leave my room in the morning, I'll set the alarm for early, so you'll have time to sneak back to your room before anyone else is up and around."

"Good thinking," Katherine said sleepily. "Any chance you're ready for bed now?"

Marcus smiled. "I assume you're referring to sleep and not anything else."

Katherine nodded. "Sleep. Anything else will have to wait until I recover from tonight."

Chapter 6

Katherine woke to the sound of the alarm clock on the nightstand. She hit the off-button and looked at the time. *Four-thirty? Well, there shouldn't be anyone up to see me heading back to my room.*

She was about to give Marcus a kiss when she smelled something. *That smells like coffee brewing.* She looked over and saw that Marcus wasn't in bed with her. She sat up and saw him at the mini-bar, making coffee for her.

"Good morning," she said.

"Good morning, Sweetheart. Sleep well?"

"Wonderfully," she replied, throwing off the covers and getting out of bed. She was wearing the panties and halter she had worn the night before. Her shirt and shorts were in her chair at the table. She stretched for a minute, then got dressed. When she joined Marcus, he gave her a kiss and handed her a cup of coffee.

"That was sweet of you. Thanks!" Katherine sipped her coffee, enjoying the feeling of the hot liquid running down her throat.

"Any time," Marcus said. "Feeling better this morning?"

"I. Feel. Wonderful!"

"Not sore or anything?"

"Not any more. But last night was a different matter altogether."

"You should go if you want to make sure you're not seen leaving. Some of the technical crewmembers head for the studio early. In fact, you should take the stairs to the lobby and come back up on the elevator. With that cup of coffee in your hand, no one will suspect a thing."

"You're so smart," Katherine purred. "Good plan. See you at breakfast?"

"Can't wait. I'll probably get dressed and go camp out in the lobby to do some writing until you come down. This time of day, it's just as quiet down there as it is here."

"I'll meet you down there." Katherine gave him a kiss and headed for the door. Marcus stuck his head into the hallway. Seeing no one, he gestured for Katherine to head for the stairs racross the hall. She whispered, "Don't forget your phone," before she crept out and then disappeared through the door across from Marcus' room. Marcus waited until the door to the stairs closed all the way before returning to his room to get dressed, grab his phone and briefcase, and go downstairs.

Over the next week, Katherine and Marcus continued their clandestine rendezvous in Marcus' suite. Whether they ate in his room or at one of the local restaurants, Katherine always took the stairs from the lobby to their floor and waited just behind the door until Marcus signaled that the coast was clear. The next morning, she'd exit the same way. So far, they had they received no strange looks from any of the cast and crewmembers staying at the hotel.

With the shooting schedule intensifying for the final week of filming, they had less time together, but they knew they'd be spending ten days together in Tennessee starting at the end of the week. Katherine had to be in Hair & Make-up well before dawn each day, and shooting ran until after nine each night.

Katherine was loving her new scenes. As the cast rehearsed the scene where Derek's character killed Sierra's character, and Katherine's character killed Derek's character, there was a touch of sadness as the cast knew that this was the final scene involving all of them. There was one additional scene left to film, and it involved only Katherine and a group of extras.

The cast rehearsed under the watchful eye of C.J. When he was satisfied that they knew what to do, and the stunt coordinator was convinced that no one would get hurt, C.J. decided it was time to see how it looked through the cameras. Once the assistant holding clapperboard was out of view, C.J. called, "Action!"

Derek knelt on the catwalk, attaching the detonator to the bomb. The catwalk was only four feet off the ground and surrounded by mats, but in post-production, the scene would be edited to look like the catwalk was five stories above a huge room filled with vats of combustible hyper-cooled liquids.

Katherine and Sierra approached Derek from his blind side, but he heard the deck plate of the catwalk rattle and leaped up. Seeing Katherine, he appeared to backhand her across the face, knocking her down—and onto a mat that kept her from getting injured. She pretended to be stunned. Sierra rushed forward, drawing her weapon, and she and Derek struggled. Sierra lost her grip on her pistol, and it bounced off the catwalk and fell to the floor below. As Derek got the upper hand in their struggle and threw Sierra over the railing—and onto the mats just out of view of the camera—he didn't see Katherine get up and rush at him. She picked up a prop wrench from Derek's toolkit and appeared to strike him in the back of his head. He slumped forward, but then he straightened and spun around. Katherine appeared to hit him again across the side of his head, and he stumbled. She moved closer, and he grabbed the wrench. As he tore it from her grip, he stood over her and raised his hand. Still in a bent-over position, Katherine grabbed his knees and yanked. He lost his balance, and flailing wildly, pitched backwards over the railings—and onto the mats close to where Sierra had landed.

"Cut!" C.J. shouted. He looked over to the camera operators, and they each gave C.J. a thumbs-up. C.J. had the video monitors rewind the scene so he could watch it again. Four cameras caught the action, and C.J. was pleased. "Print! That was perfect! Let's set up for the last scene."

The last scene, which had no dialogue, was Katherine sitting on the rear deck of an ambulance, being checked out by paramedics as police officers questioned her. C.J. filmed the scene in the soundstage parking lot, surrounded by police cars with their lights flashing red and blue in the setting sunlight. The camera pulled back, taking the close-up of Katherine's face to a wide shot. On cue, four coroner's assistants took out two stretchers with body bags on them, and then a bomb squad technician in full protective gear brought out an oversized milk can-looking container. The camera continued pulling back.

C.J. leaped up from his chair. "Cut! Print! That's a wrap, everybody! Get cleaned up and out of those costumes, and we'll meet back on the soundstage in an hour."

The cast and crew applauded. Then the cast headed for Hair & Make-up, while the technical crew began moving the sound, lighting, and camera equipment back inside. The rest of the crew either moved the police and emergency vehicles back to the parking lot or helped prepare the last remaining set for the wrap party.

When Marcus returned to the set, he packed up his script and notebook. Then he removed the back of his canvas folding chair—which had the production logo, the name of the film, and the word "Writer" stitched on the back—and put it in his briefcase as a souvenir of his work on the film. After he put his briefcase on what was left of his chair, he helped the rest of the crew move the catwalk and padded mats out of the way for the party.

The caterers arrived and began bringing in champagne, water, and finger foods for the party. They had just completed setting up when the last cast members arrived on the soundstage.

"What a great film shoot, everyone!" C.J. began. "I needed all of you to bring your A-Game, and you did. We worked hard, we had fun, and now the post-production work begins, turning all of your hard efforts into a finished product that you can all be proud of. But no matter how the audience reacts when they see what we've created, I want you to know how proud I am of all of you. Specifically, our wonderful leads, Derek, Sierra, *and* Katherine." Everyone applauded. "Our fantastic writer, Marcus." Again, everyone applauded. "And our amazing crew." C.J. singled out the department heads for photography, lighting, sound, production design, Hair & Make-Up, costume design, transportation, the stunt coordinator, as well as the producers, assistant directors, and second unit directors. The applause for these crewmembers went on for a while, and then C.J. thanked the catering company, which brought the loudest applause and cheers from the cast and crew.

C.J. continued. "I know some of you are leaving tonight, some are leaving tomorrow, and some are staying through the weekend to help break down the set and return the equipment. There will be airport shuttles leaving from here and the hotel every day, and the schedules will be posted in the hotel lobby. Okay. That's the last of the public service announcements. Let's get this party started!"

At that moment, Trish—accompanied by one of the caterers and one of the other production assistants—wheeled out a large cart with a huge cake on it. The top of the cake was decorated with the logo of the production. Trish handed C.J. a cake slicer, and he cut the first piece. The caterer took the cutter and began cutting the rest of the cake. Trish and the other assistant began handing out the cake slices.

Once Marcus and Katherine had their slices, they moved closer to each other. "Ready for tomorrow?" he asked.

"You bet," she replied. "I'm almost all packed. What time are we leaving in the morning?"

"How early do you want to get on the road?" Marcus asked.

"Before rush hour?" Katherine suggested.

Marcus nodded. "Can you be ready by six? That'll get us to my place just after eight."

"I'll be ready."

C.J. walked over with a champagne glass in his hand. He kissed Katherine on the cheek. "Great job, Kathy! You rolled with the changes and turned in a great performance. Thanks for being willing to expand your role. I hope we work together again."

"Thank you C.J.! I loved working with you on this film. We definitely need to do another one or two… or five."

C.J. turned to Marcus and gave him a hug. "Now I see why everyone loves working with you, Marc. The original script was great, the changes were great, and I think this is going to be another top-grossing film, if not an award-winner, to your credit. The next time you're in L.A., let's chat. I have an idea I'd like to talk to you about."

Marcus nodded with a smile. "You have my agent's number. Give her a call, and she'll get it set up."

C.J. nodded. "I will." Trish walked up, and he put his arm around her waist. As they started to walk away, C.J. turned back with a sly grin. "Have fun, you two." Trish giggled, and then they were gone, chatting with members of the cast and crew.

Marcus and Katherine looked at him walking away with their mouths open. "How did he know?" Katherine whispered.

Marcus shook his head. "I'm sure he saw the photo of us kissing, but I'll bet it was Trish. I caught her at the ice machine one night wearing nothing but one of C.J. T-shirts. It was obvious what they had been doing, and I couldn't resist baiting her. I'll bet she watched me like a hawk after that and saw us coming back to the hotel all the times we ate dinner together. Wouldn't have been too hard to figure out what we were up to."

"Do you think she told anyone besides C.J.?" Katherine asked.

"I doubt it," Marcus replied. "C.J. knows how gossip can ruin a film shoot. He wouldn't tolerate *anything* that could damage the film, and she knows that. I don't doubt that he had the tabloid story about us squashed. She'll keep her mouth closed as long as C.J. is making her happy."

"And if C.J. and Trish were just having a Hollywood Romance?"

"Then we'll be in the tabloids and on the Hollywood gossip shows before the premier," Marcus stated.

They stayed at the party for another hour, talking to the cast and crew who were still there. When Marcus drove them back to the hotel, they were both so full from the food provided by the caterers that they didn't want dinner.

When he parked the car, he said, "There's really no reason to keep up appearances, is there? Why don't we grab your things out of your room and bring them to my room now? We'll spend the night and leave in the morning."

"Are you sure?" Katherine asked.

"Absolutely," Marcus said.

"Okay, I accept."

They walked into the lobby, and Marcus saw one of the brass luggage carts parked next to the concierge desk. He grabbed it and maneuvered it onto the elevator. When they reached the top floor, he wheeled it to Katherine's room.

He loaded her already-packed bags onto the cart while she grabbed the rest of her things, threw them into a couple of plastic laundry bags from the closet, and then did a quick inspection to make sure she hadn't missed anything.

"All set?" Marcus asked.

"All set," Katherine confirmed.

Marcus wheeled the cart out of the room and down the hall to his room. Once he had arranged her bags in his closet, he said, "I'll take the cart downstairs and be right back. Make yourself at home."

He rolled the empty cart to the elevator, rode down to the lobby, and returned the cart to the concierge desk. When he returned to his room, the lights were off, except for the one over the door. "Kathy?" he said.

"In here," came the reply.

He closed the door and followed the sound of her voice. When he rounded the corner, he saw that the bed covers had already been turned down, and Katherine was standing next to the bed wearing nothing but a bath towel. She walked toward him and put her arms around his neck.

"I made myself at home," she purred.

She kissed him, and they held the embrace for a while. Then Katherine began undressing him. He helped, and after the last article of his clothing was on the floor, he removed her towel, picked her up, and carried her back to the bed.

"Welcome home."

When Katherine woke up the next morning, Marcus had already showered, dressed, and was loading a brass luggage cart with his bags and her bags. When he noticed that she was awake, he said. "I was hoping I wouldn't wake you."

"You didn't," Katherine said. She got out of bed and walked over to him, giving him a kiss.

Marcus ran his hands along the curves of her bare skin. "Why don't you hop in the shower while I take the bags down and load up the car?"

"Okay."

She grabbed the clothes she wanted to wear from her bag on the luggage cart. As she headed for the bathroom, she wiggled her behind and giggled.

Marcus took the bags downstairs and loaded them into the back of his SUV. Once he had them arranged so that they wouldn't shift, he locked the vehicle and returned the luggage cart to the concierge desk.

By the time he got back to his room, Katherine was out of the shower and drying herself.

"Nice view," Marcus commented, walking past the bathroom door.

"Why, thank you, kind sir," she said with her best Southern accent.

Marcus laughed as he finished packing his briefcase and started looking for anything left behind. Satisfied that everything was accounted for, he put his briefcase by the door and looked in on Katherine. She was already dressed in jeans and a T-shirt, and she was running a brush through her hair before packing the last of her toiletries into her travel case. "All packed," she said as she put the case next to Marcus' bag and slipped on her deck shoes.

Marcus just stared at her, and she finally asked, "Why are you staring?"

"Because you don't have on any make-up, other than lip gloss, and your hair isn't styled, and yet you're the most beautiful woman I've ever seen. How can one person have so much natural beauty?"

Katherine blushed. "You even like my freckles?"

"I *love* your freckles. I love everything about you. I could stare at you all day and not grow tired of the view."

Katherine kissed him, and Marcus slid his arms around her and pulled her close. After a minute, he whispered, "If we don't stop, we won't get home until after lunch."

"Okay." Katherine pulled back and gazed into his eyes. "But you owe me a raincheck."

Marcus grinned. "And in a few hours, I'll cash in that raincheck…"

He grabbed the two bags by the door, and they rode the elevator down to the lobby. It was ten minutes before six when Katherine stopped at the coffee bar to fix herself a large cup. Marcus grabbed a bottle of water and dropped the keycards to his two rooms and Katherine's room off at the front desk. Then they walked together to his car.

Once they were in the car, Marcus took out his cell phone and called a number. "Grant, it's Marc. I'm leaving this message at six o'clock on Thursday morning. I'm just now leaving Norcross, and I should be home by eight-thirty, depending on the I-24 traffic. I emailed the grocery list for Mariana yesterday, and she should be at the house before I get there. If she's not, call me, and I'll grab breakfast before I arrive. Oh, and don't forget, I'm bringing a house guest with me, and she'll be there until next weekend. Anyway, that's all I can think of at the moment. Let me know when you get this message, and I'll see you later this morning. Bye."

Marcus pulled out of the hotel parking lot and headed for the Buford Highway to I-285 west.

"Who are Grant and Mariana?" Katherine asked.

"Grant Billings is my estate manager," Marcus explained. "With me being gone for weeks at a time, I don't like the house just sitting empty. He manages the landscaping crew that comes once a week, the housekeeping crew that comes twice a week, and Mariana Perez, my cook, who comes five days a week when I'm in town and does all the grocery shopping. His office is opposite the garages, and it's the security center for the estate. In addition to his other qualifications, he has extensive experience in private security."

"Isn't that expensive?"

Marcus nodded. "Yes, but if you're going to live in a house that big, you'd better be able to afford the upkeep and the staff it takes to keep it pristine."

"When do the housekeepers come?"

"Mondays and Thursdays, but I had them come yesterday, instead, so they wouldn't bother us until after the weekend."

"And Mariana does your cooking?"

"Except for weekends, unless I'm throwing a party and need her. I'm actually a good cook, so she makes sure I have enough things to eat during the weekend, and then she's there on weekdays. Sometimes, I get so busy that I forget to eat. She makes sure that doesn't happen. She's one of the reasons directors like to have retreats at my place."

"What?" Katherine sounded intrigued.

"When a director wants me to write a script for him, it's hard for us to stay focused for the weeks it takes to refine the initial ideas into a draft script that can be taken to the studios to green-light the project. There are too many distractions in Hollywood. A lot of directors have cabins in Montana or Utah where they can go to focus. But after word got out about Mariana's cooking, and because my place is whole lot more interesting and comfortable than some remote cabin in the woods, I host them for… oh, anywhere from two to four weeks as we brainstorm ideas, draft key scenes, and complete the first draft of the script. Obviously, the script continues to get refined as the studio makes changes, the producers make changes, and A-List actors who get cast in the project demand changes."

"Who have you had to your house to work on these projects?" Katherine asked.

As Marcus took the I-75 north exit, he told her the directors, producers, and even actors who had stayed at the house before.

"I can't believe you've had all those people stay at your home," Katherine said.

"Some of them have stayed multiple times," Marcus said.

"It's part of the service I offer, beyond just writing a script for them. It's why I'm more expensive than most writers, but the directors and the studios seem to think I'm worth it, even if the Screenwriter's Guild thinks my rates are too high. Besides, it helps pay for my home."

"And you still find time to write novels?"

"Writing isn't hard. I can crank out a first draft in less than a month. It's the research and thinking about the book that can take twelve to eighteen months. Some ideas come to me completely formed, but that's rare. It usually takes a while for the ideas to percolate before I can start writing, and once I start, I can draft it quickly. Then it goes to my editors while I start work on my next project. It really is a full-time job. You'll understand when you see my office at the house."

Katherine finished her coffee and leaned back in her seat, enjoying the scenery as they drove through northern Georgia toward the Tennessee border. Shortly before crossing the border, Grant returned Marcus' call and confirmed that he got the message and that everything was ready for their arrival.

Katherine loved the change in landscape as they drove into the Appalachian Mountains. Ninety minutes after getting on I-75, Marcus took the exit for I-24 west and headed for Chattanooga. Traffic in Chattanooga wasn't bad when they reached the city, and soon they were past downtown, snaking along the Tennessee River, past Lookout Mountain, to the ridges on the eastern face of Raccoon Mountain.

Marcus exited I-24 and headed northwest. They drove through two neighborhoods filled with mansions, but Marcus kept going. After several minutes, he turned west off the road and approached a huge gate. Marcus pressed a button on the center console of the SUV, and the gate opened. "We're here," he said as he drove through the gate. "Welcome to Buchanan Manor."

Chapter 7

Katherine sat up in her seat so she wouldn't miss the view. The driveway headed up to the top of a ridge and wound down the other side. The trees were so thick that she couldn't see anything else. Then she saw the clearing ahead. As they got closer, she saw the house. When they reached the clearing and left the trees behind them, Katherine's jaw dropped.

The house that Katherine had seen in the online photos sat in the center of a large open space in front of her, but those photos hadn't prepared her for what she saw with her own eyes. The house was immense, and it had an all-stone exterior with bay windows along the ground level and multiple chimneys sticking up along the roof. An archway to the right led to the guest parking and the garages, and in the center of the circular drive leading to the front door were the two cannons she had heard so much about. Between them stood the flagpole, with a massive American flag flying at the top.

"Why don't we enter through the front door so I can give you a proper tour," Marcus suggested. "We'll use the garage entrance later."

"Okay," Katherine said, still in awe of the scene in front of her.

Marcus parked the SUV, turned off the engine, and came around to Katherine's side. He opened her door and helped her out. He pointed at two cars parked on the other side of the archway to their right. "Grant and Mariana are here already." He pushed a button on one of the remotes hanging on his keychain, "But just in case they left the alarm on…"

Marcus unlocked and opened the front door, which was a massive four-inch-thick oak door that was as wide as two doors and had large iron bands that appeared to connect to the hinges. Katherine would have thought that a door that heavy would be hard to open, but it swung open effortlessly and silently.

Katherine stepped inside… and into another world.

The entry was a two-story cavernous space that ran the full depth of the home from the front door to the fireplace in the center of the back wall. Exposed beams arched over the space like the ceiling of a gothic cathedral. Two massive, curved staircases—one on either side—framed the entryway. These curled up to a bridge in the center, spanning the width of the space and connecting the north wing and the south wing of the second floor. The entryway, and the foyer between the stairs, had marble floors, and there was an inlaid compass rose design in the center of the foyer, which showed that the front of the house faced east.

Past the stairs was a large, formal sitting area, with a massive fireplace in the center of the far wall, flanked by two-story windows overlooking the pool and the backyard. The flooring of the sitting area was hardwood covered with an oversized Persian rug. Two round casual dining tables sat in front of the windows, surrounded by chairs.

There was so much to see just in the entryway that Katherine didn't know where to look first. But she smelled something cooking, and her stomach began rumbling.

"Let's check on breakfast first, and then I can show you the rest of the house," Marcus suggested. "The tour could take quite some time."

Katherine just nodded and followed Marcus through the foyer and the sitting area. The kitchen was to the right of the sitting area in the north wing of the house. Standing in front of a massive double gas range and oven combination was an attractive older Hispanic woman. She turned when she saw Marcus and Katherine.

"Welcome home, Mr. Marc," she said with a beautiful accent. She looked at Katherine. "And welcome to the Manor House, Miss Katherine. I've seen several of your films, but you are even more beautiful in person than Mr. Marc described." She gestured to the stools along the island across from the range. "Please, sit. Breakfast will be ready in..." she glanced at the timer, "two minutes. Coffee?"

"Yes, please," Katherine said, taking a seat at the island.

"None—"

"Yes, I know, Mr. Marc. No coffee for you. Orange juice."

"Thanks, Mariana."

Marcus smiled as Mariana brought over a large mug of piping hot coffee and a tankard filled with orange juice.

"Mariana is from Caracas, Venezuela," Marcus explained. "She and her husband had one of the finest restaurants in the city, but when he passed seven years ago, she sold it and retired."

"But I got bored," Mariana interjected.

"Right," Marcus continued. "So, she started catering parties. That's how we met. Leigh, my late wife, fell in love with her cooking and asked if she'd be interested in being a private chef. Mariana agreed, and she's been working here ever since."

"And if you stayed here more, Mr. Marc, I could feed you more," Mariana said as she took the fresh-baked pastries out of the oven. She drizzled icing on them, placed them on a platter, and set the platter down in front of Katherine and Marcus. "All the restaurant food you eat... it's no good. You need more home cooked food."

Mariana handed Katherine and Marcus plates, utensils, and linen napkins. "How do you like your eggs, Miss Katherine?"

"Kathy, please, Mariana. Any way is fine for me."

Mariana nodded. Then she looked at Marcus. "Your usual, Mr. Marc?"

"Yes. For both of us," Marcus said.

Mariana smiled and began preparing the eggs.

"What's the usual?" Katherine asked, taking one of the pastries and placing it on her plate.

"Ham and cheese omelet," Marcus replied. "But believe me when I tell you that she can prepare *anything*, anyway you want it."

Katherine had finished the first pastry and was reaching for a second when Mariana slid the omelet onto her plate. Then Mariana started working on Marcus' omelet.

Katherine took a bite. "Oh, my God, this is wonderful! Thank you, Mariana!"

"You're welcome, Miss Kathy," Mariana said as she cooked.

"I should warn you," Marcus said. "We're going to have to do a lot of hiking while you're here. Mariana's cooking is very healthy, but there's so much of it that you can't help putting on weight."

"Eating is a celebration of life," Mariana said, bringing Marcus his omelet. "It is an expression of love. You don't want to skimp on love, do you Mr. Marc?"

"Of course not, Mariana. Of course not."

As Mariana started cleaning the kitchen, Katherine finished her breakfast and looked around. The kitchen was immense. The island could seat six, and had a large triple sink in the center. Katherine realized that the dishwasher must also be in the island, after seeing Mariana place the dirty dishes below the countertop. All of the counters were tan granite, and the cabinets were all dark oak. The huge refrigerator and freezer unit was covered in the same paneling as the cabinets. There appeared to be a butler's pantry past the stove on the left, and the vent hood over the stove matched the shape of the fireplace in the sitting area.

Katherine spun around and looked out the windows covering the back of the house. She saw the pool house and pool, and she saw the manicured lawn stretching back to the tree line west of the house.

"How large is the clearing around the house?" she asked.

"About two acres," Marcus replied.

Katherine looked past the kitchen at what appeared to be the den, filled with russet leather chairs and couches. The entertainment center filled the far wall, where the fireplace was, and the largest TV Katherine had ever seen was just above the mantle. The room was decorated with nautical paintings and furnishings.

As Katherine looked back to the sitting area, she saw that the nautical theme seemed to run throughout the house. The painting above the sitting area fireplace, which was at least seven feet high, was of a lighthouse with a sunset in the background.

"I'm detecting a nautical theme for this house," she said to Marcus.

"Everywhere but in my office," Marcus confirmed. "Leigh loved all things nautical, so I decorated this floor of the house for her. The art upstairs is mostly traditional landscapes—English, Scottish, Welsh, and Irish. I hope you like the decor."

"I love it. It seems perfect for the style of the house."

"Medieval royal hunting lodge?"

Katherine laughed. "Well, now that you mention it…"

"That's what the original owner was going for, but he also wanted a house that would last forever. He went a little nuts making this the most durable and safe home possible. That front door? It's not solid oak, and the iron bands are purely decorative. The front door is steel with an oak veneer. Granted, the oak is over an inch thick on the inside and outside of the door, but the core is almost two inches of steel. It can stop most projectiles fired from a gun, it cannot be rammed open when locked, and any explosive charge strong enough to put a dent in it would also obliterate the entire entryway of the house."

"Why did he want that?"

"No clue," admitted Marcus. "The house isn't wood framed. It's steel framed, and the foundation goes way down into the ground. This house can withstand a direct hit from an F4/F5 tornado, a Category 4 or 5 hurricane, and an earthquake of at least 8.0 in magnitude. All of the floor and ceiling support beams are steel. The stone facing on the outside is four inches thick, the underlay is twice as thick as normal, the outer walls are all filled with fire resistant and mold resistant spray-foam, the wood framing on the inside to hold up the drywall and wood paneling is wrapped and spray-foamed, and the drywall is double thick and mold and fire retardant. All of the inside walls, ceilings, and floors, are also spray foam filled, making every room just as insulated as the exterior, in addition to being virtually soundproof. If you're downstairs, you cannot hear what's happening upstairs, no matter how loudly someone is walking or playing music or watching television. With the exception of the entry and foyer, all of the rooms have hardwood floors covered in rugs. There's no carpeting, except in the theatre downstairs. And even though the windows all look like hand-blown glass, that's just the inside layer. Those are triple-thick storm windows that are fire retardant and impact resistant. Believe me, the house is like a fortress."

"And the original owner just died?" Katherine asked.

Marcus nodded. "The first floor was almost finished, and the second floor had been started. The north wing was done, but I was able to make some changes to the south wing, where my office and bedroom are located. And I also axed much of what was planned for the backyard because it was just too much. As it is, this house is too much for one person, but Leigh and I put so much into it when we furnished it that I can't part with it. I'm hoping it'll be filled with more people someday…"

Marcus stood. "So, where do you want to start the tour? Do you want to start down and work up, start up and work down, or see the rest of the house and save this floor for last?"

"Let's save this floor for last."

"Okay. Let's start downstairs."

As Marcus led Katherine to the basement stairs, which were right underneath the stairs leading up to the second floor, a rugged, ex-military-looking man entered the front door. "Good morning, Boss!"

"Good morning, Grant. Meet Katherine Delaney. Kathy, this is Grant Billings, my estate manager."

"Pleased to meet you, ma'am," Grant said.

"Likewise," Katherine said, shaking his hand.

"Boss, do you want me to bring in the luggage and pull the SUV into the garage?"

Marcus nodded and tossed Grant the keys. "Yes. Thank you, Grant. That's very kind of you. Put everything in the master."

"You got it, Boss."

Grant headed for the front door. Marcus pointed out the elevator in the far corner of the sitting area, and they headed down the stairs.

When they reached the basement, the center space below the entryway and sitting area was a lounge with several poker tables in the center and movie memorabilia on the walls. Marcus opened the double-doors on the south side, showing Katherine the most organized storage room she had ever seen. Shelves formed three rows filled with Christmas decorations and other holiday decorations, as well as furniture and other odds and ends. It looked more like a movie studio property warehouse than the storeroom of a private residence.

“There’s an emergency shelter in the back right corner,” Marcus pointed out, “courtesy of the original owner.”

He led her to the north side of the basement. “Here’s the theatre,” he said, opening the door and turning on the lights. The theatre was huge and could easily seat thirty people comfortably in the oversized leather recliners. There was a popcorn maker, cabinets filled with snacks, and two refrigerators, behind the concession stand.

Next to the theatre was the mechanical room, where all of the water heaters and air conditioning units were located. The gas, water, and electrical connections were also located in the space.

They then took the elevator up to the top floor. There were two rooms in the south wing: the upstairs den, overlooking the back yard, and the game room, overlooking the front driveway. Both had sliding pocket doors to keep sound from spilling into the sitting area downstairs. On the other side of the bridge, in the north wing, were the guest rooms. There were six altogether, and a sliding pocket door separated the wing from the bridge to keep any noise downstairs from disrupting someone upstairs. Four of the guest rooms were the same size, but the two at the far end were larger.

“If you and the boys end up living here, these will be their rooms,” Marcus said as he showed her the two larger bedrooms.

“Does every bedroom have its own fireplace and bathroom?” Katherine asked.

“Yes,” Marcus answered. “As well as individual climate controls. There are seven bedrooms and seven full baths in the house, there are two locker rooms with showers and toilets in the pool house, and there are three half-baths on this floor, four half-baths on the first floor, and six half-baths in the basement.”

“Good heavens!”

Marcus shrugged. “This was a house designed for entertaining, and believe me, when I have parties, or the poker club comes over, or when directors come here to work on scripts, those extra bathrooms come in handy."

They walked down the north stairs to the main floor. On the north side of the front door, there were two rooms with a hallway between them leading to the dining room. One was the lounge, and one was a wine-tasting room where the wine racks were located. The bar in the lounge had a fifteen-foot-long model of a three-masted warship from the 1700s at the top. The space was covered in dark wood paneling, and there were paintings of old sailing ships on the walls.

As Marcus led her past the wine room and the lounge, they entered the largest dining room Katherine had ever seen. She remembered the photos of the room from the online article she read, but it was more impressive seeing it in person. There were two parallel dining tables that could each seat twenty guests. There was a fireplace at the far end, and above it hung a painting of a castle surrounded by knights and ladies. The center of the wall opposite the windows was covered with a mural of a European harbor filled with sailing ships from the 1700s. The wainscoting around the room was white, and the walls between the paneling and the crown molding were crimson. There were three large chandeliers hanging in the center of the room, and Katherine realized that all of the rooms on the main floor had very high ceilings.

"Where did you get these tables?" Katherine asked.

"They came with the house," Marcus replied. "They were custom made for the space, so I asked that they be included with the purchase." Marcus pointed behind them. On either side of the entrance they passed through were two large, matching china and crystal cabinets. "Those cabinets also came with the house. Between them, they hold fifty complete place settings with every conceivable serving piece needed for any kind of formal party."

"Do you ever use it?" Katherine asked.

Marcus nodded. "I host a couple of charity dinners each

year in here. One includes an auction, which is held down in the theatre. The other is just a dinner and cocktail party. I've hosted a couple of Christmas events here, too. You should see this place decorated for the holidays."

Marcus led her out the side door of the dining room to a corridor that ran the length of the north wing, from the garage to the sitting area.

"The laundry is down there by the garage and the den, and this hallway runs just behind the kitchen."

He then led her across the sitting area to the south wing. Facing the front of the house was the library and study, which was a huge room filled with bookshelves and paintings, tufted leather reading chairs, and small tables with their own reading lamps. It had a large bay window overlooking the circular drive.

Across from the library was Marcus' office, and it was one of the most impressive offices Katherine had ever seen. It had a corner fireplace, deep wood paneling and bookcases, and large writing desk and computer desk, and artwork with historic military themes.

Next to Marcus' office was another office that also had a fireplace in the corner. "This would be your office, or whatever you want to use it for, if you come and live here," Marcus said. "The original owner had designed the library and these two offices as a single space with the master bedroom beyond, but I didn't like that design. I wanted separate spaces for the offices with a corridor running the length of this wing matching the north wing. I think it flows better."

As they exited the second office, Katherine pointed to the closed door across the hall. "What's in there?"

"Ah, that. I call it the arsenal, but it's my weapons collection. The implements for the cannons outside are in there, along with swords, pistols, knives, and rifles from throughout history."

"Can I see it?" Katherine sounded excited.

"Sure." Marcus opened a panel next to the door, entered a code, and placed his hand on the blue screen inside. "Biometric lock," he explained.

The door clicked, and Marcus opened it. Katherine entered the room and looked around. The room was filled with gun cases and display cases filled with antique firearms, lever-action carbines from the old west, firearms from the early-mid twentieth century, and modern firearms. The cannon implements stood in the far-right corner, and there were regimental flags and drums in the other corners.

Katherine looked at each of the cases closely, fascinated with the collection. "Are they real?"

"Yes," Marcus said. "And they can all be fired, although I only keep ammo for some of the modern guns and the cannons."

Marcus led her out of the arsenal and closed the door. Once he heard the locks engage, he turned to the double doors to his left. "Welcome to the master suite." He opened the doors and let her enter.

As she entered the room, she realized that no photos of the rooms in the south wing had been in the article she read online. "How come none of these rooms were photographed for the article I saw?"

"These rooms are private, and I didn't want them photographed," he explained. "These rooms are where I live and work. The other rooms are for entertaining." Then he showed her around the master suite.

The bedroom was immense. The bed was centered on the far wall, between two large windows, with a huge oriental rug underneath. There were three sitting areas, all on oriental rugs with matching designs. Two of them consisted of two matching chairs with side tables, and the third consisted of a couch and coffee table. There were two fireplaces on the wall facing the front of the house with windows on either side, and a bay window in between. On the right, next to where Grant had placed her and Marcus' luggage, there was the short hallway leading to the master bath, with two huge walk-in closets on either side. The closets had built-in dressers, cabinets, shoe cubbies, and hanging racks that were all enclosed behind glass cabinet doors. One of the closets was filled with Marcus' clothes. The other was empty.

"That was Leigh's closet, right?"

Marcus nodded. "It took me two years before I finally cleaned it out. Now, it's just a reminder that this house is empty."

The master bath had clearly been designed for two people, because there were two of everything. There was a water closet on each side with a brass plaque on each door—one said "Captain" and one said "First Mate." The counters next to the water closets had double sinks and vanities, with a linen closet at each end. There was a freestanding tub just past the center of the room that could fit two people, a fireplace on the other side of the tub, and behind the fireplace was a walk-through shower that was big enough for three people to use at the same time. The cabinetry and the countertops matched the kitchen, the floor was marble, and it was the most beautiful bathroom Katherine had ever seen.

"This part of the suite was built to Leigh's specifications," Marcus explained. "All of the fireplaces in the house are gas logs. That way we don't have to carry lumber into all of the rooms during the cold months. Not that you'll ever feel chilly in this house when it's cold outside. It's too well-insulated."

He led her back into the bedroom. Like the other rooms on the main floor, the ceilings were very high, but this room had exposed beams running the length of the room. The bed was a large mahogany-framed king bed. The headboard and footboard had wooden posts that corkscrewed up to a laurel crown cap at the top. It was beautiful, and suddenly Katherine wanted nothing more than to crawl into it.

She heard a sound behind her and turned to see Marcus closing the double doors and locking them. "I believe I owe you a raincheck…"

Katherine smiled. "Only if you light those fireplaces. I've always wanted to make love by firelight."

Marcus walked over to his nightstand on the left side of the bed and pushed two buttons. She heard the flu in each fireplace open. He pressed two more buttons, and the gas logs roared as the flames turned on. He then walked over to the windows and closed the blinds and curtains, blocking out all light except for the fires.

They undressed quickly, and then Katherine walked over to Marcus. Standing in the firelight, she looked incredible, and Marcus was immediately aroused.

"Slow down, Marc," she purred. "I want to savor this moment."

"So do I," Marcus said, gently brushing a strand of hair away from her face. "But some parts of me didn't get the memo."

Katherine slowly sank to her knees. "Then we'll just have to do something about that."

Marcus didn't argue.

They never made it to the bed.

They started near the fireplace, and then they moved to the couch in between the fireplaces. Next, they moved to the chairs to the right of the bedroom door and then to the third sitting area to the left of the bedroom door. They finally ended up in the shower, making love on the bench that ran the length of the shower while the rain showerheads made it feel like they were outdoors in a rainstorm.

After they washed away the sweat and the smell of sex,

they got dressed. Marcus turned off the fireplaces, closed the flus, and opened the curtains and blinds.

They emerged from the bedroom shortly before noon. As they entered the sitting area, they heard Mariana call out, "Mr. Marc? Miss Kathy? When do you want lunch?"

"What are we having?" Marcus asked as they approached the kitchen.

"I can make sandwiches, I can make enchiladas and tamales, I can make a salad with any kind of protein you want added… I also have plenty of lump crabmeat, so I can grill steaks with an Oscar topping."

Marcus grinned at Katherine. "See? I told you she could make anything. Do you have a preference?"

Katherine had to think about it for a moment. "Can we have the enchiladas and tamales for lunch, and then have the steaks Oscar tonight?"

"Does that work for you, Mariana?" Marcus asked.

Mariana beamed. "Give me thirty minutes, and then come back here with your appetites."

Marcus nodded and then turned to Katherine. "Would you like to relax in the den or the sitting area?"

"Let's go into the den," she suggested.

They sat on the couch facing the fireplace and the television. "I can't get over how beautiful this place is," Katherine said as she snuggled next to Marcus. "I feel like I'm the only guest at a country resort in northern England."

"I feel that way, too, after coming back from a film shoot or book tour," Marcus admitted. "This house has everything I could ever want, except for someone to share it with. And it would be nice to have kids here, too. There's so much to do to keep boys busy. Did you see the horse ranch we passed just before turning into the gate? They teach western and English riding for all ages. I go there every now and then, when I feel like visiting the horses."

"It's probably easier to go there to ride than it is to have your own stables and horses here," Katherine remarked.

"Absolutely. Trust me, I thought about building a barn and stables so I could have my own horses, but the cost, the upkeep, the care and feeding of the horses, the staff it would take to keep the horses exercised and healthy… it just didn't make sense with the amount of traveling I do. But I'm a patron of the stables down the road, so it helps them out, and I save a mint by not having my own horses here. Do you ride?"

Katherine nodded. "Most of my life, but not as much lately. The boys have ridden, and I know they love riding. If we do move here, I can see us all spending a lot of time over at the stables."

"Would you like to ride while you're here?"

Katherine's eyes lit up. "Can we?"

"Of course! Pick a day, and we'll go over there. The weather should be perfect for it."

Katherine smiled. "Thanks, Marc. But I don't have my boots with me."

"We can take care of that," Marcus assured her. "There's a tack store a couple of miles from here that carries western and English riding gear and apparel. We can get you set up however you want."

"Perfect, thanks!" Katherine looked out the window. Then she asked, "Apart from what you've already done, do you have any other changes planned for the estate?"

Marcus shook his head. "Nothing major. If you and the boys move here, I'm sure there will be some redecorating—especially in their bedrooms, but I don't see any other building projects. The Gazebo over by the waterfall that runs past the master bedroom was the last structure we built, and it'll probably be the last structure I ever build here… unless something happens to change that."

Katherine looked over Marcus' shoulder and out the

windows, noticing part of the back porch she hadn't seen before. "That's quite an outdoor kitchen you have out there."

"That's something I added to the plans… that and the porch that covers the entire patio and the front of the pool house, to keep the heat down and the rain off the walkway. We can grill on the indoor range, but if we want to smoke something or grill a lot of food for a pool party or a gazebo party, or if it's the weekend and Mariana's not here, I use the outdoor kitchen. There's something relaxing about eating outdoors—listening to the wind in the trees, the babbling of the waterfall ad the stream, and watching the eagles, hawks, and owls hunting on the property—that's so peaceful."

Katherine cocked her head to one side, and her head jiggled slightly. "Are you my boyfriend or a real estate agent?"

Marcus laughed. "I guess I *am* trying to sell you on living here. Tell you what. I'll just let you enjoy it however you want to, and then you can tell the boys whatever you truly feel about the place."

Katherine put her head on his shoulder. "I really love being here. Thanks for inviting me."

"Thanks for accepting my invitation."

They sat quietly, enjoying each other's company, until Mariana called and told them that lunch was ready.

CHAPTER 8

After their lunch had settled, Marcus offered to show Katherine around the property. She didn't have hiking boots with her, but she did have a good pair of walking shoes. Once Marcus had changed into his hiking boots, he led her down the north wing corridor to the garage. They passed the laundry room and the mudroom across from the dining room and next to the garage entrance.

When Katherine entered the garage, she saw Marcus' SUV at one end. Next to that was a large, comfortable-looking sedan. The third garage bay was empty, but the fourth bay had three golf carts. Two were electric, and one was gas powered.

Marcus explained what the golf carts were for. "We use the largest electric one to shuttle people to the house at parties, since some cars have to park quite a ways away. We use the smaller electric one to run up to the gate for the mail and packages. The gas one has more power, so we use that when we have to go into the woods or along the trails that lead up the west ridge."

Marcus grabbed the keys to the gas-powered golf cart. They pulled out of the garage, and Marcus drove around the front of the house first so Katherine could take a closer look at the cannons.

Both cannons, mounted on garrison carriages, sat on concrete pads so they wouldn't sink into the ground from their weight.

"You really shoot them?" she asked as she walked around them.

"I really shoot them," Marcus confirmed. "Not with live cannon balls or anything. Just blanks. It's great at 4th of July parties or on New Year's Eve."

Katherine looked at the cannonballs stacked in pyramid shapes next to each cannon. "What are those for?" she asked, pointing.

"Decoration," Marcus said. "They're welded together, so you couldn't load one of them into the cannon if you wanted to."

"Do you have cannon balls for the cannons that *can* be fired?"

Marcus nodded. "In the arsenal, next to the implements for the cannons. A wooden chest holds the powder charges and the safety equipment. There are four cannon balls in there, too."

"Would you ever shoot them," Katherine asked as they walked back to the golf cart.

"Good lord, no! Not unless we were under attack, which is not likely to happen around here."

"Why not?"

Marcus chuckled. "Let me tell you a little something about cannons. Have you ever played golf?"

Katherine nodded. "I'm not good, but I've played."

"And when you hit the golf ball on hard ground, what happens?"

"It keeps bouncing down the fairway."

"Right. Cannonballs do the same. If I fully elevated the barrels so the cannonballs would clear the ridge between the house and the gate, the cannonball would travel close to two miles in the air before it hit ground. But unless it hit something else, like trees, a house, or a ridge, it would keep bouncing for another ten miles. And if it hit a large rock or something equally hard, it would ricochet off, and there's no telling where it would go. The damage could be catastrophic. And if I kept the barrels low so the cannonballs couldn't clear the ridge, the cannonballs might sink into the ground, they might ricochet straight up, or they might be deflected back toward the house. No, I'd never fire the cannonballs unless there was an emergency so extreme that it warranted the risk."

Marcus drove the golf cart toward the south wing. A stream wound its way along the south end of the property. As it passed near the master bedroom windows, it formed a natural waterfall, then meandered toward the northwest, disappearing into the trees. There was a bridge that crossed the stream above the waterfall, one that crossed the stream below the waterfall next to the gazebo in the back yard, and a third bridge that crossed the stream closer to the trees. Marcus drove over the bridge above the falls.

"I'm glad the original owner left the stream alone," Marcus said. "Sitting on the back porch or in the gazebo, listening to the water, is one of my favorite things to do when I want to just clear my head."

He drove toward the southwest corner of the clearing, where there was a wide trail heading west. "This is the main trail that heads up the ridge. All of the walking trails branch off and come back to this one. This is the only trail we can take the golf cart on, and even then, it can't make it all the way up the ridge. The terrain is too rocky starting just past the halfway point."

They drove about fifty feet into the woods, and Marcus had to stop to open a gate that crossed the trail.

"What's that gate for?" Katherine asked after Marcus had pulled forward and closed the gate behind them.

"There's a fence around the house to keep wildlife from getting into the living areas of the property. It goes from the front gate, along the driveway, and around the entire clearing.

Once past that gate, we're in nature's domain, and we have to share the ridge with the deer, foxes, bears, and other critters that call the mountain home."

"You don't have a fence around the entire property?"

Marcus shook his head. "Parts of the property line are inaccessible due to the terrain. Fencing-in the living areas was the best compromise."

"Have you seen bears up here?" Katherine sounded nervous.

"A time or two." Marcus lifted his shirt, and Katherine saw the holster. "Don't worry. I'm prepared. Nothing's going to harm you up here."

Katherine nodded. They rode for another ten minutes, and then they arrived at a clearing. Four trails branched out from the clearing in different directions. Marcus stopped the golf cart and turned off the engine.

"We walk from here. Are you ready for a bit of a climb?"

Katherine leaped out of the golf cart. "You bet."

Marcus grabbed the binoculars from their holder on the dashboard. Then he reached under the golf cart's canopy and extracted two walking sticks. He handed one to Katherine. "You'll want this."

Katherine smiled as she accepted the polished stick with a leather wrapped grip near the top. "You think of everything, don't you?"

"I try."

Marcus' phone rang, and he answered it. "Hi, Grant. What's up? No, we're at the upper clearing, heading for Pinnacle Rock. I've got two GPS trackers with me, so you should be able to track where we are and where the golf cart is. It did? That's great. Can you put it in the den for me? Thanks!"

Marcus hung up. "That was Grant, obviously. A package I've been waiting for just arrived." He handed Katherine a chain with a disk hanging from the bottom. "Put this around your neck.

It's a GPS tracker, so we can find you if you wander off."

Katherine put the chain around her neck and saw Marcus doing the same with another chain.

Marcus gestured toward the trail on the left. "Shall we?"

Katherine nodded and walked with him toward the trail.

The trail stair-stepped up the ridge. When they reached the plateau of each step, Katherine looked around at the scenery. She could see the house in the distance, and as they got higher, she could see beyond the ridge that crossed between the house and the road. Eventually, she was able to see the horse farm that Marcus had mentioned.

The farther they walked, the rougher the terrain became, making Katherine grateful for the walking stick. Giant boulders blocked their path, and soon they had to scramble up the rocks to keep going.

When they reached the summit, Katherine couldn't believe the view. She could see Raccoon Mountain clearly, and she could see where the Tennessee River flowed between the ridge they were on and the mountains to the west. But when she turned around to look east, the view below her took her breath away.

"Welcome to Pinnacle Rock, the highest point and the western edge of my property." Marcus pointed out the key points of interest. "To the north is where the Tennessee River comes around Raccoon Mountain from downtown Chattanooga. That's downtown to the right of the bend over there." Marcus handed Katherine the binoculars so she could see.

"That's Lookout Mountain straight ahead. The railroads and rail museum that made Chattanooga famous are hidden on the other side. To the south, is Georgia, and a little ways past the border to the southeast is the Chickamauga Battlefield, which is a national park. I love the history of this area as much as I love the landscape."

Katherine looked through the binoculars at all of the sights. From some of the hiking trails she'd walked with the boys in

California, you could see the Pacific Ocean in the distance, but the view from Pinnacle Rock was truly breathtaking. Mountains, trees, and the Tennessee River surrounded her, and below her, she saw hawks, falcons, and Bald Eagles riding the air currents as they hunted.

"It's so beautiful up here," she said in awe. "I see why you don't want to leave."

She heard a cry from above and looked up in time to see two hawks circling each other.

"Those are Red-tailed Hawks, my favorite. We also have Red-shouldered Hawks on the property. Closer to dusk, the owls start hunting, and if we sit out on the patio or the gazebo after sunset, you can see them silhouetted against the night sky. There are a number of Great Horned Owls on the property, as well as Barn Owls, which are also my favorite. I've seen Barred Owls and Screech Owls, and I even saw a Snowy Owl once, but they're rare in these parts."

They stayed up there for thirty minutes, enjoying the view, before Marcus suggested heading back down before dusk. Katherine reluctantly agreed.

"We can come back here any time you want. We can also explore some of the other trails. You can see the nests and perching trees of various birds of prey along the northern trails."

"I'd love that," she said.

When they reached the golf cart, Marcus returned the binoculars to the holder on the dashboard and put the walking sticks back underneath the canopy. Once Katherine was seated, they started back down toward the house.

When they reached the clearing, Marcus crossed the stream on the bridge near the tree line and headed around the clearing, past the pool house, to the garage.

When they entered the house, Katherine smelled food cooking.

"Is that you, Mr. Marc?" Mariana's voice called from the

kitchen.

"It's us, Mariana."

"Go wash up. Dinner's almost ready. Where do you want to eat?"

"Do you have a preference?" Marcus asked Katherine.

"How about the patio?" Katherine suggested.

"The patio, Mariana," Marcus called.

"Okay, Mr. Marc."

Marcus gestured for Katherine to follow him into the mudroom. They took off their shoes and socks, and then they washed their hands in the large utility sink on the left wall next to the laundry room. They dried their hands and walked barefoot to the kitchen.

"I'll go get our shoes," Marcus said. He disappeared across the house, heading to the master bedroom.

Katherine entered the kitchen from the hallway and sat at the island.

"How was your hike, Miss Kathy?" Mariana asked as she began plating their dinner.

"It was wonderful, Mariana, thank you. I've never seen views like that before."

"Mr. Marc loves going up to Pinnacle Rock. I think he'd stay up there if he could. He gets lots of ideas for his books up there."

Marcus entered the kitchen from the sitting area a moment later. He had his deck shoes on, and he knelt to put Katherine's on.

"Thank you."

"You're welcome."

"Go to the patio table," Mariana said. "I'll bring the food out."

"We can help, Mariana," Katherine said.

"No, no, no. You go sit. I'll bring the food."

Marcus led Katherine out one of the three patio doors.

Mariana had already set the round table just outside the kitchen. There were candles glowing in the center, and a bottle of wine already opened next to two glasses.

"Mariana insists on letting the wine breathe before serving," Marcus said as he held Katherine's chair for her. She sat, and he pushed her chair closer to the table before sitting next to her. He poured the wine and handed Katherine her glass.

"Here's to your first night here," he said, raising his glass.

"The first of many, I hope," Katherine said. She sipped the wine and found it excellent.

Mariana brought out a basket of steaming hot bread and a butter dish. She disappeared back into the kitchen and returned with their salads. A minute later, she brought their entrée, which was a large beef filet Oscar-style, meaning it was covered with grilled asparagus, lump crabmeat, and hollandaise sauce.

Katherine inhaled the aroma. "This smells so good!"

"Mariana bakes all of the bread from scratch, even the hamburger and hotdog buns and sandwich breads. Her hollandaise sauce is unique, but fantastic."

"I hope you enjoy everything, Miss Kathy."

"I'm sure I will. Thank you, Mariana."

Mariana beamed.

"I'll take care of the dishes, Mariana," Marcus said. "You can head home anytime you're ready."

"Thank you, Mr. Marc. What do you want for breakfast?"

Marcus glanced at Katherine, who shrugged. "Surprise us."

"Okay. Good night, Mr. Marc, Miss Kathy."

"Goodnight, Mariana," Marcus said.

Mariana disappeared back into the kitchen, and Marcus and Katherine began eating dinner.

"I can't believe how good that was," Katherine said when she finally pushed her plate away and leaned back in her chair, holding her wine glass. "I thought lunch was great, but this was better than what you get at most restaurants. I see what you mean about having to do a lot of hiking to keep from gaining weight."

"It's a small price to pay to eat like this," Marcus said, finishing his last bite. "The mantra of this place is, Work Hard, Play Joyously, and Eat Exceptionally."

"That's great!" Katherine giggled. "So, what's on the schedule for tonight?"

"That package that arrived earlier has some new movies I ordered. We can watch one or two of them in the den… or in the theatre downstairs. It's quite an experience."

"I'm game."

Marcus stood and started clearing the dishes. Katherine drained her wine glass and stood to help.

"I've got this," Marcus said.

"Hey, I may feel like I'm at a private resort, but I'm not going to act like I am. Whatever you're doing, I want to do it with you. Okay?"

"Okay. Thanks, Kathy."

They set the dishes on the island. Marc began cleaning them as Katherine went back to blow out the candles, cork the wine bottle, and bring it and the butter dish back inside.

"Where do you want the wine and butter?" she asked.

Marcus pointed to the counter to the left of the Island. "Wine bottle there, butter in the fridge."

Katherine put the wine bottle next to two other corked bottles. She went to the fridge and opened it. It was flawlessly organized, but she couldn't tell where the butter went. "Where does the butter go?"

"Sorry, there's a compartment in the door, third shelf from the top."

Katherine found it and put the butter dish inside. "Do you want me to bring in the placemats from outside?"

"Yes, please. They go in the hamper in the laundry room."

Katherine went out and got them. She locked the patio door when she came back in, and then she went to find the hamper, which was just inside the laundry room. When she got back to the kitchen, the dishes were done and the island had been wiped down. Marcus wasn't there.

She was about to call his name when she heard a sound coming from the den. She walked in there, and she saw Marcus opening a package.

"The new movies?" she asked.

Marcus grinned. "Yes. Come and see."

She walked over and looked into the box. Then she looked up at Marcus. "What? You bought all my movies?"

Marcus nodded. "Yep! The entire catalog of your films that are out on disk. I'm still waiting for the television show boxed sets to arrive. But if you don't want to watch one of them, I have plenty of others to choose from."

Katherine looked at him suspiciously. "Suppose we *were* to watch one of my movies, which I rarely do. Which one would you choose and why?"

"Well, *The Spy Upstairs* isn't out yet, so I can't choose that one." He looked through the more than twenty disks in the box. He finally selected one and held it up. "This one."

"Why that one?"

"Because you play a Texas country girl, and for some reason, that's how I like to think of you."

"You know that was filmed in Canada, don't you?"

Marcus chuckled. "I'm familiar with the production company. All their films are set in the states but filmed in Canada. Wasn't this one filmed in Alberta? Kind of a strange substitute for Central Texas, especially since Texas has its own film industry."

"It was the heat," Katherine said. "We'd be sweating too much shooting a summer movie out there, and no one wanted to risk a heat stroke. That part of Canada is equally flat, but much cooler."

"That makes sense," Marcus said.

Katherine took the disk and held it up. "You do know I'm not a country girl, don't you? I'm a California city girl through and through?"

"And yet here you are in the Tennessee Mountains. So, it begs the question: were you just acting in this film, are you acting now, or is your big-city girl persona the real act?"

Katherine snorted in amusement. "Fair question. You don't really expect me to answer it, do you?"

Marcus just grinned. "Why don't you pick out another movie?"

Katherine looked at his movie collection. "Where do you keep *your* films?"

"The ones I wrote?"

She nodded.

"The shelf with the glass door. I like *those* movies protected."

While Katherine looked for the shelf, Marcus said, "I'm going to turn on the security system."

He walked over to the security monitor on the wall next to the den's hallway entrance. He checked to make sure that Grant and Mariana had left the grounds, and then he entered the code that would lock down the estate. The system confirmed that the estate was secure.

"The doors and windows are now all locked, as is the main gate and the back gate. There are motion sensors and pressure sensors throughout the clearing, but the motion and pressure sensors inside the house are turned off, except on the second floor. I'll turn on the rest of the inside sensors once we go to bed."

Katherine held up one of Marcus' older movies. "I forgot you wrote this one. It's one of my favorites. Can we watch it?"

Marcus smiled. "Of course."

Marcus turned off the lights in the north wing and led Katherine down the stairs to the theatre. Just inside the theatre door, there was a cabinet containing a multi-format videodisk player that could hold up to fifteen disks. He loaded the two movies into the system.

"Do you need anything to drink?" he asked. "And if you need to use the restroom, there are four on this side of the basement, on either side of the theatre entrance."

Katherine decided to use the restroom, and Marcus did the same. When Marcus came out of the half-bath, he saw Katherine standing in front of the bar along the west wall of the poker lounge. She was happy to see that the liquor cabinets all locked.

"Looking for something in particular?" he asked.

"Just looking. You've got quite a selection here."

"You should see what's kept in the lounge and wine room upstairs," Marcus said. "I may not be a big drinker, but I know how to take care of my guests."

She followed Marcus back into the theatre. Looking around the room, she pointed toward the front. "How come all of the other seats are single occupant, but that's a double occupant seat?"

"Because that's our seat," Marcus replied. He grabbed two bottles of water from the fridge and led her down to their seat. She noticed that the room sloped down toward the screen so no one's view was blocked by the head of the person in front. Their seat was situated so they could look at the screen dead center without having to tilt their heads back or forward. It was the perfect location.

He placed the waters in the cup holders at each end and then motioned for her to sit. He showed her where the controls were to adjust the footrest, since all of the seats in the theatre could recline. Once she had the seat the way she wanted it, and Marcus had set his seat to match, he picked up a large remote control from the small table next to his side of the seat.

"This controls the entire theatre," he explained. "This button turns down the lights in the card room. This button turns down the lights in here." He pressed the button, and the lights slowly began to dim. Floor lighting turned on to help see where the aisles were.

Marcus pressed another button on the lit-up remote, and the projector turned on. A menu appeared, showing the titles of the two disks loaded into the player. "Which movie first?"

"Yours," Katherine answered.

Marcus selected that movie. "Let me know if it's too loud or too soft. I can adjust that, too. Oh, and be warned. This theatre has a surround sound system that will blow your socks off."

The movie started, and Katherine snuggled up next to Marcus. He put his arm around her shoulder, put the remote back on its table, and leaned back to watch the film.

Nearly three hours later, the movie ended, and Marcus turned the lights up slightly.

"So, what do you think of the theatre?" he asked.

"It's incredible. The seats are great, the screen is huge, and that's the best sound I've ever heard." She looked at Marcus. "But I didn't recognize several of the scenes in the movie. I've seen it a dozen times, but I swear those scenes weren't in it."

"This is the Director's Cut," Marcus explained. "It comes the closest to my original script. I have the studio's theatrical release, too, but I usually prefer the extended versions."

"I can see why," Katherine said. "There were a couple scenes that I never quite understood before. Seeing the additional footage helped those scenes make sense to me."

"If you really want to understand the story, you should read the novel."

"I assume you wrote it."

"I did."

"Did you base the script on the novel, or is the novel based on the script?"

"This script was based on one of my novels," Marcus replied. "It originally had a different title, but we re-released the novel when the film came out, using the title of the movie and the movie poster artwork on the front cover. It hit the bestseller list twice—once under each title."

"Do you have a copy of it?"

Marcus nodded. "I have a few paperback and hardback copies of all of my books in the storeroom. You're welcome to any that you want."

"Thanks."

"Ready to start the next movie?"

"Do you really want to see it?" Katherine asked.

"It's you, isn't it? Why? Don't you like watching your own movies?"

Katherine took a deep breath and shook her head. "I can't watch one without remembering what was happening while shooting it. I either end up reciting the dialog along with the film, or I start giving a running commentary about what was happening and all the little flaws that were never edited out."

Marcus laughed. "I think the commentary would be interesting."

"Then start the film, and don't say I didn't warn you."

Marcus dimmed the lights and started the movie.

He quickly discovered that she *wasn't* kidding. But he was fascinated listening to her stories. He was glad he had already seen the movie before, because otherwise he wouldn't have heard any of the dialogue.

When it came to the love scene, Marcus pointed to her back. "I don't remember that mole."

"That's not me," she said. "That's a body double. I don't do nude scenes anymore."

"Good editing," Marcus commented. "I wouldn't have known if you hadn't told me… and if I hadn't already seen you barebacked before."

At the end of the scene, Marcus whispered, "We did it better."

"Every single time," Katherine agreed. She gently traced her finger up and down his arm. "If you want, we can do it better now."

"While the movie is playing?"

"Why not?"

Marcus couldn't think of a good reason.

When the movie was over, Marcus turned the lights on low so they could find their clothes and get dressed. "Well, that was fun," he said.

"Yes, it was," Katherine agreed. "I'd rather make love than watch one of my movies anyway."

"I like both, but let's not do both at the same time again. I can't tell if you're talking to me or if it's the movie."

Katherine laughed. "I didn't think about that. I can see how it could get confusing."

"Especially when your character in the film kept yelling, 'Stop!' I wasn't sure if I should really stop or keep going."

Katherine nodded. "I'm glad you kept going. And I was able to check something off my bucket list tonight. I finally had sex in a movie theatre."

"*That's* on your bucket list?" Marcus asked. "What are you, seventeen?"

"It's an old list," Katherine defended herself. "I had forgotten about it until just now."

Marcus led her to the rear of the theatre. He removed the disks from the player, put them back in the cases, and then led her upstairs. When they reached the main floor, he turned off the downstairs lights and asked, "Would you like a nightcap?"

"Sure."

"Wine or something stronger?"

"Stronger."

He led her to the lounge and offered her a seat. "Let me put the disks back in the den, and I'll be right back." He turned on the lounge lights, illuminating the paintings and the ship model above the bar, and disappeared down the hallway.

He returned a moment later. "What's your pleasure?"

"What do you have?" she asked.

"Do you like scotch?"

"Sure."

"Then I've got a treat for you." He motioned for her to join him at the bar. He walked around the bar and over to a cabinet with brass mesh doors. He unlocked the door, opened it, and removed a wooden case that said "The Macallan 40" on it.

"Is that what I think it is?" Katherine asked.

Marcus nodded. "Forty-year-old single malt scotch."

"What did that set you back? I've heard those bottles go for more than twenty-thousand dollars apiece."

"Not a penny. This was a gift from the studio when one of my films won best picture, best original screenplay, best director, best sound design, best original score, best cinematography, best film editing… and… best visual effects. Sadly, it came in second in all the acting categories, but at least I got this bottle of scotch."

"And your own Oscar," Katherine said. "Where do you keep your awards, by the way? I didn't see them with the movie memorabilia downstairs."

"They're in my office," Marcus, taking out two crystal tumblers from behind the bar. "I have a display cabinet in there for my film and book awards."

He poured a finger width of scotch in each tumbler and slid one tumbler in front of Katherine. "Remember, you sip this, you don't chug it. This is meant to be savored."

"I know this scotch is aged in casks, but in what year was it actually bottled?" Katherine asked, picking up the tumbler and staring at the liquid inside.

Marcus looked at the bottle. "Five years ago."

"Do you realize it's older than I am?" she noted.

"And just as smooth and breathtaking as you are," Marcus stated.

Katherine smiled and raised her glass to him. She took a sip. "Oh, my holy God!"

Marcus took a sip. "It's something, isn't it?"

"It's... it's... spectacular. I don't have the words. Hell, I need a professional writer to help me describe how great this is." She took another sip and held it on her tongue for a moment. She closed her eyes with a look of almost reverence as she swallowed.

"More?" Marcus asked.

Katherine shook her head. "No, you've spoiled me enough already."

Marcus put the bottle back in its case and put the case back in the cabinet. Then he led Katherine to the sitting area. They sat on the couch facing the lighthouse painting over the fireplace. The lights in the sitting area and entryway were low, but the painting was illuminated with its own lights, making the sunset in the background glow.

They sipped their scotch and stared at the painting.

"Is that an original?" she asked.

"Yes. There are canvas prints of that painting—much smaller, of course—but that's the original. It went up for auction when the artist died several years ago, and for some reason, no one was bidding on it. I think the size intimidated most of the bidders. I got it for a steal."

"You're a bit of a wheeler-dealer, aren't you," Katherine asked.

"You can't survive in this world if you pay retail prices for everything," Marcus replied. "My mother and her sisters were master negotiators, and a little of it rubbed off on me. If I paid retail for this house and the furnishings, I couldn't afford to live here in a hundred years. Maybe three hundred. But I struck good bargains, I was lucky with my bidding, and now I have all of this for far less than any of it is worth. Money is too hard earned in this business to waste it. When I spend it, it has to be for the right things or the right reasons."

"And what about all those meals you bought us in Atlanta?" Katherine asked.

"They were all for the right reasons."

"What reason?"

"I was falling in love with you, and I wanted to spend more time with you. What better reason could there be?"

Katherine smiled. "Well, I'm glad. I'm glad we met, I'm glad we started going out, I'm glad we… took things to the next level, and I'm glad I'm here with you, even though it all still seems like a dream."

"Me, too. And if this is a dream, don't wake me."

They finished their drinks. "Let me wash these," Marcus said, taking Katherine's tumbler, "and then let's retire for the evening."

She handed him her tumbler and followed him into the kitchen. She sat at the island while he hand-washed and dried the tumblers. After returning them to the bar, he turned off the lights in the entryway and sitting area. Small lights appeared on each riser of the staircases leading to the second level, and four single spotlights—hidden in the beams along the ceiling—came on to provide low lighting so the house wouldn't be pitch black.

Once they reached the bedroom, Marcus closed and locked the doors. He entered a code into the security panel, activating the motion and pressure sensors in the basement and the main level of the house.

"We're secure now," Marcus told Katherine. "If you leave the bedroom before morning, make sure I turn off the sensors downstairs, or you'll set off the alarms."

Katherine nodded. She pointed at her luggage. "Where

should I put these?"

"In your closet," Marcus replied. "I'll help you.

He helped carry her bags into the empty walk-in closet. "Feel free to unpack and put your things wherever you want."

As Katherine started unpacking, Marcus grabbed his bags and took them into his closet. He unpacked, put away the clean clothes, and put the dirty clothes into the hamper.

"I have a hamper in here for any clothes you want washed," Marcus called out. "I'm sorry, I forgot to put the one for that closet back in there when I emptied it out."

"No worries," Katherine called back. She walked into his closet with a handful of clothes. "Just put these in the basket?"

"Yes," Marcus said. "I can wash them tomorrow or over the weekend; or if you can wait until Monday, one of the cleaning crew will handle it. They do all the laundry on Mondays."

"I'll let you know once I see how much clean clothing I have left."

Marcus finished unpacking and then walked to the other side and leaned against the doorway of Katherine's closet. "Finding places to put everything?"

Katherine looked up and smiled. "Oh, yes. Too many."

She emptied her last bag and moved the empty luggage to the far corner of the closet. Then she carried her toiletry case to the bathroom. Marcus showed her the drawers and cabinets where she could put everything.

Once they were dressed for bed—Marcus in his sleep shorts and Katherine in the pink outfit she wore at The Four Seasons in Atlanta—Marcus showed her one more feature in the bathroom.

"Remember the ambient lighting that the bathroom at The Four Seasons had?"

"Sure."

Marcus pressed one of the light switches. The lights in the bathroom and closets turned off, and ambient lighting appeared underneath the bathroom counters and the closet dressers and cabinets. "That'll provide enough light to keep you from bumping into anything if you have to get up in the middle of the night, but it shouldn't be so bright as to keep you awake."

"Thank you!" Katherine said. "I always get disoriented for the first couple of nights I'm sleeping in a new place. This'll help. How come I didn't see them this morning?"

"I didn't have them turned on," Marcus said. "One switch turns off the lights only, and the other turns off the lights and turns on the ambient lighting."

"I'm going to have to learn a lot of light switches and security controls, aren't I?"

"You'll get used to it. There may be a lot of things you have to learn, but each one was designed to make sense."

Marcus removed the decorative pillows and tossed them on the couch before turning down the covers. Katherine crawled into the bed, and Marcus joined her. As he turned off the bedroom lights, she said, "The sheets are so soft."

"That's why I love them," Marcus said. "I stayed at a hotel in New York that used these sheets, and I made a note of what they were. I went online and found them, and now they're the only sheets I use. They're on every bed in the house."

Katherine snugged up close to Marcus. "Thanks for such a great day."

"The first of many."

"I love you, Marc."

"I love you, Kathy. Sleep sweet."

"You, too."

CHAPTER 9

The next morning, Katherine woke to find that she was alone in the bedroom. She looked in the bathroom and the closets, but Marcus wasn't there. She took a quick shower, got dressed in jeans and a T-shirt, and made the bed. She glanced at the security control panel on the wall next to the door, and the screen indicated that the alarm system was off. She opened the doors and decided to look for Marcus in his office.

The office was empty when she arrived. *I hope he doesn't mind if I look around a bit.* Copies of all of his books and screenplays were in the bookcases flanking the credenza behind his desk. Next to the fireplace, there was a sitting area with two small couches and two chairs, all covered in russet tufted leather. Across from his desk, there were two more chairs like the ones in the sitting area, and behind them was an oversized cabinet that had all of Marcus' awards.

She saw two Academy Award statues, one for Best Original Screenplay and one for Best Adapted Screenplay. There were three Golden Globe Awards for Best Screenplay. There were also three Emmy Awards for Outstanding Writing for a Limited or Anthology Series or Movie. Then she saw two other awards. *I had no idea he has won two BAFTA awards for Best Original*

Screenplay. On the lower shelves of the cabinet, she saw his literary awards and the awards for reaching Best-Seller status. There were quite a few of these awards, since Marcus had been writing popular novels for over 20 years.

Most of the artwork in the office depicted scenes from American history, including the Revolutionary War, the War of 1812, the War Between the States, and the Old West. There were several display cases containing Scottish and military memorabilia, including a collection of cannonballs.

Katherine looked around for another minute, and then she walked across the hall to the Library and Study. The room had the same russet tufted leather chairs and small couches as the office and the den, and in addition to the nautical art, there were two beautiful old English landscapes.

She heard a sound coming from the kitchen, so she headed there next. Mariana was busy cooking, but there was no one else around.

"Good morning, Mariana," she said as she sat at the island.

"Good morning, Miss Kathy," Mariana said happily. "Mr. Marcus had to run a quick errand, and he said he'd be back in thirty minutes. Your breakfast will be ready in five minutes. Would you like some coffee?"

"Yes, please."

When Mariana brought the coffee, Katherine took a deep breath and asked. "So, tell me, Mariana. You've known Marc for… what, seven years? I've only known him for a couple of months. What's he like when he's here at home?"

Mariana beamed. "Mr. Marc is the nicest man you'll ever meet. Oh, if only you could have seen him when Miss Leigh was still alive. He was such a happy person then. Now… he's more serious, but still just as kind. He cares about other people like no one I've ever met. At Christmas, he invites my entire family and Mr. Grant's entire family over for either Christmas Day or Christmas Eve, just to make certain that we can celebrate the holiday with our family… and I think so he won't be alone. Miss Leigh's children never come see him, now that she's gone. They have their own lives and their own families. He won't say it, but I know he misses having family around. It's a big house without someone to share it with."

"What do you do when he's away on tour or on a film shoot?" Katherine asked.

"Mr. Marc lets me keep up my catering business when he's away. He even lets me use the kitchen here to do the cooking for my catering. Occasionally, he sends me photos and descriptions of food he eats when he travels to see if I can duplicate it, so I do a lot of experimenting with recipes for him."

"That's amazing."

"Yes, it is. He takes care of me, and I take care of him… when he's here."

Mariana brought over a breakfast of individual spinach and feta quiches, sausage links, and fresh baked biscuits. Mariana also brought a dish with honey, butter, and strawberry preserves.

"Thanks, Mariana. This smells wonderful."

"Eat, before it gets cold," Mariana encouraged her.

Katherine was half way through breakfast, when she heard Marcus enter from the garage. "Mariana, is Kathy up yet?"

"I'm in the kitchen, Marc," Katherine called back.

Marcus entered, looking happy. "Great! I see you're eating. I was hoping you wouldn't wait until I got back."

"Where were you?" Katherine asked, finishing her biscuit.

"I noticed one of the tires on the SUV was going flat, so I ran out to get it changed. Turns out two were going flat, so it took a little longer than planned. Everything's good now."

He sat next to her as Mariana brought him a mug of tea.

"Have you eaten already?" Katherine asked.

"Yes, I ate before I left. Mariana would never let me leave the house without eating."

"She really looks out for you, doesn't she?"

"Someone has to," Marcus replied with a grin. "Otherwise, who knows what bad habits I'd pick up?"

Katherine finished her breakfast. "So, what's on the schedule for today?"

"Whatever you want," Marcus said. "We can go into the city, we can go riding, we can go hiking again, we can swim, we can do something else, or a combination of any of those. What's your pleasure?"

"Can we go riding?"

"Of course. And afterwards, I'll take you somewhere so you can get a proper pair of hiking boots. You'll need them before we go back to the west ridge again."

"And I can still get my riding gear at that tack shop before we go to the stables?"

Marcus nodded. "We'll get you whatever you need."

"When can we go?" Katherine sounded excited.

Marcus looked at his watch. "The tack store opens at nine, so we can go anytime. Can you be ready in ten minutes?"

"You bet! Are you going to change?"

"I'm going to put my boots on and grab my hat, but they're in the mudroom."

"All I need to do is put on my shoes, since I'm buying boots at the tack store."

Marcus smiled. "Well, go grab them, and let's get out of here!"

Katherine kissed him and then ran to the master bedroom.

"Why didn't you tell her where you really went, Mr. Marc?" Mariana asked softly, as she started washing Katherine's dishes.

"Because I'm not ready for her to know about that," Marcus said. "I need to know that she's truly sold on living here before springing that surprise on her. Besides, it won't be ready until Tuesday or Wednesday of next week. No sense telling her about something that isn't ready yet, is there?"

"Maybe, maybe not. It never hurts to give her more than one reason to stay here."

"You'd like it if she and her sons moved here?"

"Of course, Mr. Marc. It's no good to see you alone. Oh, you stay busy, but it's not the same as being happy. You need to be happy."

Marcus nodded.

A moment later, Katherine entered the kitchen. "I'm ready."

Marcus smiled at her. He stood and said, "Mariana, we'll be back around one this afternoon."

"Lunch will be ready when you are ready," Mariana said pleasantly. "Have fun riding."

They arrived at the tack store in less than fifteen minutes. It was immense, and Katherine couldn't decide if she wanted western or English riding gear.

"Do you ride for pleasure, or do you ride for sport?" Marcus asked.

"I used to ride for sport, but now I ride for pleasure."

"What kind of boot are you more comfortable wearing?"

"English," said Katherine. "I can wear them with other clothes. But I like wearing western boots, too. I can dance in those."

"And do you want clothes to match the boots or boots to match the clothes?"

"What do you mean?" Katherine asked.

"Would you ever wear English boots with jeans, or do you prefer English riding pants? And do you wear western boots only with jeans, or would you wear them with a skirt?"

"All of those, I guess."

Marcus laughed. "Then it looks like you're getting both English and western boots and clothing today. You'll have to decide what you want to change into to go riding."

Finding a pair of English riding boots proved easy. She preferred black, and she only had to try on four pairs before finding one that fit her feet and leg length properly. The boots were so well made that she could tell they wouldn't require much break-in time.

Finding the right western boots was harder. She found several that fit, but she couldn't decide which design she liked the best.

"You said that you wear them with a skirt, right?"

"Right," Katherine replied.

"And do you wear them inside or outside of your pants?"

"Both."

"Then get a pair that looks good against your leg for all to see, rather than a simpler design," Marcus suggested.

Katherine finally settled on a pair, and then she found a tan and a black pair of English riding pants, a very flattering pair of jeans, and a couple of tops.

"Should I get a helmet or a hat?" she asked.

"That's your call," Marcus said. "I wear a western hat, but you need to do what's comfortable to you."

She picked out a western hat similar to the one Marcus was wearing. "Looks like I'm going western today."

Marcus grinned.

Katherine went into one of the dressing rooms to change into the clothing she planned to wear riding. Marcus took the opportunity to pay for her purchases without her knowing.

When Katherine returned, Marcus was struck by how beautiful she looked in her outfit. "Who's a big-city-girl now?" he joked when she walked up to him.

She blushed. "Okay, *maybe* I'm a bit of a country girl at heart."

"And that makes me love you even more," Marcus said. He took the clothes she'd arrived in, placed them in one of the bags with the rest of her purchases, grabbed the bags, and led her to the door.

"Wait, I haven't paid yet," Katherine protested.

"Already taken care of," Marcus said.

Katherine stopped. "You didn't have to do that, Marc."

Marcus faced her. "I wanted to. I like doing things for you, and I think it's been a long time since you've had someone who did things for you from the heart." He gave her a kiss on the cheek. "I did it because I love you."

Katherine smiled. "Well… okay… but don't think you're going to pay for everything while I'm here."

"If you insist," Marcus agreed. "Shall we go?"

Katherine walked with him to the parking lot. *What a sweet thing to do. But I can't let him keep doing everything for me. We should be partners in this relationship.*

Marcus had called ahead, and two horses were already saddled for them when they arrived at the stables. The owner, Ted Johannsen, was Marcus' good friend. He gave them a quick safety briefing and an overview of the ranch and trails.

The owner clearly recognized Katherine, but he tried not to show it. He ended the briefing by saying, "Marc knows the layout of the place and which trails are best for whatever adventure you're looking for, so you're in good hands. If you need anything, just let me know."

"I will. Thank you," Katherine said sweetly.

Marcus helped Katherine onto her horse. Then he mounted his own. "What are you in the mood for? Easy, fast, hilly, twisty?"

"I'd like to do some open field running, but mostly I just want to be out in nature, looking at the sights and enjoying being on a horse again."

Marcus pointed north. "There's a ridge over there with a great view. There's also a stream at the base, and on the other side, there's a pasture, where we can let the horses run for a bit."

"Let's go!"

As they left the stables behind, Katherine felt exhilarated. *No rules, no style points or deductions for not doing things perfectly, just the joy of being on a horse again. I wish I had done western riding from the beginning. This is the life.*

They crossed the stream and then headed up the path to the top of the ridge. Marcus was right. The views were amazing. They rode down the other side to the meadow. Once there, Katherine encouraged her horse to run, and it obliged. Marcus took off after her. He caught up, and the two raced across the open field, laughing and cheering each other onward. After a while, they rode to the top of the ridge again, dismounted, and walked the horses for a while.

When they finally reached the stream at the bottom of the ridge, they stopped to let the horses drink. "That was a blast," Katherine said. "Thanks!"

"Glad you enjoyed yourself," Marcus said. "This place is open every day from March through October, unless it's raining or snowing."

"Do you get much snow here?"

"Not that much in the city and the lower elevations," Marcus replied as they headed back toward the stables, "but the higher peaks get a fair bit. It usually snows at the house at least once a year, but it melts quickly. We've only had one serious snowfall since I've lived here. It snowed for three days, and it didn't melt for a week. I have a great photo of the house in the snow, and it's lovely."

"Are the winters cold?"

"December, January, and February are typically below freezing, but usually it's just chilly. The summers are mild, too. We rarely get above the mid-90s in the middle of summer, and there's always a breeze. We definitely have four distinct seasons here."

"I see why you call this place heaven."

"Especially now that you're here."

When they returned to the stables, Marcus dismounted and walked around to help Katherine dismount. She leaned down and kissed him, and then she slid out of the saddle into his arms.

"Thank you for bringing me here," she said.

"My pleasure," Marcus answered.

One of the ranch hands took their horses and led them back to the barn. Katherine stopped off in the office to get information about their youth riding programs and summer riding camps. Then she and Marcus walked back to the car.

"Where to next?" she asked as they pulled onto the main road.

"Hiking boots," Marcus replied.

"Right. Lots of boots today."

"It's the nature of the area. You need the proper footwear for whatever activity you're enjoying."

He drove east to the other side of downtown and then turned south on I-75. A mile later, he exited the interstate and pulled into the parking lot of a major outdoor, camping, and fishing equipment store.

"What should I be looking for?" Katherine asked, when she saw their selection of hiking boots.

"I know you hike in California," Marcus said, "but for here, I'd recommend waterproof, good ankle support, and deep treads that can handle dirt, rocks, and any other terrain."

Katherine tried on several pair before finally deciding on one. She bought the boots and three pairs of boot socks.

"I guess I'm all set now," she said as they left the store.

"Is there anything else you'd like to see while we're out?"

Katherine thought about it for a moment. "No, there's no sense in trying to do everything all at once. Let's pace ourselves."

"Good plan." Marcus got back on the interstate and headed back to the house.

As they passed the bend in the Tennessee River that curled around downtown, Marcus asked, "Do you like riverboats?"

"Sure."

"There's a riverboat cruise that leaves from the pier downtown. It has a daylight sightseeing tour, which is incredible when the leaves are turning, and a sunset cruise that's perfect year-round. Would you like to check it out while you're here?"

"That sounds like fun. Yes!"

As they drove past downtown, Katherine said, "If you don't mind me asking, just how *did* you get the house and land around it for so cheap? I went online after I saw the photos of your house, just to compare the price-per-square-foot with other large houses in the area, and no matter how I do the math, the cost is astronomical."

Marcus chuckled. "Curiosity got the better of you?"

"Well… yes."

"Okay. It's simple. The original owner had all of the land inside the clearing zoned as a single-family dwelling, and the rest of the land, including the ridge between the house and the gate, zoned as a wildlife preserve. If it's inside the fencing I told you about, it's residential, and the rest isn't. That means that the land cannot be broken up and developed any more than it is now. No developers could subdivide the land and build more houses on it, and no one can build another house or houses in the clearing, including me. I can build a guesthouse, but it has to be connected to the main house, either by a covered walkway or an enclosed walkway. Plus, the house wasn't finished. Basically, no one else wanted it. Most of the mansions in the area are northeast of town along the river, and that's where everyone wants to either build or buy. But I wanted the mountain, not the river, so I threw a low-ball bid on the property, just to get things rolling, and much to my surprise, there were no other bids. The state didn't care what the property sold for; it was all profit to them, since the land reverted to the state when the original owner died, so no one complained when I got it all for less than the cost of the house. And I had enough money left over to finish and furnish the place. I estimate that it's now worth about eight times what I paid."

"And the operating costs are low?"

"From a utilities perspective, yes. It's the most energy efficient residence in this part of the state. There's little upkeep required on the bulk of the property, other than keeping the hiking trails clear of branches and other debris, and clearing out the dead undergrowth periodically. The real ongoing costs are the landscapers, the cleaning crew, Mariana, and Grant, but I can't maintain the place without them."

"And what happens if something happens to you?" Katherine asked.

"I guess it goes to Leigh's kids, although I don't think they want it. They never came for a visit before Leigh passed, and they didn't stay here for the funeral. They'll probably just sell it and split the proceeds."

"You don't sound thrilled about that."

"I'm not," Marcus said. "I'd rather pass it to someone who loves the place as much as I do, but unless I get a new family somewhere, I don't see that happening. I wouldn't mind having it converted into something for charitable use, but what charity could take advantage of the layout? I've had my attorneys look into some possibilities, but nothing jumps out at me. Who knows? Maybe I'll think of something…"

Katherine understood—in that moment—that Marcus could never be happy living anywhere else, and that any future with him would have to be in Tennessee, not California. *This complicates things, but if this relationship is right, we'll find a way to make it work.*

They pulled into the garage shortly before one that afternoon. After they removed their boots and put on their deck shoes, Katherine took her purchases back to the master bedroom, and Marcus went to find Mariana.

"Ah, you're back, Mr. Marc," Mariana said. "Did Miss Kathy enjoy herself?"

"I think so," Marcus said.

"What do you want for lunch?"

"Any chance of having crab cakes?" Marcus asked.

Mariana gave him an amused look. "Of course you may have crab cakes, Mr. Marc. What do you want with them?"

"Whatever you think is best."

"Okay. Oh, and before I leave today, can you go over your schedule for after Miss Kathy leaves? I need to know how many catering jobs I can take on between now and the end of the year."

"Of course," Marcus said. "I should have done that yesterday."

"No worries, Mr. Marc. Today is fine."

"I'll go print out the schedule right now."

"Thank you!"

Marcus left the kitchen and headed for his office as Mariana started working on lunch.

Marcus had just sat down and put his phone on his desk when he heard Katherine walk past. "Kathy?"

"Marc? Where are you?"

"In the office," he said.

She stuck her head in and smiled. "What are you doing here?"

Marcus gestured for her to sit across the desk from him. "Mariana wants to know my schedule for the rest of year, so she can confirm which catering gigs she can take."

"She told me that you let her do catering when you're travelling, and that you let her use the kitchen here."

"It's better than her own kitchen, and it's not being used when I'm gone, so it seemed like a great way to help her out."

Katherine leaned back in the chair and watched as he turned on the computer, pulled up the calendar that she and he had made in his hotel room in Norcross, and printed it off.

"You really are a wonderful person," she said as he took the schedule off the printer.

"It's more fun to be nice to people, don't you think?"

"I do." Changing the subject, she asked, "What's for lunch?"

"Crab cakes."

"I should have guessed. That's a staple for you, isn't it?"

Marcus nodded with a grin. "I judge every restaurant by how good their crab cakes are, and none are better than Mariana's."

He started typing on the computer.

"What are you doing now?" Katherine asked.

"Checking availability for the sunset river cruise. Looks like there's an opening for two this Sunday night. Seven o'clock. Want me to reserve the tickets?"

"Yes!"

Marcus booked the cruise and printed out the tickets. "Anything else you want me to check on while you're here?"

"I can't think of anything at the moment," Katherine said. "I just want to be with you."

"And I just want to be with you," Marcus said.

They gazed into each other's eyes. Marcus turned off his computer, walked around the desk, and placed his hands on either side of Katherine's face. He kissed her, and she reached up and put her arms around his neck. He reached down, put his arms around her waist, and pulled her to her feet.

When Marcus finally pulled away, Katherine asked, "So,

Mariana and Grant won't be around all weekend?"

"No, we'll have the entire estate to ourselves from tonight until Monday morning."

"Good. I want to do things that normal couples do… and I don't want us to be disturbed."

"That can be arranged." Marcus smiled at her.

They heard Mariana calling from the kitchen. "Lunch is ready."

"Let's not keep her waiting," Katherine suggested.

"Good idea."

Marcus left his cell phone on his desk when they left the office and walked to the kitchen. When they arrived, Mariana was plating the crab cakes on a bed of mixed greens with homemade remoulade sauce and two wedges of lemon.

Marcus placed the printed schedule on the island. "Here's the schedule, Mariana."

"Thank you, Mr. Marc." Mariana pointed to one of the round tables on either side of the sitting area fireplace. "Go sit at the table, and I'll bring the food over."

Marcus and Katherine complied, and soon Mariana had brought over placemats, utensils, napkins, their plates, and glasses of iced tea. Then she was back in the kitchen, cleaning everything.

"These are so good," Katherine said.

"Told you hers were the best."

When they were finished eating, Mariana came and took their plates. "Do you like pork, Miss Kathy?"

"I love pork," she replied.

"Good. It's what's for dinner."

Katherine laughed silently as Mariana scurried back to the kitchen with the dishes.

CHAPTER 10

That evening, once Mariana and Grant had left and dinner was finished, Marcus and Katherine went for an evening swim. Katherine didn't wear her swimsuit, but that didn't matter, since they were all alone.

"Is this a saltwater pool?" Katherine asked, as she felt invigorated by the heated water against her bare skin.

"Yes, it is," Marcus replied. "And being heated, it can be used year-round. I like to swim laps in the morning when I'm here. It's a great way to start the day, and the saltwater is better for the skin and the hair. I don't need all those chemicals."

"How come you don't have a hot tub?" she asked.

"The chemicals. The pool is healthier, it can hold a lot more people, and it has hidden waterjets that can be turned on and off to give the pool more of a spa feel."

A wicked grin appeared on Katherine's face. "Show me."

Marcus activated the jets. Katherine swam over to the closest ones. The water level was low enough so she could stand up with her head above the water. She leaned back against the side of the pool, and she started giggling as the jets stimulated her more sensitive areas.

Marcus swam over to her. "Enjoying yourself?"

Katherine put her arms around him and kissed him, wrapping her legs around his waist. It didn't take long for him to be aroused by her passionate embrace and the waterjets shooting water directly at his lower extremities.

They made love in the pool, and Katherine found the sensation of being nearly weightless incredible. It allowed them to try positions that would be too difficult to attempt in the bedroom.

When they finally went back inside the house to wash off the salt, they ended up making love in the shower, followed by a lengthy session in the bed—by firelight. Katherine seemed to be unable to get enough of Marcus, and Marcus did his best to oblige. When they had finally exhausted themselves, and Marcus turned off the gas logs in the fireplaces, Katherine lay as close to him as possible, as if she were afraid that he would suddenly disappear.

The next morning, they woke up close to the same time, and Katherine suggested that they swim laps before breakfast.

"You want to swim laps… naked?" Marcus asked.

"Why not? No one's going to see us."

"Okay."

They swam laps for thirty minutes and then jumped into the shower together, where they shared a quick lovemaking session. After that, they got dressed, and Marcus cooked breakfast.

"I'm not as good as Mariana, but I think you'll like it," Marcus told Katherine.

After breakfast, they hiked up to Pinnacle Rock again. Katherine appreciated how much easier it was to reach the summit in her new hiking boots. They also hiked some of the other trails on the property. Marcus had packed a lunch to take with them, so they didn't get back to the house until after four in the afternoon. They went swimming again, showered, and put on matching bathrobes and slippers that Marcus had hanging in the closet, which rivaled the robes at The Four Seasons.

Marcus and Katherine made dinner together that night. After the leftovers had been put away and the dishes washed, they sat in the den, enjoying a bottle of wine.

"How long have you been divorced?" Marcus asked.

"Eight years," replied Katherine. "Sometimes it seems much longer, and sometimes it seems like only a few months ago."

"Would you ever consider getting married again?"

"Are you asking if I think about getting married, if I want to get married, or if I want to get married to you?"

"Yes."

Katherine looked at him. "Is that a proposal?"

"It's an inquiry… for the moment."

"Do *you* ever think about getting married again?"

"I asked first," Marcus reminded her.

"Okay," Katherine began. She took a deep breath and let it out slowly. "Yes, I have thought about it. Yes, if I were with the right person, I'd want to get married again. And even though we haven't been together very long, yes, I think you're the right person. Now, answer my question, please."

"Yes, I think about it, but I haven't met the right person… until now."

"So, you *are* asking me to marry you?"

"Would it be a problem for you if I were?"

"You know I could never say 'yes' unless the boys approved of you. We've talked about that before."

"I know," Marcus said. "But if you didn't have to worry about what the boys thought, or if the boys didn't… disapprove, would you want to marry me?"

Katherine looked him in the eyes and said, "There's nothing in this world that I want more than to marry you, Marc Buchanan."

"And would you consider wearing a ring before the boys approved of me, if I were to get you one?"

"A promise ring or an engagement ring?"

"I think it would definitely be considered an engagement ring," Marcus replied.

"Yes," Katherine stated.

Marcus smiled. "That's all I wanted to know. Conversation to be continued."

"When?" Katherine demanded.

"Wednesday," Marcus said, "and then again in November."

"What happens Wednesday?"

Marcus shook his head. "You'll find out on Wednesday."

Katherine groaned, grabbed the decorative pillow next to her, and smacked Marcus in the back of the head with it. "That's not fair."

"I could have just said November," Marcus pointed out.

"Okay, okay." Katherine kissed his cheek. "I'll wait for Wednesday."

When they went to bed later, they didn't bother putting anything on, after they removed the robes. They realized that they preferred the feeling of skin on skin, even if they weren't making love.

Over the next several days, Katherine and Marcus spent their time enjoying each other's company. Katherine loved the sunset riverboat cruise on Sunday. The colors of the sky and the lights reflecting on the water were beautiful.

On Monday, they toured Lookout Mountain, the railroad museum, and some of the other tourist destinations in the area. On Tuesday, Marcus drove Katherine to the Chickamauga Battlefield in Georgia, just south of the city. He kept her up late watching movies in the theatre downstairs, so she'd sleep late on Wednesday morning.

Marcus left the house at seven on Wednesday morning. He

had an errand to run, and he didn't want Katherine knowing about it. He moved so quietly that Katherine never felt him get out of bed and never heard him turn off the alarms and leave the bedroom.

He returned just after eight-thirty, and found that Katherine was still in bed. He got undressed and crawled in bed with her. He snuggled close and held her in his arms as she slept.

When she finally woke up just after nine, Marcus was smiling at her. "Good morning, sleepyhead," he said.

"Good morning," Katherine responded. "What time is it?"

"Nine-ish."

"Humpf. I didn't think I'd sleep this late." She sounded groggy. "Why didn't you wake me?"

"I like watching you sleep."

Katherine propped herself on her elbow and gave Marcus a kiss. "How long have you been awake?"

"Since six-thirty."

"And you've been watching me the whole time?" She didn't sound groggy anymore.

Marcus chuckled. "No, I actually got up and left for a while. I came back thirty minutes ago. You were still asleep, so I got back to bed to be with you."

"And watch me sleeping."

Marcus nodded.

Katherine lifted the covers. "And undressed, too?"

Marcus just grinned.

"Is that an invitation?"

"Not necessarily," Marcus replied. "I just didn't see any reason to get in bed fully dressed."

Katherine looked confused. "Where did you go?"

"To get you a little something."

"You didn't have to do that," she said, sitting up. "You've done enough already—too much, in fact."

Marcus sat up, too. "I can always take it back if you don't

want it."

Katherine stared at him for a moment. "Well, I don't want to seem ungrateful. Maybe I should see what it is first."

Marcus turned on the bedroom lights, and then he handed her a small, royal blue sack with gold lettering on it. It was a name, but Katherine didn't recognize it. Inside was a package wrapped in matching blue paper with a gold ribbon. She opened the package, and inside was another package, only this package was slightly smaller and wrapped in crimson paper with a gold bow. Katherine looked at Marcus curiously, then she opened the smaller package.

Inside was a cardboard box. She opened the box, and inside was a leather-covered box with a small clasp on it. She took a deep breath, let it out slowly, and opened the clasp. The top of the box split open to reveal a ring inside.

Her hands trembled as she looked at it. The diamond sparkled with fire as the light refracted from the perfectly cut facets of the stone. Smaller, deep green emeralds flanked the diamond on either side. The band was yellow gold.

Katherine took the ring out of the box, so she could take a closer look at it. She noticed an inscription on the inside of the band, which read, *You Write the Words in My Heart*, followed by the date. She looked up at Marcus, her eyes filling with tears. "Is this what you were talking about when you said our conversation from the other night would be continued today?"

Marcus nodded. He put both of his hands around her hand and the ring. "Katherine Delaney, with the understanding that your sons have to give their approval before it's official, will you marry me?"

Katherine couldn't hold back the tears any longer. She nodded. "YES! Yes, I'll marry you... based on the stipulated conditions." She giggled as Marcus took the ring and placed it on her finger. It fit perfectly.

"How did you do that?" she asked.

"Do what?"

"Buy a ring that doesn't have to be resized?"

Marcus smiled and wiped the tears from her eyes. "First of all, I didn't buy this ring. I had it made." He held up the bag. "This jeweler does custom work only. Second, I've seen you wear a ring on this finger before, so I traced the inside loop of that ring and photographed it on a grid that the jeweler gave me, so he could match the size perfectly."

Katherine stared at the ring in awe.

"Do you like it?" Marcus asked.

Katherine threw her arms around his neck and kissed him. "I absolutely love it!"

It was two hours before they finally emerged from the bedroom, and by then it was nearly time for lunch.

Mariana was about to say something about them missing breakfast, but she took one look at the ring on Katherine's finger and just smiled. "I see Mr. Marc finally gave you the ring."

Katherine looked at Mariana open-mouthed. "You knew about this?"

Mariana nodded. "I knew last Friday morning when Mr. Marc met with the jeweler, and I knew again this morning when Mr. Marc went to pick up the ring. He's been nervous about giving you that ring for days."

Katherine looked at Marcus, who appeared to be blushing, although it was hard to tell with his beard.

"Anyway," Mariana continued. "You missed breakfast, which is not good. I'll get started on lunch. You must eat!"

As Mariana began scurrying around the kitchen, Katherine asked Marcus, "So, who else knows about our engagement?"

"Well, Grant knows, of course. And Julia and Frankie know. I haven't told anyone else. Have you thought how you're going to tell Greg and the boys?"

"I think I need to do that face-to-face, once I get back to L.A.," Katherine said. "It doesn't feel right to do it over the phone or on a video chat. I think it needs to be more personal."

"If you want to include me when you tell them, just let me know," Marcus offered. "I can be on the phone or on a video chat. Your choice."

Katherine smiled. "I think that's a good idea. They need to keep getting used to seeing you before they meet you in person in November."

"That's what I was thinking, too."

The rest of the week went by too fast for Katherine. She was scheduled to fly out on Saturday morning just before noon, change planes in Atlanta, and arrive at LAX at three-thirty in the afternoon. Greg and the boys were coming to the airport to pick her up, and she looked forward to seeing them. She hadn't been back to Los Angeles in almost four months—even though she talked to the boys several times a week via video calls on her cell phone—and as much as she missed home and the boys, she found it increasingly difficult to pull herself away from Tennessee and Marcus.

"When do you leave for your book tour?" Katherine asked Friday night when she and Marcus were alone in the den.

"Tuesday morning. Early."

Katherine nodded. "I'm supposed to land at three-thirty Pacific Time tomorrow. That's six-thirty here. It'll take over an hour to gather my luggage and drive home, so why don't we plan to have the video call at five-thirty Pacific, eight-thirty here. Is that too late for you?"

"No, it's perfect. But let's not use cell phones for this. I can set up a video conference on our computers. Your computer has a camera and microphone, doesn't it?"

Katherine nodded.

"Good," Marcus continued. "That way the video quality will be better, and it'll be easier for me to see all of you at the same time. I'll email you the link."

"Thanks."

Marcus looked at her. "Are you nervous about going home?"

"No. The problem is I'm not sure L.A. will seem like home. I love this place, and I love you. Anyplace you're not just won't feel like home anymore."

Marcus nodded. "Well, at least we'll be able to talk on the phone or on video calls until I get out there. I know we'll probably have to schedule the calls a day at a time, but I don't want to go a day without hearing your voice or seeing your face."

"Me neither," Katherine said.

Marcus pulled her close to him.

"When you take me to the airport tomorrow," Katherine began, "I want you to drop me off outside. Don't come inside to see me off. If you're there, I'll never be able to get on that plane."

"Are you sure?"

"No," she admitted. "But… please. I don't want to go, but I have to. Okay?"

"Okay. I understand."

They sat silently for a while.

"What time do we have to leave in the morning?" Katherine asked.

"Nine-thirty."

Katherine looked at the clock on the wall. "That's in twelve hours. We don't have a second to waste."

She kissed him, and he held her tight. Then he pulled away, stood, and picked her up in his arms. He carried her to the master bedroom, closing the door behind him with his heel.

Marcus had already pulled the SUV around to the front door and was loading Katherine's luggage, when she emerged from the master bedroom with her travel case.

"Did you check everywhere to make sure you weren't leaving anything behind?" Marcus asked when she joined him outside.

"I think so."

"Everywhere in the closet? The mudroom?"

Katherine nodded.

"And you remembered to pack all of the information you gathered this week about Chattanooga? The riding programs and camps? The private schools? All that?"

"It's all packed," Katherine confirmed.

Marcus looked down and saw that Katherine was wearing her engagement ring. He smiled and packed her travel case in the back with the rest of the luggage.

Katherine got into the front seat, as Marcus activated the alarm and locked the front door. When he got into the SUV, he said, "It's going to be very strange around here without you."

"At least you're only here for another couple of days."

"But I'll be all alone here for the rest of today and all of tomorrow. I don't even remember what it's like to be completely alone in this house."

Katherine reached out and put her hand on his. "Hopefully, you won't have to be alone here much longer."

Marcus looked at her and nodded. He started the engine and headed for the gate. Katherine turned around in her seat and watched the house behind them, until the ridge and trees hid it from view.

When they reached the airport, Marcus unloaded her

luggage, while Katherine had all of the bags checked at the curbside check-in. As each piece was being tagged and moved to the conveyor, Marcus hugged and kissed Katherine.

"Have a safe flight, and I'll see you online this evening."

He could see the tears brimming in her eyes. Knowing the conflict she was struggling with, he simply said, "Go. We'll be together again soon enough."

Katherine nodded, wiped away the tears from her eyes, gave him a quick kiss, and turned and entered the airport terminal.

Marcus watched her go, until she disappeared in the crowd. He got back in the SUV and drove home.

When he pulled into the garage, he heard a chime that told him he had a text message. He looked at his phone and saw the message was from Katherine.

"Marc, I love you more than words can say, and I've had more fun in the months that we've known each other than I've had for the rest of my life combined. I love you, and I miss you already. I'm looking at my ring, and it helps me know that I have a piece of you with me always. I'll see you soon. Kathy."

Marcus sent a quick response, and then he headed for his office to work on the novelization of *The Spy Upstairs*, submerging himself in work to avoid the loneliness he felt so strongly.

CHAPTER 11

Katherine's plane landed at LAX a few minutes before three-thirty local time. Her flights had been smooth and uneventful, but inside she was a wreck. Between missing Marcus, looking forward to seeing the boys, and trying to find the right words to explain that she was engaged to a man the boys had never met and what that meant to the three of them as a family, she found it hard to relax and enjoy the flight.

As she waited for the cabin door of the plane to open, she sent a quick text to Greg. *"I'm here."*

Greg responded almost immediately. *"We're at baggage claim, waiting for you."*

Katherine then sent Marcus a text to let him know that she arrived safely.

He responded a moment later, letting her know how much he loved and missed her.

The cabin door finally opened, and Katherine exited the plane, walked up the jetway to the terminal, and followed the signs to the baggage claim area. As soon as she exited the secure part of the airport for arriving passengers, and approached the baggage claim carrousels, she heard two familiar voices shout, "Mom!"

She looked around and saw Jack and Ben running toward her. She hugged and kissed them both. "Oh, I've missed you two."

"We missed you, too, Mom," both boys said.

Greg caught up to the boys a moment later. Katherine smiled and gave him a kiss on the cheek. "Hi, Greg. Thanks for picking me up and bringing the boys with you."

"They've been looking forward to this for days," said Greg. He looked at her closely. "My God, you're glowing! I guess Tennessee agrees with you."

Katherine beamed.

As the boys led the way to the carousel, Greg noticed the ring on Katherine's finger. "What's that?" he asked, pointing to her left hand.

Katherine held up her hand so Greg could see the ring.

"You're engaged?!" he whispered.

Katherine nodded happily.

"That's wonderful, Kate." He gave her a quick hug as they walked. "Do the boys know?"

She shook her head. "I'm telling them after we get home. I'm having a video conference with Marc, and we're going to tell the boys together. Marc knows that the engagement isn't *official* until the boys approve, which I hope they do."

"When do they get to meet him in person?"

"He'll be here in November at the end of his book tour. But they've already seen him on a video call, they'll see him again tonight, and we're trying to set up more video calls while he's on tour, so they can get used to seeing him."

"Wow. I'm so happy for you, Kate. You know, if you move to Chattanooga, I'll almost be as close to you there as I am here from my place in Santa Barbara… or at least the drive will be about the same. You'll have to let me know one way or another as soon as you can. It'll help determine where I should look for a house."

"The boys will love that," Katherine noted. "When are you moving to Atlanta?"

"I have to be there by the first of February. Originally, we were supposed to be there before Thanksgiving, but then someone remembered that it's a lousy time to be moving people right before the holidays. I'll have to make a few house-hunting trips between now and then, but that's all the traveling I'll have to do before the move."

"Any new projects in the works?"

"Several actually," Greg admitted. "Business is booming."

"Any parts for me?"

Greg laughed. "Are you going to continue acting?"

"Of course. I'm not going to suddenly become a housewife, you know."

"Just checking," Greg said, chuckling. "And there are a few parts you might want to pursue. You know, we were hoping to bring Marc onboard to write a couple of scripts for us, but his agent let it slip that he's up for the head writer spot on a film franchise reboot and may be tied up with that for a couple of years. We're hoping to hear back before February, but it'll be a shame to miss out on tapping into his talents."

They arrived at the carousel and waited for the luggage to arrive.

"How many bags do you have with you?" Greg asked.

"Six," was the reply. "No, seven. I forgot I had to buy another bag for some things I bought out there… including some gifts for the boys. Plus, I have several copies of Marc's books."

Greg brought Katherine up-to-speed on how things had gone with the boys while she was away, including school and their after-school activities. When the carousel lit up and began turning, they all moved closer to watch for Katherine's bags.

Since she had flown first class, her bags came out of the conveyor first, and Greg and the boys grabbed each one as it passed. Then they all rolled her bags out of the terminal to

Greg's car.

On the ride home, Katherine was struck by the difference between the hustle and bustle of Los Angeles and the easy pace and wide-open spaces of southeastern Tennessee. It made her miss Marcus and Chattanooga even more. When they pulled up to her house, it seemed so small, and for the first time since she had bought it, it didn't feel like home at all.

Greg stuck around while Katherine gave the boys their gifts and then went upstairs to unpack. When she came back downstairs, it was thirty minutes before her call with Marcus. She called the boys over and sat them down.

"What's that?" Jack asked, pointing to the ring.

"We're going to talk about that," Katherine said. 'But first, I wanted to let you know that we're going to be on a video call with my friend Marc Buchanan in thirty minutes."

"He's the one you started dating, right? The one on a couple of the calls we had with you?" Jack asked.

"That's right, Jack. He wants to see the two of you again. He's going to be here in November, and we're all going to get together while he's in California, but he wants both of you to get used to seeing him before the first time he comes over."

The boys nodded, and Greg just smiled in the background. "I'm going to head out," Greg said. "It's a long drive home, and I want to get there before dark."

Katherine got up and walked him to the door. "Thanks again for everything, Greg."

"You're welcome, Kate. Good luck with the video call and the announcement."

Katherine grinned nervously. Greg left, and she walked back to the den where the boys were waiting.

"Tell us about where Mr. Buchanan lives in Tennessee," Jack asked.

Katherine tried to describe the house, but finally she had to pull up the architectural magazine article on the computer and show them the pictures.

“Wow, he lives there?” Jack asked.

Katherine nodded. “And believe me; the pictures don’t come close to showing you how wonderful it is.” She told them about what all she had done while she was there, including the hiking and horseback riding.

She looked at the clock and saw that it was almost time for the video call.

“I’m hungry,” Ben said.

“Can you wait a little while?” Katherine asked. “We’re going to be chatting with Marc in a couple of minutes. After that, we’ll eat. Okay?”

Ben agreed, and Katherine activated the video link that Marcus had sent her. A moment later, Marcus’s face appeared on the screen.

“Hi, Kathy,” he said with a huge smile on his face.

“Hi, Marc,” Katherine said. She pulled the boys in closer. “You remember my sons, Jack and Ben? Boys, say ‘Hello’ to Mr. Buchanan.”

“Hi, Mr. Buchanan,” the boys said.

“Mom just showed us pictures of your house,” Jack added. “Wow!”

Marcus laughed. “It’s a bit empty, now that your mom’s gone.”

Katherine interrupted. “Shall we tell them?”

“Go ahead,” Marcus said. “They should hear it from you.”

Katherine nodded. She took a deep breath and let it out slowly. “Jack, Ben, you know that Marc and I started dating while we were working on my movie in Atlanta. We got… close, and after I went to visit him at his home in Tennessee, we got even closer.” She showed the boys her ring. “Marc has asked me to marry him, and even though I said ‘yes,’ it was understood that it can only happen if the two of you approve. What happens to me affects both of you, so we all have to be in agreement, okay?"

The boys nodded. "So, you'll be our new dad?" Jack asked.

Marcus grinned. "You'll always have your real dad, and nothing will ever change that. I certainly don't want to change that. You can think of me as an additional dad, or you can think of me as an uncle, or you can just think of me as your mother's husband. It's really up to you. But know this. I love your mother, and I'll love both of you for as long as I live."

"Do we have to move to Tennessee?" Ben asked. "I've never been there."

"Well, that's part of what we need to decide," Katherine said. "Marc will be here at the first of November, and he'll be in L.A. for several weeks. We'll all be getting together, here and at his apartment in Marina Del Ray, and if things go well, we'll all fly to Tennessee together to stay with him at his house for Thanksgiving. That's when I'll need for both of you to either approve of the marriage and the move to Tennessee, or tell me you don't want to move out there and be a family."

The boys nodded.

Katherine kissed them both. "Okay, boys. Why don't you go upstairs while I saw goodbye to Marc, and then we'll make dinner."

"Bye, Uncle Marc," Jack said.

"Bye, Jack."

"Bye," Ben said.

"Bye, Ben."

Once the boys had left the room, Katherine said, "I think that went well."

"Did it? I don't think Ben's too keen on the idea."

"He loves his father and doesn't understand why we divorced. It'll take him a little longer to come around, but he will."

"Okay, I'll rely on you to help me there."

Katherine nodded. "What did you do after you got home?"

"Just working on *The Spy Upstairs*. I'll be spending all day tomorrow and Monday doing the same. Writing keeps me from feeling lonely."

"Don't forget to eat," Katherine reminded him.

"Did Mariana put you up to saying that," Marcus joked.

"No, but she's right, you know. You need to take care of yourself when you're alone."

"Yes, *Dear*."

Katherine laughed. "Well, I better figure out dinner for the boys. I love you!"

"I love you," Marcus said.

"Can we talk Monday?"

Marcus nodded. "Let's talk early. I'll be packing and getting ready to fly out before dawn on Tuesday."

"Okay. Talk to you then."

"Bye, Kathy."

"Bye, Marc."

The video call ended, and Katherine shut down the computer and headed for the kitchen to see if there was any food to cook or if she needed to order food to be delivered.

She checked the pantry, the refrigerator, and the freezer. *Pizza delivery it is.*

Over the next two days, Marcus wrote and rewrote chapters of the novel for *The Spy Upstairs*, trying to bring the book and the way the film was shot closer together. As he wrote, he couldn't help but think about Katherine's performance, and he constantly had to remind himself that the novel was not about her character alone. There were two other lead characters and a host of secondary characters that deserved proper treatment in the story.

By Monday evening, he had accomplished a lot, but he knew he needed to stop and get ready for his trip. He shut down his computer and walked down the hall to the master bedroom, so he could begin packing for two months-worth of travel.

Marcus had given Mariana the day off, so he grabbed a quick bite from the kitchen and ate it over the sink. Then he went to his office and packed up his laptop and a few other things he needed. When he returned to the bedroom, he lined up the bags next to the front door, and then he went to bed.

The next morning, he showered, dressed, and grabbed a pastry from the kitchen. A few minutes later, the gate intercom sounded. It was the airport shuttle. He opened the gate from the security panel, and then he started moving his luggage next to the driveway. The shuttle pulled up to the house, and the driver helped Marcus put the luggage in the back. Marcus locked the front door, activated the alarm, and took his seat in the shuttle. The driver headed out the gate and toward the airport.

Katherine woke early—her body still on Eastern Time—and lay in bed. She tried to get back to sleep, but she was wide-awake. And she was used to Marcus lying next to her. She finally got up and started making lists of everything she had to get done that week.

She got the boys up, made them breakfast, and drove them to the private school they attended about ten minutes away. After she dropped them off, she went to her yoga class. She stopped by the grocery store on the way home, and then she started the laundry as she checked messages, returned calls and emails, and rearranged her bookshelves to make room for Marcus' books.

She talked at length to her agent, not only about her engagement to Marcus, but also about potential upcoming parts. Katherine asked her agent to keep an eye on Greg's production company, relaying his comments that there were projects starting after the first of the year with parts that she should pursue. Her agent promised to keep Katherine informed, then she congratulated Katherine on her engagement again and ended the call.

Katherine's life was settling into the same routine she had before her film shoot and her vacation in Tennessee—mom, housekeeper, and actress-between-jobs. She went hiking several times along the hills around her house, but whether she was by herself or with the boys, it didn't feel the same. She found herself thinking about the mountains of Tennessee, the trees, the birds, and the views of the valleys and rivers. And she thought about being with Marcus.

The elements that comprised her everyday life were all too familiar, but Katherine couldn't shake the feeling that it would never seem completely normal again.

Marcus landed in New York on time. He changed clothes in the men's room, grabbed his luggage from baggage claim, and met the limo waiting to take him directly to one of the largest bookstores in the city for his first signing of the new tour. His latest novel was being released that same day, and according to Julia, the line of people waiting to meet him and get a signed book was wrapping the building already.

When the driver pulled up to the bookstore, Julia was waiting for him. The driver looked back and said, "I'll take your luggage to your hotel, and then I'll be back here at six to pick you up. You have a reception at your hotel at seven-thirty."

"Thanks," Marcus said.

The driver got out and came around to open Marcus' door. Marcus grabbed his briefcase and stepped out of the car. He gave Julia a kiss on the cheek as the crowds recognized him and began cheering. He waved, and Julia led him inside the store as the driver pulled back into traffic.

Once the crowds waiting for Marcus were allowed into the store—all of whom were required to have wristbands distributed the previous week—the five levels of the bookstore quickly filled to capacity.

In the center of the first level of the store, a platform had been set up with speakers at every corner. His editor from the publishing company introduced Marcus, and as the crowd went wild, she handed him the microphone. He waved to the people surrounding him on the ground level, and the people pressed against the railings on the upper levels. Marcus then stepped up to the lectern and started reading pages from his new book. His voice was amplified, so he could be heard throughout the store.

Julia and the people from his publishing company finished setting up the signing area while he was reading. Cases of books were stacked behind the signing table, and velvet ropes were set up to keep the queue organized and moving so the crowd wouldn't completely disrupt the bookstore's normal operations.

When Marcus was finished with his reading, the crowd went crazy. Marcus was escorted to the signing table, and bookstore employees took their positions to help patrons from all five levels of the store get through the signing lines as quickly and safely as possible.

At a quarter to six, Marcus signed the last two copies of his new book. The cases of books were all empty, and everyone with a wristband had received their copy. Marcus leaned back, took a sip of water from his bottle, and looked up at Julia and his editor.

"That went well," he said.

"That was fantastic," Julie and his editor gushed.

His editor continued, "You have five more signings here in the city, and I expect they'll be just as successful."

Julia asked, "Are you ready for the reception tonight?"

"Tell me again who's attending?" Marcus asked, standing.

"Fans who paid handsomely for the privilege of attending," his editor answered, "along with key staff from your publisher and some of our distribution partners."

"What's the attire?"

"Put on a coat and tie, and you'll be fine," Julia said.

"Will there be food, or will I have time to eat before it starts?"

"Dinner will be waiting for you in your room when you get to the hotel," his editor said. "Julia and I will be up to collect you at seven-twenty. Be ready, okay?"

Marcus grinned and saluted. "Yes, ma'am!"

Marcus saw the limo pull up outside. "If you ladies will excuse me, my ride is here."

They walked him out. The driver held the door for him as he got into the back seat.

When the driver got into the car, Marcus asked, "How long before we get to the hotel?"

"Fifteen minutes in this traffic."

"Good. I need to make a call."

The driver raised the partition to give Marcus privacy as he called Katherine to tell her about the book signing.

The boys had just gotten home from school when Marcus called. Knowing that she was busy, he kept the call short.

"I just wanted to say that the first signing went well, all of the books sold out, I'm heading to a reception at my hotel, and I have five more signings in the city before I head to Boston. I miss you, I love you, and I can't wait to see you. Can we video chat tomorrow night after I get back to my hotel?"

"What time?" Katherine asked.

"What works best for you?"

"What about seven o'clock here, ten o'clock your time?"

"I can do that. I'll call you then."

"I love you, Marc."

"I love you, Kathy. Tell the boys I said 'Hi'."

"I will. Bye."

"Bye."

The next signings in New York went just as well as the first one. Marcus and Katherine had three video chats and sent lots of text messages during those five days. Julia and Gina—who represented his publisher—flew with Marcus to Boston for the next round of signings, which included two in downtown Boston and one near Harvard.

After Boston, he was driven down to Providence and then to Hartford. From there he flew to Atlanta, Miami, Nashville, and then Chicago.

He spent a week in the Windy City, doing five signings, two receptions, and taking advantage of a rare day off before heading for Dallas-Fort Worth, Houston, Oklahoma City, Kansas City, St. Louis, Portland, Seattle, Phoenix, Albuquerque, and Las Vegas. Then he had another day off before heading for San Francisco and ending up in Los Angeles, where he was going to speak at a screenwriter's conference, in addition to doing four book signings.

Marcus took advantage of the few days off built in the schedule to finish the novel for *The Spy Upstairs*. He also spent as much time as possible talking to Katherine, who has been attending auditions for a couple of films that were slated to start filming the next spring.

"Sounds like your life is back to normal again," Marcus noted on their video call his last night in Las Vegas.

"Not at all," Katherine stated. "I miss you every second of the day. The other stuff is just how I'm dealing with it, but my life is with you. *You* are my normal, now."

"I feel the same way," Marcus said. "You know I'll be in

California tomorrow and in Los Angeles in three days."

"I know." Katherine held up her calendar with the days marked off and the day he arrived in Los Angeles circled. "I can't wait."

"Neither can I," Marcus said. "Did you get the email with my schedule for when I'm there?"

"I got it, thanks."

Marcus stifled a yawn. "Sorry about that. I was up late finishing *The Spy Upstairs*."

"You're done?" Katherine was excited.

"I want to read through it one more time, but yes, I think it's done."

"I can't wait to read it."

"I'll have my publisher add you to the pre-release recipients, so you can get one of the review copies. Only a few of those are printed, so it'll be a collector's item someday."

Katherine laughed. "I know you think you're kidding, but all of your books are collector's items to me. Now, get some sleep, and I'll see you soon."

"I love you, Kathy."

"I love you, Marc. Good night."

"Good night."

The two signings in San Francisco went well, but he hardly slept his last night in the city. He was too excited to be flying to Los Angeles the next morning.

Julia and Gina met him in the hotel lobby the next morning. As the luggage was placed in the limo taking them to the airport, Julia asked, "Excited to finally be heading for L.A.?"

Marcus nodded enthusiastically.

"Looking forward to seeing Katherine again."

"More than I can say," he confirmed.

Julia had a cryptic smile on her face. "I imagine you've been keeping her updated on how well the tour has been going."

"Of course." Marcus looked at her. "But I have a question. Why are you flying to L.A.? You usually don't stay with me for the entire tour. What gives?"

"I'm taking the opportunity to meet with Frankie while we're here," Julia replied. "It long overdue, don't you think?"

Marcus smiled. "I do. Are you going to be with me in Britain and Canada in December?"

Julia shook her head. "No, but your publisher is sending someone to coordinate everything in the cities you'll be visiting. You'll be in good hands."

They all climbed into the limo and headed for the airport.

When the plane landed at LAX, Frankie was there to meet them.

"What are you doing here?" Marcus asked, giving her a kiss and introducing her to Julia and Gina.

"I'm going with you to your speaking engagement at the Screen Writer's conference," she replied. "By the way, I went by your place in Marina Del Ray to make sure that everything's ready for your arrival. The pantry and fridge are full, I adjusted the temperature for you, and I made certain that the place had been cleaned. The keys to the car we're providing are on the kitchen counter, and the car is in your usual spot."

"Thanks, Frankie."

"I've also made arrangements for the limo to wait for us at the venue. It'll take you to your place before taking Julia and Gina to their hotel, which is just down the street from the apartment."

"Perfect."

They collected their bags and went to meet the limo driver.

CHAPTER 12

They arrived at the venue a few minutes early, and the crowd waiting to get inside was huge.

"Good turnout," Frankie noted. She told the driver to pull around to the back of the building, where parking had been reserved for the limo. He pulled into the assigned space when he reached the rear, and Marcus, Frankie, Julia, and Gina got out and headed into the venue's backstage area.

When it was time for the speaking engagement to begin, Marcus stood behind the curtain, waiting to be introduced. The event organizer walked onstage, made a few announcements, and then introduced Marcus as the featured speaker, giving details of his screenwriting credits and awards. Marcus heard the applause and knew it was time to make his entrance. He stepped through the curtains and waved to the cheering crowd.

He shook hands with the event organizer, thanked him for his introduction, and then stepped up to the microphone. The crowd quieted down.

"Good morning, fellow screenwriters!" The crowd erupted again. Marcus let them clap for a moment, and then he held up his hand to quiet them down.

"And here I thought that screenwriters were a calm and

reserved bunch. I guess I was misinformed." The audience laughed. Marcus smiled, and then he continued. "The strange thing about movies is that everyone remembers who the actors are, most people remember who the director is, many people even remember who scored the soundtrack, but few people remember who the writer is. And yet, without a script, the actors don't know what to say, and the director doesn't know what to shoot. There is no film without a script. Actors bring our words to life, directors create the environment in which the actors give their performances, composers enhance the emotional impact of the scenes through music, but without a script, none of the rest of the movie exists. No vision from the director, no performance from the actors, no music from the composers… hell, the studio won't even know what to market. But we're not the ones celebrated when a movie does well, and we're often not the ones blamed when a movie tanks, although we certainly share in that blame. To most moviegoers, we're invisible. And that's as it should be. It's not our job to be in the limelight. It's our job to put others in the limelight for their great vision, their great performances, and for their great music. We provide the context for how all the other components of the movie's production can exist… ultimately to entertain and delight the audience. That's our job; that's our place; that's our role in this business. So, let's talk about how we can do that job to the best of our abilities."

Marcus spoke for an hour, giving several examples of the components of a good story, how to translate that story into a script, adapting the script to the casting and the changing vision of the director, and keeping ego out of the screenwriting process, so the writer is focused on giving directors what they want, giving actors what they need, and giving audiences what they're paying to see.

At the end of his talk, he opened the session for questions from the audience. The first person who stood was none other than C.J., the director from *The Spy Upstairs*. Marcus introduced him to the audience.

"What's your question, C.J.?"

"I thought it might be helpful if you walked your fellow writers through how you rewrote those scenes in the movie we just completed together."

"Certainly. On a film shoot, the writer must be mindful of three things: the script—meaning the story itself, the director, and the actors. Some dialogue sounds good in your head, but it sounds terrible when actually spoken by the actor. Fortunately, we didn't have too much of that to deal with in *The Spy Upstairs*. But you have to be able to tell when a scene isn't working, and then quickly come up with ideas that can improve it, without changing the story so much that you cause a great deal of re-work, or create contradictions between a scene that needs to be changed and scenes that have already been shot or will be shot later in the production. You must be able to read the frustration from the actors and the director, identify the source of the frustration, and come up with ideas on-the-fly to alleviate the frustration."

Marcus then gave a specific example from the film that C.J. had directed. "In *The Spy Upstairs*, an actress was cast who was really too good for the part the way it was written. The original story called for her death before the end of act two, but her talents would have made her a great addition to several subsequent scenes, including the climax of the film. We had been shooting take after take after take of her death scene, but I saw that C.J. wasn't satisfied with any of them. It took a while, but I finally saw that his frustration wasn't the way the scene was written or the way the actors were performing, it was that he didn't want the character to die. So, I began writing a new scene in my notebook, which I'm never without on a film set. I also had to note changes in future scenes that were needed if the character were to live instead of die, and because of this particular actress' talents, I saw an opportunity to increase the importance of her role, giving her an expanded part that, I think, made for a far better ending. Do you agree, C.J.?"

C.J. stood and said, "I certainly do."

"You see, that's part of the job. It's not 'write a script and collect a paycheck.' It's supporting the director's vision for the film, even if that means changing the script to adapt to a variety of factors that take the film in a different direction. As the writer, you have to balance preserving the integrity of the story with delivering what directors need to fulfil their vision. It's not a one-and-done proposition, it's an evolving process, and if you cannot watch your work get rewritten time and time again, this isn't the profession for you. Screenwriters exist to serve actors, directors, producers, and studios—all of whom have a say, to some degree, in the final product."

Marcus answered several other questions, and at the end of the second hour, the event organizer announced that the session was over. The audience applauded, and many of the audience members came forward to speak with Marcus privately.

C.J. came up and congratulated Marcus on his presentation. "We really need to chat while you're in town," he said several times. Marcus pointed to Frankie and told him to speak with her to set up meetings.

As the line of people waiting to see him started getting shorter, he saw a familiar face standing at the end of the line. His face broke into a huge smile. "Ladies and gentlemen, I'd like to introduce you to the actress I was speaking about earlier when I talked about the rewrites on *The Spy Upstairs*. This is Katherine Delaney, the actress who did *not* die at the end of act two."

Marcus motioned for Katherine to come forward as the remaining audience members applauded.

"What are you doing here?" he asked when she reached him.

"Frankie and Julia called me and arranged this."

Marcus looked over at his agents and smiled. He then

looked at the audience members, held up his hand, and said, "Excuse me for a moment." He kissed Katherine.

Katherine smiled when the audience cheered, and she stayed next to Marcus as he finished answering the one-on-one questions.

Once the audience members had left the auditorium, Marcus hugged Katherine and then introduced her to Frankie, Julia, and Gina. They took turns oohing and aahing over Katherine's ring.

"That was the first time I've ever heard you speak in front of a crowd," Katherine said. "You were great! It seemed so natural and effortless."

"Thank you! I used to be terrified of speaking in front of people," Marcus said. "But after you do it enough times, it gets easier. And it's not the first time I've delivered this particular presentation. It's my standard Screenwriter 101 lecture, there are other presentations I give depending on the nature of the workshop or group I'm presenting to. It's good to give back to the youngsters coming up behind you, don't you think?"

"I do," Katherine confirmed. "That's why I work with acting workshops and community theatre between gigs. I think teaching makes us better at our craft. If we understand it well enough to teach it, then we should understand it well enough to do it properly."

"I couldn't agree more. So, what are your plans for the rest of the day?" Marcus asked.

"Greg has the boys until tomorrow night," she said, "so I was hoping to spend the day with you and come to your book signing tomorrow. Julia already reserved my wristband."

"Terrific! How did you get here? Did you drive?"

"Frankie sent a car for me."

"There's room for all of us in the limo," Frankie said. "We should head out."

The limo took Marcus and Katherine to Marcus' apartment, which was located close to the ocean, Santa Monica, LAX, Hollywood, and the major film studios. Katherine had packed an overnight bag, which Frankie had already put in the limo with the rest of the luggage. The driver helped take the luggage out of the trunk and bring it inside the apartment building.

Once the luggage had been loaded into the elevator, Julia said, "We'll be here at nine in the morning to collect you for the signing."

"We'll be ready," Marcus promised.

The Limo left to take Julia and Gina to their hotel, and then take Frankie back to her office.

Marcus inserted his key into the elevator control panel, and the elevator doors closed. When they opened again, they were in an enclosed foyer outside Marcus' apartment. He removed the luggage from the elevator, retrieved his key, and opened the apartment door. He gestured for Katherine to enter while he brought the luggage inside the apartment.

Katherine looked around his place. It was an open-concept loft that had an amazing view of Marina Del Ray. As she continued looking around, she counted three bedrooms, each with its own bathroom. She joined Marcus in the largest bedroom, just as he was placing the last piece of luggage next to the closet door.

"This is beautiful, Marc. I had no idea. Your agent rents this place for you?"

"It's mine to use whenever I'm in town. Frankie's firm owns the building and allows their screenwriters to live in the apartments while they're working on films or in town for meetings, but since I'm their top earner, and I'm out here all the time, they reserve this apartment just for me. I don't keep any personal items here, but no one else uses the place when I'm not around."

"Wow," she said. She looked at her watch. It was one-thirty in the afternoon, but she wasn't hungry at all. She just wanted to be with Marcus. "So, we're on our own until tomorrow morning?"

Marcus grinned as he walked over and stood in front of Katherine. "It seems so. Is there something in particular you wanted to do today, Miss Delaney?"

Katherine threw her arms around his neck. "You know there is." She started to kiss him, but then she looked around. "Can anyone see us through these windows?"

"Only if it's dark outside and the lights are on inside," Marcus replied.

"Good. It'll be interesting to do this in the sunlight."

He leaned in for the kiss, and she jumped up and wrapped her legs around him. He carried her over to the bed. They were undressed in no time, and they soon gave in to the passion and longing they had both been feeling during their month apart.

"Wow," Katherine said, panting as she snuggled next to Marcus. They were both sweating and breathing heavily from what they had just shared together. The afternoon sun shown on them as they lay there, feeling deeply satisfied.

"Is that how good it's going to be *every* time we're away from each other for a while?" she asked.

"I don't know, but it'll be fun to find out," Marcus answered. He looked at her. "I'll bet you're hungry by now. Want me to whip up something?"

"Sure, if you let me help."

"Okay," Marcus agreed. "Why don't you put on a shirt, and I'll put on some shorts. I don't like cooking naked. Too much risk of hot spatter."

Katherine laughed and got out of bed. "I think I brought one of those with me." She pulled out a T-shirt from her bag that had the riverboat logo on it from the sunset cruise they had taken on the Tennessee River. "Look familiar?"

Marcus nodded in appreciation as she put the shirt on and fluffed her hair out. "It looks perfect on you."

He grabbed a pair of sleep shorts from one of his suitcases and pulled them on. After he closed the blinds, they exited the bedroom. "Why don't you see what's in the fridge and the pantry, and I'll adjust the blinds in here," he suggested when they reached the living room.

Katherine walked into the kitchen as Marcus lowered the blinds and adjusted them so light could come in, but no one could see them. Then he joined her.

"Find anything that you want?" he asked.

"It looks like Frankie had a few meals prepared for us already. They're in those foil pans stacked on the lower shelf of the fridge. Why don't we try some of those?"

Marcus opened the fridge and looked at the selection. "Steak Diane with Roasted Potatoes, Tortellini Alfredo with Chicken, Grilled Mountain Trout Almandine with Potatoes Au Gratin, Shrimp Scampi over Angel Hair Pasta… Do any of those sound good?"

They each selected an entrée, and while Marcus read the heating instructions, Katherine started making a salad for them.

They ate their salads at the dining table while the entrées were heating. When the timer went off, Marcus cleared their salad dishes and brought back the entrées. The food was excellent and was soon finished. Marcus cleared the table and cleaned the dishes and utensils. He brought over a bottle of wine and two glasses, and joined her on the couch that faced the marina. Her poured the wine into the glasses and offered one to Katherine.

"What a view," she said, watching the sunset over the

ocean.

"It's one of the few things I like about L.A.," Marcus said. "I love the ocean. I just wish I didn't have to be in California to be near it. It's so crowded out here, and I find I just don't like crowds anymore."

"I know what you mean. When I landed in L.A. after leaving Tennessee, I started feeling claustrophobic… like I was trapped in a sea of people and drowning. It took a week before that sensation started to fade."

"So, when do I get to meet the boys?"

"Tomorrow, when you take me home. We can pick up the boys, take them to their favorite place—that'll earn you some points with them—and have a fun evening together. Then we can get together this weekend and spend a day with each other."

"Any thoughts on what we should do on that day?"

"Go to Anaheim," Katherine replied.

"Why there?"

"The theme parks. The boys love going there."

Marcus nodded. "So where exactly *is* your place?"

"Woodland Hills. It's just north of here in the San Fernando Valley."

"That's the opposite direction from Anaheim, isn't it? Here's a thought. Why don't you and the boys come over the night before, stay here, and then we can get an early start together. It'll save us a lot of backtracking. Then, depending on how the day goes, you can either go home from here that night, or you can all spend the night and go home the next morning."

Katherine smiled. "I like that idea."

"You can do the same thing the night before we fly to Chattanooga for Thanksgiving," Marcus suggested.

Katherine nodded. She finished her wine, put her glass down, and rested her head on his shoulder. "I'm so glad you're here."

"I'm glad you're here with me," Marcus said. He put his

glass down, turned her head toward him, and kissed her. She put her arms around his neck and pulled him closer.

Soon, her shirt and his shorts were on the floor as they made love on the couch, bathed in the light from the sunset.

The next morning, Marcus and Katherine were waiting in the lobby of the apartment building when the limo pulled up. Julia rolled down the rear passenger window and waved. Marcus and Katherine got in the back seat, and the limo pulled into traffic, heading for the bookstore.

"Here's your wristband," Gina said, handing the paper band to Katherine.

"Thanks," Katherine said. She peeled off the cover from the sticky part of the paper and put the band on her wrist. "How does a book signing work?" she asked.

"People should already be queuing outside the bookstore for the signing. We'll let in the first group of people with wristbands, and I'll introduce Marc," Gina said. "Marc will then read a selection from the new book. While he's doing that, I'll be getting the signing area set up to make sure we have all of the books handy. Once Marc is finished with his reading, he'll sit at the signing table, and the bookstore staff will help manage the queue, so the signing doesn't disrupt the store's entire business. Then we'll let in the second group and so on until everyone finally gets inside the store. If we keep the lines moving as predicted, we should run out of books to sign, and people waiting in line, at the time the bookstore advertised. Then we do it again tomorrow at a different location."

"What are you going to be doing while I'm signing?" Marcus asked. "You're welcome to sit with me in the signing area."

"I think I'm going to mingle with the crowd," Katherine

replied. "I want to experience this from the point of view of your fans. Once you sign *my* copy, I'll probably stay near the signing area until you're done."

When they pulled up to the bookstore, Katherine was amazed at the size of the crowd already lined up around the block. "Is this normal for one of your signings?" she asked.

Julia nodded. "Marc's a big draw, and his fans love him."

When Marcus emerged from the back of the limo, the crowd went wild like they had in New York. Marcus waved, and the bookstore manager escorted Marcus, Julia, Katherine, and Gina into the store.

"Is there anything I can get for you, Mr. Buchanan?" he asked.

"Just a couple of water bottles for me," Marcus replied. He looked at the others. "Do any of you need something? Kathy?"

Katherine shook her head. "Nothing for me, thanks."

The manager brought Marcus three bottles of water and then showed him the stage and signing areas.

Katherine was impressed at how organized the event was. "This is like a movie premier," she said to Julia.

"This is the equivalent of a premier for book authors," she replied. "Except that the author comes to the audience. We only hold these events in cities where there are strong sales and in venues that can handle the crowds. In cities where there aren't any bookstores that can handle the traffic, we hold the events at convention centers, in hotel ballrooms, and places like that. Marc packs them in, and it's one of the reasons why he's my favorite author. He never forgets the fans, and he makes each one feel appreciated for taking the time to come see him and buy his book. If it weren't necessary to keep the lines moving, I think he'd get up and hug everyone who comes out."

At ten o'clock, the doors opened, and the bookstore staff herded the crowds into the queue. There wasn't enough room in the store to hold everyone who had shown up, so Marcus had agreed to do a reading every ninety minutes, so no one missed out hearing him speak.

Katherine stood at the end of the first queue allowed into the store. She looked down at her wristband, and for the first time noticed that it was color coded with a time and the number of books purchased printed on it. *I guess that lets everyone know when to arrive, when they can enter the store, and how many books they purchased in advance to have signed.*

From her place at the end of the line, she saw the manager introduce Marcus. When Marcus took the stage, Katherine was surprised at the reaction from the crowd. Marcus was gracious as he accepted their applause and cheers. Then he stepped up to the lectern, opened the copy of his book that Gina had placed there, and began turning the pages until he found the section he wanted to read. The crowd went silent, waiting to hear him.

When Marcus started reading, Katherine was mesmerized by his voice, as were the others waiting in line in front of her. *No wonder he's such a big draw. If I heard an author speak like that, I'd buy everything he'd ever written.*

When Marcus stopped and closed the book, the crowd erupted with applause. Marcus waved and then took his seat at the signing table. The line started to move, and Katherine couldn't wait to reach Marcus.

When she finally arrived at the table, Marcus grinned at her. He took a book from the stack and wrote in it. He handed the book to her and said, "It's time for my next reading. Why don't you sit with Julia, and I'll be back shortly."

Marcus got up and headed for the stage to read to the next group of fans who had been allowed inside the store. Katherine sat next to Julia and opened the book to look at the inscription. It read, *"To my Darling Kathy, whose love changed my life in ways I could never have imagined. I love you with all my heart. Marc."* Below that was Marcus' autograph.

She saw him looking at her from the stage. She put her hand

over hear heart and mouthed, "I love you, too."

The signing ended right on time, and the limo was waiting to take Marcus and Katherine back to his apartment.

"What do you two have planned for tonight?" Julia asked.

"We're getting together with my sons," Katherine replied. "They've been waiting to meet Marc ever since we told them that we're engaged."

"That sounds like fun," Julia said.

Gina looked at Marcus and said, "Tomorrow is Friday, and you have one signing and then a reception. You have the weekend off, and Monday you're taping several segments for local news stations and radio stations all day. Then you have signings on Tuesday, Wednesday, and Thursday, and then this tour will officially be over. In December, there's the European and Canadian tour. Are you still good with that schedule?"

"I am," Marcus confirmed.

"Good. I won't be traveling with you in December, but another one of our event coordinators will, so you'll be in good hands."

"I appreciate all that you've done to make this tour so successful," Marcus said.

Julia spoke up. "I know you have some meetings lined up with Frankie the week after next, but I hope you take the time to relax before Thanksgiving."

"That's the plan. Kathy and I are taking the boys to Anaheim this weekend to spend the day at one of the theme parks."

Julia grinned, "I wouldn't exactly call that relaxing, but it should be fun. I thought you only liked the Florida theme parks."

Marcus shrugged. "When in California, you do what the Californians do."

The limo arrived at Marcus' apartment, and Marcus and Katherine exited. They went upstairs so Marcus could change clothes before they headed to Woodland Hills to pick up the boys for dinner.

Traffic was heavy as they drove to Katherine's house, and when they arrived, the boys raced out the front door to greet their mother. Greg followed close behind.

"Hi, Marc," he said, shaking Marcus' hand.

"Hi, Greg! It's been a while. How have you been?"

"Doing well," Greg replied. "Congratulations, by the way."

"Thanks! I hear you're moving to Atlanta."

"After the first of the year. I hope Kate and the boys move to Chattanooga with you. I'll still be able to see the boys on a regular schedule that way."

"I know they'd love that," Marcus said. "And you'll always be welcome at the house."

Greg looked surprised. "Thank you for that, Marc."

"Hey, I'm not trying to replace you or keep you from the boys. They're your sons and always will be."

Katherine brought the boys over to Marcus. "Forgive the interruption," she said. "Marc, this is Jack, and this is Ben. Boys, this is Marc Buchanan."

Marcus shook hands with the boys. "I'm happy to finally meet you both."

"Are you really taking us to Anaheim this weekend?" Ben asked.

"That's the plan," Marc replied.

"Cool!" Jack said.

Greg looked at his watch. "I need to head home. Bye, boys."

"Bye, Dad!" they said.

"Bye, Kate."

Katherine gave him a hug. "Thanks for helping out this week."

"Happy to do it," Greg replied.

After Greg left, Katherine showed Marcus around her house. She pointed out the books he had given her on her bookshelves, then she made sure the boys were ready to leave. She helped the boys into the back seat of Marcus' car and gave Marcus the directions to the restaurant.

The evening turned out to be very enjoyable for Marcus. The boys were in a talkative mood and not only told Marcus everything about themselves, but they asked some good questions.

At one point during dinner, Jack asked, "So… I have a question, Uncle Marc. Mom and Dad dated for two years before they got engaged. You and Mom have only dated for a few months. Why did you two get engaged so much faster?"

Marcus glanced over at Katherine, who just smiled and shrugged.

Realizing that she wasn't going to help him answer the question, he replied, "I can't speak for your mother, but here's what I think. When you've never been married before, you're still trying to learn what you like and what you don't like about the people you're dating. You're also trying to understand what it is you're looking for in someone you want to spend the rest of your life with. But you never really know what it's like to be with someone until you've been with them for a while, and by then it's sometimes too late. It's when people discover that the person they're with is not the right person for them that divorces happen. Your mother and I have both been married before, and we learned a lot from the experience. We both knew exactly what we were looking for, and we recognized it in each other from the beginning. That's why it didn't take us long to know we had found the right person. Does that make sense?"

Jack looked unsure. "I think so. So… you were married before? What happened."

"She passed away several years ago."

Jack looked embarrassed. "I didn't know that. Are you still sad about it?"

Marcus nodded. "I probably always will be. She was a wonderful person."

"Did you have kids?" Ben asked.

"She had two children from her first marriage—a boy and a girl. I adopted them when they were a little older than you two are. They're both grown now and have families of their own. One lives in Texas, and the other lives in Connecticut. I don't see them very often. They don't like to travel much."

They spent the rest of the evening talking, laughing, and eating. By the time they got back to Katherine's house, Marcus felt the evening had gone well.

"Boys, say goodnight to Marc and then go upstairs and get ready for bed," Katherine said when everyone reached the front porch.

"Goodnight, Uncle Marc," Jack said.

Goodnight, Jack."

"Goodnight… Uncle Marc," Ben said.

"Goodnight, Ben. I'll see you both this weekend."

The boys scampered inside the house. Katherine looked at Marcus and smiled. "Did you have a good time?"

"I did. Do you think they had fun?"

"Yes, I do. And thank you for how you talked with them tonight. You didn't talk down to them once, but you chose your words so they'd understand what you were saying. You handled their questions well."

"Trying to learn from past mistakes. This weekend will be the real test."

Katherine moved closer to him. "Will you have time to talk tomorrow?"

"Probably not until after the reception. It might be late. Is that okay?"

"I'll be awake, no matter how late it is," she replied.

"When are you and the boys coming over on Saturday?"

"Is mid-afternoon okay?"

"That's perfect," Marcus told her. "I'll cook dinner."

"And I'll help," Katherine said.

"And you're still okay with going to Anaheim on Sunday?"

Katherine nodded. "Monday is a school holiday—teacher's workshop, or something like that." She glanced at the front door. "Do you want to come inside for a while?"

Marcus heard Jack calling for his mother. "I'd better go," Marcus said. "I'll call you tomorrow. If I get a break earlier, I'll text you before I call."

Katherine put her arms around his neck and pulled him closer. She kissed him, and Marcus put his arms around her and held her tight.

"I love you," she whispered.

"I love you," he said.

Jack called out again, and Marcus let her go. She waved and disappeared into the house. Marcus got into his car and drove back to his apartment in Marina Del Ray.

CHAPTER 13

Anaheim was a blast. They got an early start on Sunday, allowing them to reach the theme park before it got crowded. They found a great parking spot, and the gates opened just as they walked up to the ticket window to pick up their passes.

Katherine and Marcus had a time keeping up with the boys, who wanted to see and ride everything—multiple times. The lines didn't have too long of a wait, so they were able to do most of what they wanted to do. By the time they left that night, they were stuffed and happy, and the boys were carrying bags of souvenirs that Marcus and Katherine had bought them.

By the time they reached Marcus' apartment, it was too late to drive back to Katherine's house, so she and the boys stayed over for another night.

After the boys had gone to bed, Marcus said, "I have to leave early in the morning, but that doesn't mean you have to. Sleep in and leave whenever you want."

Katherine thought about it and smiled. "On one condition."

"What's that?"

"That you wake me before you leave so I can get a kiss goodbye."

"Okay, but it'll be early."

"I don't care. I want to see you before you leave. We haven't worked out when we're going to see each other again."

"You know what my schedule's like this week. You could always show up at another signing event, but if you'd rather wait until the weekend, I'm free from Thursday night until Monday night. Then I have meetings on Tuesday and Wednesday with a couple of directors and producers, and I'm still trying to find time to meet with C.J. about another project. Apart from that, I'll be free until we leave for Chattanooga to spend Thanksgiving at my house."

"We should definitely get together over the weekend," Katherine said. "I'll see what the boys want to do, and we'll talk Tuesday evening and work out the details."

"Sounds like a perfect plan," Marcus said.

The next morning, Marcus left before sunrise. He woke Katherine and gave her a kiss goodbye, and then he let her go back to sleep. The limo was waiting for him downstairs, and as he climbed in the back, he realized that he had left his phone upstairs. He went back to his apartment to retrieve it and then got into the limo, where Julia was waiting for him. The driver headed for the first of several television and radio interviews he had scheduled for the day.

Julia did a great job keeping Marcus on schedule. Most of the segments he recorded lasted only ten minutes, but between hair and make-up at each station, getting the lighting and sound checked out, and waiting for the interviewer or show host to arrive, he spent close to an hour at each station before having to leave and head over to the next station on the itinerary.

By the end of the day, he was exhausted. He and Julia grabbed a quick bite to eat, and then the limo dropped him off at his apartment. When he got upstairs, the apartment was spotless. *Kathy must have cleaned before she left. She didn't have to do that.* He sent her a quick text, letting her know that he was home and about to go to bed, and thanking her for cleaning.

She texted back immediately, using the sign language emoji for "I Love You."

Marcus responded with the same emoji. Then he walked slowly to his bedroom and went to sleep.

The book signing the next day was well attended, and Marcus felt good about it as the limo took him back to his apartment. He fixed himself dinner, and after he had cleaned the kitchen, he sat down and gave Katherine a call.

"Hi, Beautiful!" he said when she answered the phone.

"Hi, Handsome!" she responded. "How did it go?"

"Yesterday or today?"

"Both. I saw your interviews, and you looked and sounded great. I didn't get to hear the radio interviews."

"I'll send you a link so you can listen online." He described how the interviews and how the book signing went. "According to Julia, the book just made the Times Best Seller list. She's beside herself, as is my publisher. I've already started jotting down notes for the second book in the series."

"It never stops, does it?" Katherine asked in awe.

"Not if I want to keep eating with a roof over my head. I've had normal nine-to-five jobs before, and they're easier on the lifestyle, but they're nowhere near as much fun."

Katherine laughed. "It's the same with my job. I guess we're more alike than I first thought."

"You've certainly seen behind the curtain of my world this week, haven't you?"

"Yes, and I wouldn't have missed it for anything."

"So, how was your day?" Marcus asked.

Katherine told him what she did after he had left the apartment the day before, what happened when she got home with the boys, and what she had done that day.

"It all sounds blissfully normal," Marcus said. "I think I could use a bit more normal in my life."

"Maybe I can help with that."

"Maybe you can. And by the way, thanks again for suggesting the theme parks this past weekend. I hadn't had that much fun since I took Leigh's kids to the Florida theme parks right after we got married."

"You're welcome! The boys and I had a great time. And speaking of great times, let's talk about this weekend."

"Okay. What do you have in mind?"

"How do you feel about sailing?"

Marcus thought about it for a moment. "Well, apart from the fact that I haven't been sailing since I was in grade school, I remember that it was fun. I've never been sailing on the ocean before. Why?"

"Well, it just so happens that a friend of mind has a twenty-foot sail boat that he lets me use when I need to be in the water and clear my head. He's out of town this weekend and reminded me that I can use the boat whenever I want. And it's docked at Marina Del Ray. The boys have been asking when we can go sailing again, and I thought this weekend would be a good time. The weather's supposed to be perfect."

"I didn't know that you knew how to sail."

"I've been sailing since I was fourteen," Katherine said proudly. "It's one of my favorite things to do."

"You can sail on the Tennessee River," Marcus pointed out.

"I know. I saw," Katherine replied.

"Well, I don't know how to sail," Marcus admitted, "but I take directions well, skipper. I'm game."

"Great! We can be at your place early that morning, head

out after breakfast, eat lunch on the water, and be back at the dock by mid-afternoon. Then all we need to do is figure out dinner."

"And y'all can stay over at my place again," Marcus suggested. "That way we'll have the whole weekend together."

Katherine agreed with Marcus' suggestion, and when she mentioned it to the boys, they loved the idea. Katherine and Marcus talked for another thirty minutes before ending the call.

The last two book signings went well, and when the limo dropped Julia off at LAX so she could take the red eye back to New York, she seemed happier than Marcus had seen her in years. "I'll see you in December," she said as she got out of the limo and headed into the terminal.

The next day, Marcus met with C.J. to discuss a new film project. Marcus promised to think about it, but he was clear that he couldn't commit to anything until his meetings the next week and in early January.

"I know," C.J. acknowledged. "I just wanted to be first in line if those projects don't pan out or get delayed."

The weekend with Katherine and the boys was a lot of fun. Katherine proved to be an excellent sailor, and Marcus did exactly what she asked him to do, helping him learn the art of sailing while allowing her to focus on navigating and avoiding the other boats on the water.

The next week, his two meetings were actually both related to the same project, rather than different projects as Frankie had led him to believe. The first meeting was with the director, who Marcus had worked with before, and the second meeting was with the production company.

The director revealed his plans for the reboot of the film franchise. "There will be three films initially, with options for more, depending on the box office take from the first three. The films will be coming out one every other year, so there will be two directors at the helm, since I'll still be in post-production on the first film when filming begins on the second one. Because we need these films to be part of a cohesive story arc, I need a single writer to preserve the integrity and connectivity between the films, and you're the only writer I know who can handle the job."

"So, you want me to write three scripts, or really one script broken into three parts, right?"

"Exactly."

"And how far have you gotten with the ideas for the three films?"

"I have specific scenes in mind, but no cohesive story tying them all together yet."

"And when do I get to know the franchise that you're rebooting?"

The director stared at Marcus for a minute. "You've already signed the non-disclosure agreement?"

Marcus nodded. "Before I agreed to the meeting."

"Very well." The director named the franchise. Marcus was stunned. This was the most successful science fiction action film franchise in history, with six films that had already topped most box office records. "Holy smokes! I had no idea you were working on *that* franchise."

"It took some convincing, but the studio finally let me have the project," the director said. "But they stipulated that, if I couldn't hire you to write it, I had to find someone equally as good, or they'd pull the plug."

Marcus sat back and stared wide-eyed at the director.

"Of course, I didn't bother to remind them that no one is equally as good as you."

Marcus laughed. "No schmoozing. You had to know I'd be interested before you called Frankie to set up the meeting."

"I did," the director admitted. "If you're in, I'd recommend spending March at your place in Tennessee, working out the overall storyline that I can take to the studio, while you finish the initial scripts."

"Who all would be coming?" Marcus asked.

"Just myself and my head of production design. I want to build actual sets on either soundstages or suitable locations, not rely on computer graphics, so we need him to tell us what's practical and affordable before we get too crazy, and it will help him get the initial designs ready to present to the studio—along with the preliminary budget."

Marcus thought about it. "March, eh? I don't have a problem with that, but there's a wrinkle."

"You haven't lost Mariana, have you?" the director asked. "I've been looking forward to her cooking for months."

Marcus smiled. "No, Mariana is still with me. It's something else. I doubt you've heard, but it looks like I could be getting married."

"Really? That's wonderful! To whom?"

"Do you know Katherine Delaney?"

"Of course. She's beautiful and talented. How did you meet?"

"She was in *The Spy Upstairs*, the film I wrote that just wrapped a couple of months ago."

"Well, congratulations," the director said. "But how does that create a wrinkle?"

"If all goes well, she and her two boys will be moving from L.A. to Chattanooga in December. That means they'll be at the house when you and your production designer arrive. The two of you will have to be on your best behavior when Kathy's sons are home, and it means that we'll have to be very careful about what we say when they're around, so they don't know what we're working on. At some point, I'll have to tell Kathy, if all goes well, but not the boys. Not yet."

The director nodded. "You keep saying, 'If all goes well.' What does that mean?"

"It means that everything is contingent on the boys approving of me, Chattanooga, and the marriage. That's why I'm out here, spending time with them so they can get to know me. Then we're flying to Chattanooga for Thanksgiving so they can see the house and decide if they want to live there."

"Hell, *I* want to live there," the director said, grinning. "They'd be crazy not to."

"I know, but you never know with kids," Marcus noted.

The director cocked his head. "Wait, you mean if the boys don't approve, the wedding's off?"

"That's right."

"Wow. I imagine you're a bit nervous right about now. Well, no matter how it turns out, we'll make March work out however you need it to, whether it's just us in the house or us along with Kathy and her kids." The director cocked his head to one side. "You know, the cast for these films could be huge…"

Marcus grinned. "Meaning there could be a role or roles for Kathy?"

The director nodded. "I'm surprised you didn't bring it up."

"I didn't want you thinking that her getting cast in the films was part of the deal," Marcus said. "But I'd like her to be considered for any part that's a good fit. It would certainly give her career a nice boost."

"Even if the marriage falls through?" the director asked.

Marcus leaned back and thought about it. "Yes, even if the marriage falls through. If she's right for the part, she should get the part. No strings attached."

"That's unexpectedly mature of you, Marc," the director commented. "Especially in this business. But it's good to know you won't let personal relationships impact your professional work."

Marcus thought about how awkward it would be if the

marriage fell through and they had to still work together. *It could happen on any number of films that I write. I can't very well quit a film project just because she got cast or might get cast.*

The director interrupted Marcus' thoughts. "So, are you in?"

Marcus grinned like a Cheshire cat, "I'm in. With the usual caveats."

"Which are?"

"I have the exclusive novelization rights to all films I work on, whether I'm the initial writer, whether I'm called in to do re-writes of someone else's script, or whether you replace me with someone else before the three films are completed."

The director waved dismissively. "Just that? Of course, I accept your caveats. It's in all your contacts, anyway. Do we have a deal?"

"We have a deal."

The meeting the next day with the production company was to formalize that Marcus would be the head writer for the first three films. They also discussed the overall vision for the three-film story arc that the studio wanted. Marcus didn't see any issues with what the studio wanted, and the meeting ended with commitments to get the contracts to Frankie by the first of December.

As the limo took Marcus back to his apartment, he called Frankie and filled her in on the two meetings.

"So, you've given your tentative commitment?" Frankie asked.

"Pending the signing of the contracts, agreement to the terms and conditions, and the usual items that you take care of for me," Marcus said. "The novelization rights must be in the contact, as does the stipulation that I get full pay and all rights, even if I get replaced as the writer before the third film wraps."

"When will they have the contracts to me?" Frankie asked.

"The first of December at the latest."

"This sounds like the most amazing opportunity that any writer I know has been offered," Frankie said. "We're talking a six-year commitment with three novels included, and that's just barely enough time to write the other novels that your publisher is expecting. You're going to be a busy boy. What does Kathy think of this?"

"I don't know," Marcus admitted. "I can't tell her. I can if we get married, but until then, I can't tell anyone apart from you."

There was a moment of silence. "I understand," Frankie said finally. "And no matter what happens with you and Kathy, congratulations on this opportunity."

"Thanks, Frankie. Talk soon."

Marcus ended the call and stared out the window as the limo headed for Marina Del Ray.

As the week of Thanksgiving approached, Marcus felt increasingly nervous. Things were great with Katherine and the boys, but he knew that, by the Friday after Thanksgiving, the boys would make their choice about him, Chattanooga, and the marriage. One dissenting vote would end things with Katherine immediately. Marcus felt helpless, but he did his best to hide this from her.

Katherine and the boys came over to the apartment on Friday afternoon, and Marcus cooked dinner. Once the kitchen was cleaned, the boys went to their room to play video games while Marcus and Katherine sat on the couch, watching the sunset.

On Saturday morning, Marcus and the boys stacked the luggage next to the door. After surveying all the rooms to make certain that nothing had been left behind, Marcus left the car keys on the kitchen counter, and they rode the elevator to the lobby. Marcus realized that he had left his phone upstairs, so he had to go back to the apartment and retrieve it.

Since Katherine had driven her car to Marcus' apartment, and since she and boys were returning a week later without Marcus, they decided to take Katherine's car to LAX. It was a tight fit getting all of the luggage in the car, but they made it work.

They parked in one of the decks and walked to the terminal. After checking in, they boarded a seven o'clock flight to Dallas-Fort Worth, where they had a one-hour layover before their next flight departed, getting them into Chattanooga at four that afternoon. Katherine wore the tan riding pants and riding boots she'd bought in Chattanooga, along with a hunter-green sweater, since it would be cold in Tennessee when they arrived.

Marcus expected to be met by the same shuttle service that had taken him to the airport before the book tour began, but he saw Grant when he reached the baggage claim area.

"Grant, what are you doing here?" Marcus asked, shaking Grant's hand.

"Welcome home, Boss. I thought you'd rather see a familiar face. I've got the SUV outside." He saw Katherine and the boys. "Hi, Kathy," he said to her. "Are these your sons?"

Katherine smiled. "Yes. This is Jack, and this is Ben. Boys, this is Grant Billings. He's Marc's estate manager. He looks after things when Marc is away on business."

"Pleased to meet you," Grant said. "Show me which bags are yours."

The carousel began turning, and soon the luggage appeared. Marcus had the most bags, since he had been traveling for two months. Katherine had two large suitcases, and the boys each had one small bag. Grant and Marcus grabbed the bags as they appeared on the carousel, and soon they had all the luggage and were walking toward the parking area.

Grant and Marcus loaded the bags into the rear of the SUV.

The boys climbed into the center seat with Katherine, and Marcus got into the front passenger seat next to Grant.

As Grant drove to Marcus' home, Marcus pointed out the features of the Chattanooga area.

"Where is everyone?" Jack asked.

"What do you mean, Jack?" Marcus asked.

"I mean, the streets aren't filled with cars. At home, the streets are always filled with cars."

"That's the beauty of Chattanooga," Marcus replied. "No crowds. Just wide-open spaces, mountains, rivers, and beauty for as far as the eye can see."

"This is only Jack's second time outside California—third time outside the L.A. area," Katherine explained. "He's never seen anything like this before. Neither has Ben."

Marcus nodded. "Then I imagine my home will be quite a shock."

"To say the least," Katherine agreed. "They've seen the photos, and they've heard me talk about it, but seeing it in person is something else altogether."

Grant pulled up to the gates.

"Where are we?" Jack asked.

"This is where I live," Marcus said as the gate swung open and Grant drove through.

Jack's eyes were as wide as saucers. Then he pointed out of the left window. "What are those?"

Grant slowed down, and Marcus looked where Jack was pointing. A family of deer was standing on the other side of the fence that separated the driveway from the protected parts of Marcus' land. "Those are deer," he said. "We see them all the time around the property. The big one is a doe, the mother, and the other three are her fawns."

"I've never seen one before."

Another deer came into view. This one was a male with an impressive rack on its head. Marcus did a quick count and saw fourteen points on the antlers. "That one over there is a buck. He's probably the father."

Marcus glanced back, and even Ben's eyes were glued to the majestic animal so close to them. The buck's head turned sharply, as if it heard a noise, and then it bounded off, followed by the doe and the fawns.

"Will they come back?" Jack asked as Grant drove toward the house.

"Probably," Marcus said. "There are whole herds of deer living in this area."

As the SUV crested the ridge that kept the house from being seen from the road, the boys were speechless. "We're here," Katherine said to them.

"This is where you live?" Jack asked as the car approached the front door.

"Yes, it is," Marcus replied.

As soon as the SUV stopped, the boys got out of the back seat… and started running straight for the cannons.

"Don't touch them," Katherine called after the boys. "They're not toys. Come back."

The boys stopped, turned around, and slowly walked back.

Marcus chuckled. "Tell you what. We'll fire the cannons while you're here. How does that sound?"

Jack's and Ben's eyes lit up. "You mean it?" Jack said.

"Can we help?" Ben asked.

"Yes, I mean it. No, you can't help, but you can watch. When you're older, I'll teach you about cannons, and then you can help. Okay?"

"Okay!"

Katherine whispered, "You're not going to use cannon balls, right?"

Marcus laughed. "Heavens, no. I'll just be using gunpowder wrapped in foil… like firing blanks in the movies, only much much louder."

Katherine smiled, looking relieved to hear that.

Grant and Marcus brought the luggage into the house. They put the boys' suitcases at the bottom of the stairs, and Marcus took his and Katherine's bags to the master bedroom.

When Katherine brought the boys into the entryway, she heard Mariana call out, "Mr. Marc, is that you?"

"It's us, Mariana," he called back.

"Who's Mariana?" Ben asked.

"Mariana is my cook. She makes sure I eat properly."

"You have a cook?" Jack didn't know what to think about that. He had never met anyone with their own cook.

Mariana walked through the foyer to greet everyone. Katherine introduced Mariana to the boys while Grant drove the SUV to the garage.

"Dinner will be ready in fifteen minutes," Mariana said. "Eat first. Tour second."

"Okay, Mariana," Marcus agreed.

Mariana scurried back to the kitchen. "Why don't you get the boys settled in their rooms," Marcus suggested.

Katherine nodded and led the way upstairs to the two rooms at the far end of the north wing. After the boys finally agreed on who would get to overlook the cannons and who would get to overlook the pool, Katherine showed them where everything was on the second floor.

"You even have your own den up here, in case you want to watch something different from what we're watching downstairs," she said.

When she and the boys came back downstairs, Marcus had the fireplace in the sitting area turned on, giving the room a warm glow. The den fireplace was also lit.

Mariana had them sit at the round table next to the sitting area fireplace as she served dinner. Once all the food was on the table, she looked at Marcus, who nodded. "I'll clean up, Mariana. Go ahead and head out. And thanks for coming in on a

Saturday. That was kind of you."

"No worries, Mr. Marc. I have plenty of food for the weekend, and I'll be back Monday morning."

"Good. We can talk then about how things went while I was gone."

Mariana beamed. "Good night, Mr. Marc. Good night, Miss Kathy. Good night, boys."

"Good night, Mariana," they all replied.

"She's nice," Ben said after Mariana had left. "Why do you have someone cook for you?"

"Because I work here at the house, and I get so busy that I forget to eat. I need someone to make sure that I take care of myself. She also does the grocery shopping."

"What does she do when you're not here?" Jack asked.

"She caters parties for other families and businesses around the city. Her cooking is very popular. She and her late husband used to own one of the best restaurants in town."

After dinner, Marcus showed the boys around his house. Katherine had already shown them the upstairs, so he showed them the main floor, except for the arsenal, and then he took them downstairs to see the theatre.

"You have a movie theatre in your basement?" Jack asked. That was something else he had never seen before. "Can we watch a movie tonight?"

Marcus looked at Katherine, who nodded. "Sure, we can. Kathy, why don't you show the boys where the movies are and help them pick one out?"

Katherine smiled. "Okay."

It took a while to find something age appropriate that both boys could agree on, but Katherine finally helped them find the right movie. As she handed it to Marcus, she whispered, "I don't remember you having any children's movies when I was here the last time."

"I checked out what you had on your movie shelf the first

night I came over, and I ordered what I could remember, along with a few other films that were supposed to be similar."

"Ah, using the house tour as a chance to do some intelligence gathering, eh?" Katherine grinned as she jiggled her head slightly.

"Of course, I did," Marcus confirmed. "I want this week to be perfect for the boys… and you."

"Nicely played, Marc. Nicely played."

Marcus led everyone downstairs and loaded the movie into the player in the back of the theatre. Then he showed the boys where the bathrooms were. When they came back, Jack asked, "So, where can we sit?"

"Anywhere you want, except for that double seat in the middle of the third row," Katherine told them.

The boys raced down to the front row and sat in the center seats. Marcus led Katherine to their usual seat. She showed the boys how to adjust the footrest and recliner controls, and then she sat next to Marcus. A couple of minutes later, the theatre was dark, the movie was playing, the boys were mesmerized by the size of the screen and the sound from the audio system, and Marcus and Katherine were snuggling and kissing in their seat.

After the boys were in bed, Marcus and Katherine retired to the master bedroom, where Marcus had already lit the fireplaces. As he checked the alarm system, he said, "I'd better not set the inside motion sensors and pressure sensors, in case the boys get up in the middle of the night and start exploring."

"Good idea," Katherine said.

The next morning, Marcus took everyone to the stables so they could ride horses. The boys had a great time, and Katherine was surprised at how fearless they seemed while riding. She was grateful that the stables had several pintos for smaller riders.

On Sunday, Marcus and Katherine packed lunch and took the boys hiking up to Pinnacle Rock. The boys were used to hiking in the hills between their house and the ocean, but they had never hiked in real mountains before. The views from the top of Marcus' property were amazing, and when the boys saw bald eagles and hawks for the first time, they were speechless.

"I've only seen one at the zoo," Jack said in awe.

"There are hundreds in the area," Marcus told him. "Some of them even have nests on the property. Same with the hawks."

"And don't forget the owls," Katherine said.

"You have owls?" Ben asked. "Mom gave me a book about a baby owl who was friends with a squirrel. I've never seen a real owl."

Marcus nodded. "You can see and hear them at night, if you're outside."

Jack looked up at Marcus and Katherine. "I love it here."

When he turned back to look at the birds, Katherine held up one finger, letting Marcus know that he had one vote.

Marcus gestured toward Ben, and Katherine shrugged. Ben's vote was still uncertain.

They stayed for another thirty minutes, watching the birds and the boats on the river in the distance, and then they hiked back down the ridge and returned to the house.

CHAPTER 14

Monday morning, after Mariana made the boys pancakes, Ben asked, "Can we go outside and play?"

"Sure," Marcus replied. "Just don't go outside the fence unless your mother and I are with you, okay?"

"Okay." Ben headed for the patio door.

"When are you going to fire the cannons?" Jack asked.

Ben stopped and turned around so he could hear the answer.

"We can do it today, if you'd like."

Both boys nodded enthusiastically.

"How about after lunch?"

"Okay." Both boys exited the patio door and were soon playing in the backyard and inside the trees between the yard and the fence.

"What do you have to do to get the cannons ready?" Katherine asked, standing next to Marcus and watching the boys play.

"Not much. I have two powder charges already made. Everything else I need is in the arsenal. It's cleaning the barrels afterwards that takes a little effort."

"Want some help with that?" Katherine asked.

Marcus looked at her. "It's dirty work. Did you bring some

clothes you don't mind getting ruined?"

"I have some things that I won't miss if they get messed up," she replied.

Marcus nodded. "If you're sure, then I can always use the help."

"Is it like cleaning a regular firearm?" Katherine asked.

"Yes, except you don't have to disassemble anything. It's just one long barrel with a large hole at one end and a small hole at the other. But we have to clean it thoroughly, and then dry and oil it before putting the covers back on."

"Why?"

"Because the cannon uses black powder, not regular gun powder, and the residue turns into sulfuric acid that'll eat away at the inside of the barrel, making it unsafe to use."

"Ah. Got it. I look forward to you showing me how it's done."

After lunch, Katherine followed Marcus to the arsenal to get the cannon implements and supplies. They carried them outside, put them in their proper place on the cannon carriages, and then Katherine brought out the boys.

"I'm going to explain what I'm doing as I'm doing it, okay?" Marcus said.

Katherine and the boys nodded.

Marcus removed the cover over the muzzles and vent holes. He inspected the inside of each cannon barrel with a flashlight, and then he used the implements to clean and prepared the barrels for firing.

Marcus walked back to the wooden chest sitting on the grass twenty-five feet behind the cannons, unlocked it, and put on two leather welders' gloves. Then he pulled out a leather satchel that went over his shoulder. He placed two aluminum-foil-wrapped packages into the satchel, grabbed a smaller satchel, put it over his other shoulder, and closed the chest.

He walked to the front of the first cannon, keeping his body behind the muzzle. He removed one of the foil-wrapped packages. "This is the powder charge. You have to be extremely careful when handling this." He placed the powder charge just inside the muzzle. Then he grabbed another long pole and rammed the charge, making certain that it was all the way at the back. Then he did the same thing with the other cannon.

Marcus used a long metal pick to stab a hole in the powder charge through the vent hole. He inserted the primer and attached a lanyard to the primer in the first cannon's vent hole. He stepped back until most of the slack in the lanyard had been taken out. He surveyed the area in front of the cannons and looked back. "Cover your ears."

Katherine and the boys covered their ears with their hands. Marcus placed a couple of earplugs in his own ears. Then he shouted, "Fire in the hole!" He yanked on the lanyard, and a moment later, the cannon erupted, and a fifty-foot tongue of flame shot out of the muzzle.

Marcus moved to the second cannon, used the pick to break open the powder charge, inserted the primer, attached the lanyard, and shouted, "Fire in the hole!" He yanked the lanyard, and the second cannon erupted just like the first one.

Marcus removed his earplugs and turned back toward Katherine and the boys.

"Did you enjoy that?"

The boys were speechless. Katherine was giggling, but her eyes were even wider than her sons' were.

"That was COOL!" Jack and Ben cried when the shock of what they had just seen wore off. They started jumping up and down with joy.

Marcus held up his hand to keep them from running forward. "What did I say you do after every time you shoot the cannon?"

"Clean the barrel," Jack said.

Marcus cleaned the inside of the barrels. He then motioned

for Katherine and the boys to join him.

"We need to make sure that no grass, leaves, twigs, or trees are burning. Will you help me?"

They all nodded and Marcus had them stand in a line and walk forward, looking for anything smoking. He stamped out a couple of leaves and twigs that appeared to be smoldering, and he recovered the remnants of the original foil wrappings of the powder charges.

Marcus let the boys get close to the cannons, but he wouldn't let them climb on them. When they finally went to the backyard to play, Marcus showed Katherine how to thoroughly clean, dry, lubricate, and then seal the cannons so they were safe from the weather and any critters looking for a place to live. Then she helped clean and take all of the implements and supplies back into the arsenal.

Once everything was put away, Marcus called Grant in the estate office. "Can you turn on the sprinklers in the cannon zone for ten minutes? Thanks, Grant!"

Marcus saw Katherine's quizzical look and explained, "There's always the chance of a slow-burning ember that could start a brush fire. Whatever we might have missed out there, the sprinklers will take care of. That's why the sprinklers in front of the cannons are in a separate zone, and they're positioned to water down the whole area."

Marcus took everyone horseback riding again on Tuesday, and Wednesday he let the boys do whatever they wanted. They spent most of the day playing online video games with their friends in California.

On Wednesday afternoon, Mariana was busy cooking Thanksgiving dinner and packaging everything so it could be reheated easily the next day. She wrote detailed notes, and

Katherine was with her reviewing those notes to make sure she understood everything. She also took the opportunity to sample most of the dishes.

"This dressing is amazing," Katherine said after tasting the traditional cornbread casserole.

"That is Mr. Marc's recipe," Mariana said. "It's the only dressing he likes, and I make it at least once a month for him when he's home."

"Marc's recipe?"

"It's based on a recipe from a restaurant I used to eat at with my parents," Marcus said, entering the kitchen. "I loved their dressing so much that I figured out how to duplicate it. I've been making it, or having Mariana make it, ever since."

Marcus inhaled the smells of the kitchen deeply. "How long before the bird is done?"

"Thirty minutes," Mariana replied. "You want me to carve it for you?"

"Please," Marcus replied. "You know how I butcher turkeys. Beef, I can slice. Pork, I can slice. Turkeys and chickens, I butcher."

"No worries, Mr. Marc. I'll take care of you."

"And make sure you get out of here early tonight," Marcus said. "I want you to enjoy the long weekend."

Mariana smiled. "I will, Mr. Marc. Don't worry."

Marcus walked into the den and sat on the large couch.

"Is there anything else you need to tell me?" Katherine asked Mariana.

"No, I'll leave all of the instructions on the counter next to the range. It should all be easy."

"Thanks, Mariana.

"You're welcome, Miss Kathy. And in case I don't see you before I leave, I hope you and the boys will be back here soon to stay."

Katherine smiled and nodded. Then she joined Marcus on

the couch.

"Two days," Marcus said when she wrapped her arms around his. "Our entire future will be decided in two days, and then y'all are leaving the next morning. Frankly, I'm terrified that I'll never see you again."

Katherine squeezed his arm reassuringly, but inside, she was wrestling with the exact same fears. She had no idea what decisions the boys were going to make, and she didn't feel comfortable asking them before Friday.

They sat in silence, each wresting with their worst fears.

Thanksgiving was a happy day, in spite of what loomed the next day. Marcus and Katherine handled the cooking while the boys played in the back yard. Marcus set the table while Katherine called the boys inside and told them to get cleaned up.

Katherine served the plates, but the food was set out buffet-style, in case anyone wanted seconds. Dessert wouldn't be served until later in the afternoon.

And there was so much food that Katherine knew they'd be eating leftovers up until she and the boys flew home on Saturday.

After Marcus expressed his gratitude for Katherine and the boys joining him for Thanksgiving, everyone started eating. As expected, the food was incredible, and they all ate entirely too much.

After lunch, the boys went upstairs to play video games while Katherine and Marcus put the food away and cleaned up.

"I have so much nervous energy right now that I feel I should be outside chopping lumber… except that all of the fireplaces use artificial logs."

"I know Marc, and I'm sorry," Katherine said. "I know this must be hell for you, but you know why it's important to me."

"I know," Marcus said. "I don't agree that this is the right approach, but I understand."

That night, after the boys were asleep, and Marcus and Katherine had retired to the master bedroom, Marcus found himself unable to bring up what was happening the next day. Evidently, Katherine wasn't able to bring it up either. Unable to break through the silence, they went to bed.

For Marcus, who usually had no trouble falling asleep, it was the worst night of his life since the day that Leigh died. No matter what he did, he couldn't sleep, so he finally got up, pulled on his robe, and quietly left the bedroom. He went to his office to finish outlining the next book in his espionage series.

The next morning, Katherine woke from a terrible dream and found that Marcus was gone. She put on her robe and went to his office, anticipating that he'd be there. He was.

She crept in so she wouldn't disturb his train of thought, and she sat down in one of the chairs across from his desk. She waited for him to stop typing.

When he finally realized that she was there, he swiveled around to face her.

"You look like hell," she said with a sympathetic expression on her face. "Couldn't sleep?"

Marcus shook his head.

"Wanna talk about it?"

"What's the point?" Marcus said. "I don't want this to end, and you're placing the decision in the hands of your sons. It is what it is."

"Marc…"

Marcus held up his hand to stop her. He shook his head, letting her know that no further discussion was needed or wanted.

Katherine slumped in her chair, realizing just how badly Marcus was taking the situation. Not knowing what else to do, she stood and headed back to the bedroom to get dressed.

The boys spent the day either playing outside or playing video games upstairs. Marcus stayed in his office, leaving Katherine alone for most of the day. She wanted to be with Marcus, but knowing he was facing the very real possibility that this was their last day together, she understood why it pained him to be with her. He was pulling away, even though the final decision had not yet been made.

Marcus did have dinner with Katherine and the boys, but no one said much, and even the boys felt that something was off. After dinner, Katherine decided it was time to sit down with each of the boys. She decided to talk to them one at a time, instead of both together, so one wouldn't influence the other's decision.

She knocked on Jack's door, and when he told her to come in, she entered his room and closed the door behind her. "Can we talk, Jack?"

Jack nodded and paused his game. "What's wrong with Uncle Marc?" he asked. "He seemed so sad today."

"He knows we're leaving tomorrow," Katherine said. "He enjoyed having us here this week, and I think our leaving is making him sad."

Jack nodded.

Katherine continued, "Do you remember when I told you that Marc and I want to get married, but I told you that it would only happen if you and Ben agreed to us becoming a family and moving here?"

"Yes," Jack said.

"Well, today is the day I need to know if you want us to become a family and live here, or if you don't."

"What do *you* want, Mom?" Jack asked.

"I want whatever is best for you and your brother," Katherine replied. "I'm your mother, and anything I want for myself comes second to what's best for you two."

"Well, I want you to be happy with Uncle Marc," Jack stated. "And I want to live here. L.A. is too crowded… and too weird. I love it here. Besides, isn't Dad moving to Georgia?"

"Where did you hear that?" Katherine knew that Greg hadn't told the boys, in case it swayed their decision one way or the other.

"He said something to Uncle Marc the night we met him for the first time at our house. I figured I wasn't supposed to know, since no one has said anything, but I know what I heard."

"That's for your father to talk to you about," Katherine said, not wanting to confirm or deny Greg's plans.

Katherine stood. "Thanks for letting me know what you want. Don't stay up too late. We're leaving very early in the morning, and I want you packed before you go to bed."

Jack stood and gave her a hug. "Okay, Mom. I promise."

Katherine walked to the door. "I love you."

"Love you, too, Mom."

Katherine walked across the hall to Ben's room. Once she had entered his room and sat down across from him, she asked him the same question that she had asked Jack.

"I like… Uncle Marc," Ben said, "but he's not Dad. And there aren't any people my age close by that I can play with. It's nice here, but I want to go home. Dad's there, and I have friends there to play with."

Katherine closed her eyes and tried to hold back the tears. The bubble of happiness that she had been living in ever since she and Marcus had started dating started crumbling all around her.

"Mom? Did you hear me?"

Katherine nodded and opened her eyes. She forced a smile. "I heard you, son. Don't stay up too late. We're leaving early in the morning, and you still have to pack."

"Okay. 'Night, Mom."

Katherine stood. "Good night, Ben. I love you."

"You, too, Mom."

Katherine gently closed Ben's bedroom door and walked to

the end of the corridor. She closed the sliding pocket door so the boys wouldn't hear anything that she and Marcus might say to each other downstairs.

She walked down the stairs and heard Marcus in his office, typing. She couldn't face him at the moment, so she went into the den and sat in one of the chairs… and wept.

Marcus began to wonder what was taking Katherine so long to come find him and let him know what the boys had decided, even though he was fairly certain that he would have heard already if it were good news.

He left the office and listened. He heard a noise coming from the den and walked in that direction. As he rounded the corner from the sitting area to the kitchen, he saw Katherine in the den, crying.

He walked up to her and sat in the seat beside her. He didn't say anything. He just waited for her to deliver the verdict.

"One vote yes, and one vote no," she was finally able to say.

Marcus had been prepared for that, but the words hit him harder than he expected. "Ben?"

"Does it matter?" Katherine asked. "What's done is done."

"So… what does this do to *us*? Do we try to make this work long distance? You know I can't move to L.A. My life is here in Tennessee."

"And my life is in California. Besides, you know long-distance relationships rarely work." Tears were still running down her face. "There can't be an us anymore."

Marcus was suddenly angry, and even though he felt no desire to lash out, he couldn't stop what he said next. "So, this really was just a Hollywood Romance, wasn't it? As soon as the filming ends and reality sets back in, what seemed like love turns out to be just infatuation—born in the moment and quickly faded?"

"No!" Katherine exclaimed. "I'd never do that—especially not to you. This wasn't a Hollywood Romance. This was… *is* real."

"Really," Marcus said. "Then why did you just say that there's no longer an us anymore? Am I the only one who's willing to fight for this relationship?"

Katherine glared at Marcus. "Fighting for *us* means fighting with my son, and that's a line I won't cross."

Marcus just shook his head. "And when is it *your* decision what happens to you… to us?"

Tears poured down Katherine's face. "I really do love you, Marc."

"I love you, too," Marcus stated. "And yet you're ending this relationship, instead of helping your son live with the changes *you're* making so that you and I can continue. That's what parents do, you know. The help their children deal with change."

Marcus' words cut like a knife. "You think I'm being a bad parent?" Katherine demanded.

"Not at all," Marcus said, his voice softening a bit. "It's obvious that you've been a great mother for the boys. But from my perspective, you've abdicated your happiness and my happiness. Did you even try to reason with him to lead him to the right decision for all concerned?"

Katherine started to protest, but Marcus knew that further discussion was pointless. She had made up her mind. He stood. "I have some work to do in the office. You should go to bed. The shuttle will be here early to take you and the boys to the airport." As he turned to leave, he said, "I'll see you before you leave tomorrow."

Marcus left the den and disappeared into the sitting area. A moment later, Katherine heard his office door close. Katherine looked around at the empty room, and then she began weeping uncontrollably.

Katherine finally stopped crying and went to bed. Marcus heard her walk past the office door. He knew he had not handled things well, and he regretted what he had said to her. Getting angry with her was the last thing he ever wanted. He wanted to apologize to her, but he couldn't find the words to express his shame and his sorrow for his reaction.

He moved over to one of the couches in his office and stretched out, trying to think of how he could have dealt the situation better. Eventually, he drifted off to sleep.

He was awoken several hours later when he heard someone knocking at his office door. He stood and opened it. Katherine stood there, looking down at the floor. "The airport shuttle is here, and I don't know how to open the gate and turn off the alarm."

"I'll take care of it."

She nodded and walked back to the bedroom to get her luggage. Marcus opened the gate, deactivated the alarm, and turned on the lights along the driveway and in front of the house. Then he followed her to the bedroom. "Do you have everything?" He couldn't think of anything else to say.

"Yes." She brushed past him and headed for the entryway.

The boys came downstairs with their bags a moment later. They said goodbye and thanked Marcus for letting them come and visit. Jack gave him a hug, but Ben held back and stayed next to Katherine.

When the shuttle pulled up in front of the house, Marcus helped put the luggage in the back. Katherine helped the boys into the van, and then she turned to look at Marcus one last time. In that look, she saw the indescribable pain and guilt he was feeling, and she understood what had caused his reaction the night before.

She wanted to say something. She wanted to help him understand that she made the only decision she could make. She wanted to try one more time to help him see that the boys had to come first. But no words came to her. Finally, she hung her head, turned, and climbed into the van.

Marcus stood on the front patio, watching the van disappear over the ridge, taking the love of his life away from him forever. He walked back into the house and headed to the bedroom to shower and change clothes. As he passed the bed, he saw something sitting on Katherine's night table. He walked toward it and recognized it as the leather box that had contained her engagement ring. Standing over the box, he saw the facets of the diamond catch the light from the hallway.

He sat down on the bed and held the ring, staring at it and praying for a way to turn back time, so he could find a way to keep her in his life.

CHAPTER 15

Katherine began crying as soon as they drove through the gate at the end of the driveway. Jack noticed immediately.

"Why are you crying, Mom?" he asked.

"I said goodbye to Marc," she replied softly.

"But it's just for a month, right? Just until he's back from his book tour? We're coming back in December to live, right?"

"No, Jack, we're not."

Jack looked confused. Then he became angry. He turned to Ben. "What did you do?"

"I told Mom that I want to live in California with Dad and my friends," Ben stated. "She told me it was my choice."

"Stupid! Do you know what you did? You made Mom leave the man she wants to marry… for you! And you can forget about living close to Dad. He's moving to Georgia after Christmas."

"What? He never told me that."

"He never told me, either. I overheard him mention it to Uncle Marc. He was looking forward to us moving out here so he could still see us on weekends."

Ben looked at Katherine. "Is that true, Mom?"

"That's for your Dad to talk to you about," Katherine said. She didn't want Ben feeling like he had to change his mind until Greg confirmed that he was moving.

"And when do you play with the kids in our neighborhood?" Jack demanded. "We play sports after school, and then you play video games until bedtime. You never go outside and play."

Ben squirmed in his seat. "Mom said I could choose whatever I wanted, and I want to go back home."

"Stupid!"

"Don't call your brother stupid," Katherine said, wiping the tears away from her eyes.

The flight to Dallas left Chattanooga at six o'clock. Katherine and the boys had a ninety-minute layover, and then their flight to LAX landed at ten-thirty local time that morning. Katherine never said a word from the time she boarded the plane in Chattanooga until after the plane landed at LAX, and even then, she didn't say much.

Katherine's body felt like it was afternoon, but it was still morning as they collected their bags and walked to the parking area. Once everything was loaded into the car, Katherine drove home. The boys weren't speaking to each other, so it was a very quiet ride.

I was just after noon when they pulled into their driveway. Katherine unlocked the front door, and then she opened the trunk. The boys grabbed their bags and ran inside the house. Katherine took out her bags, closed the trunk, locked the car, and followed the boys inside. She could hear Jack yelling at Ben and Ben shouting back.

Might as well let them get it out of their system. Jack needs to come to terms with what happened... just like I do.

However, for the first time, she had doubts about how she handled the situation with the boys… and with Marcus.

The first week they were back in California was difficult for everyone. Jack and Ben had nothing civil to say to one another, and Katherine's days and nights were filled with overwhelming sadness as the full impact of what she had done to Marcus began to sink in. Each night, after the boys went to bed, Katherine curled up on the couch, stared at the tabloid photo of her and Marcus kissing, and then she cried herself to sleep.

She had no idea that Jack was listening and watching.

Nor did she know that Jack called his dad for help.

On Thursday afternoon, Greg called Katherine.

"Hi, Kate! Welcome back."

"Hi, Greg. What's up?"

"I was wondering if you'd let me take the boys this weekend. I missed them over the holidays, and I want to spend time with them."

Katherine was surprised. "Um… sure, that'll be fine."

"Good. I'll pick them up tomorrow afternoon, and then have them back on Sunday around dinnertime."

"Perfect," Katherine said. "I'll have them ready for you."

"Thanks, Kate. I'll see you tomorrow."

Katherine hung up and stared at the phone. *It's strange enough that he wants to see the boys, but it's even stranger that he didn't ask how things went last week. Does he already know?* She looked up at the ceiling, trying to see through it into the boys' rooms. *One of them must have called Greg, and I bet it was Jack. What's he up to?*

She stood and walked up stairs to tell the boys that they were spending the weekend with their father.

Greg pulled into the driveway at five-thirty on Friday evening. The boys had been fighting, and they still weren't ready to go.

Katherine had been crying, and even though she had flushed her eyes to hide the fact from Greg, her eyes were still bloodshot and swollen when she opened the front door. Greg took one look at her and knew.

"What happened?" he asked as he entered the house. "Tell me about Tennessee."

"I guess you already know." Katherine sat down and looked away from her ex-husband.

"I want to hear it from you, Kate."

Katherine took a deep breath and let it out slowly. "Marc and I are… over. Jack wanted to stay out there, but Ben wanted to come back here. He didn't want to leave you or his friends."

"He doesn't know that I'm moving?" Greg was incredulous.

"That's for you to tell them, not me," Katherine snapped back.

Greg was flabbergasted. "You little fool! Don't you think Ben would have made a different decision if he knew I'm leaving?"

"I didn't want anything influencing his decision," Katherine defended herself. "It had to be his choice, not my choice and certainly not your choice."

Greg shook his head in utter shock. "So, you just left Marc? You just walked out of his life?"

"I had to put the needs of the boys first," Katherine countered. "I don't expect you to understand."

"You're damn right I don't understand," Greg snapped. "You found love again, you found happiness again, you found the perfect place to raise the boys away from all the nonsense out here, and you just walked away?"

Katherine threw up her hands. "Why is that so hard for you

to understand? My whole life is those two boys. They come first, no matter what. Marc understood that."

"Did he really?" Greg lowered his voice. "Look at me Kate."

She looked at him with swollen, bloodshot eyes, and he saw tears brimming on her lower eyelids. "You still love him, don't you?"

"What are you talking about?"

Greg snorted. "I know I don't always pick up on visual cues, as you so eloquently pointed out in our divorce, but I can see this a mile away. You left a man that you're still deeply in love with."

Katherine's eyes flashed anger. "And so what if I do? It doesn't change anything."

Greg stared at her in disbelief. "You love him, and he loves you… or at least he did before you walked out of his life. You know, people break up for all sorts of reasons, but mostly it's because one falls out of love with the other, or one betrays the other, or—in our case—one isn't emotionally or physically there for the other. But how is a guy supposed to process getting dumped by someone he loves and who loves him? He did nothing wrong, and you left him. He did nothing but offer you and the boys a great life, a chance for love and happiness, and you left him. I can't imagine anything that would hurt a guy more than what you did."

Katherine grabbed the sides of her head and leaned back, staring at the ceiling. "It doesn't matter. It's too late. I did what I had to do."

Greg sat there, his mouth agape. "I've seen you play a lot of different roles, Kate, but never the martyr. This *noble sacrifice* you've convinced yourself that you made is a crock. All you've done is cause yourself pain… and probably caused Marc a lot of pain, too."

Katherine was genuinely angry now. "Look, Marc knew

that I could never stay with him if the boys didn't want to be there. Jack wanted to stay, but Ben didn't. He didn't want to leave his friends behind. He didn't want to leave you behind. I had no choice."

"Ben didn't want to leave his friends behind? He never sees his friends! He plays online games from the moment he gets home from school until he goes to bed. He friends could be next door or halfway around the world for all he knows. And I've seen how he interacts with his friends at school. They sit around the table and text each other and send each other funny videos to watch. They never speak directly to each other. He's plays sports, but he can do that anywhere, so don't give me that crap that he didn't want to leave his friends. He could live in Spain, and it wouldn't change how he interacts with them. And he hardly sees me that much as it is. I travel more now than I did when we were married. And after I move, he won't see me much at all if you all stay here. If he wants to see more of me, he'd be better off moving to Tennessee than living in California."

Katherine clearly didn't like the way the conversation was going. She was feeling guilty enough without Greg making it worse. "A lot changed in my life when I became a mother. I swore that I'd always be there for our children, that I'd always put them first, that no sacrifice was too great for them. I stopped accepting roles that I'd be embarrassed if they ever watched, and I reinvented the kind of actress I am. I shed the 'sex kitten' persona, and now I take on more mature roles that I'm proud to let them see. It was the right thing to do. Marc knew that I had to put them first, and he knew that they both had to agree with moving out there, or we couldn't be together."

"So, you left the fate of your future in the hands of two boys who are too young to fathom the weight of their decision? Did you even try to convince Ben to change his mind?"

"Of course not," Katherine snapped, irritated that Greg was saying the same things that Marcus had said. "It had to be his choice. If I put my finger on the scale, so to speak, to influence his decision, how would I ever know if it was his decision or mine that he made?"

"He's a nine-year-old boy, Kate! The biggest decision he's ever had to make is whether he wants pizza or chicken nuggets for dinner! And you let him be the deciding vote of your entire future? That's insane!"

Katherine shook her head. "You just don't understand."

Greg stood and walked to the foot of the stairs. "Boys, we're leaving in five minutes."

"Okay, Dad," came the reply from both boys.

Greg turned toward Katherine. "You claim that you're putting the needs of the boys first, and that's laudable. But that's not what you did here. You didn't put Ben's needs first, you put his *wants* first. That's not the same thing. Look, you're a great mother. No one would ever say differently. Heck, you're better than my mom and your mom. Both your mom and my mom put the needs of their families first, but they never put the wants of their families first over their own happiness. They knew what was best for us, and they led us to the right decisions. And if they couldn't make us see what the right decision was, they made the decision for us, because that's what parents do. They decide what's best until the child, or children, grow up and are capable of making the right decisions on their own."

"So, you think I messed up?" she accused.

Greg looked at her like she had lost her mind. "Of course you did, Kate. You let a boy who's incapable of making this kind of decision decide whether or not you're going to be happy or alone for the rest of your life. No mother in her right mind would ever do that. If you and Jack both thought that moving to Tennessee was the right thing to do, and Ben didn't see it, you should have explained it to him so he'd see that it was right. And if it's still not what he wanted, then you should have made the decision for him, because *you* know best what he needs, not him.

You claim to be putting the needs of the boys first, but you failed in this case. This was the most important decision of your life, and you left it in the hands of a nine-year-old who has no concept of the consequences of his choice. And in so doing, you hurt a man who wanted nothing more than to love you, love the boys, and make you and the boys happy in a place that's clearly a better place to live than Los Angeles."

Katherine felt the tears building. Before she could say anything, she heard the boys bounding down the stairs. She wiped her eyes and gave the boys a kiss.

"Go get in the car, boys," Greg said. "I'll be right out."

The boys raced out the front door for Greg's car. Greg looked back toward Katherine. "Look, I don't know if it's too late for you and Marc, but I do know that you need to start focusing on what the boys *need* and not just on what they want. You're their mother, and you have full custody. It's *your* responsibility to raise them to be better men than I am. And remember, boys their age change their minds all the time. If you parent based on their wants, it'll be like a ping-pong match, going back and forth again and again. *You* know what's best for them, even if, and especially if, they don't. Looking at you, even I can see that you believe living with Marc in Tennessee is what's best—for them and for you. You need to help the boys accept that."

Greg headed for the door. "I'll have the boys home before dinner on Sunday." With that, he left and closed the front door behind him.

Katherine sat alone on the couch, staring at where Greg had been standing. Against all expectations, Greg had zeroed in on why she felt so sad. She should never have left the choice entirely up to the boys, if she knew what was best for them… and what they needed. But she had, and now she was alone, and she had undoubtedly hurt the man she loved and who loved her. She started crying again.

As Greg walked to his car, he saw the boys in the back seat, fastening their seatbelts. *I know what I have to do. Kate is so stubborn, and she'll never ask Ben to reconsider his decision. She'd rather suffer in silence for the rest of her life than have to admit to this mistake. We'll, I'm not going to let that happen. I'll talk to the boys and let them know how much their mom is suffering, and I'll convince Ben that Tennessee is where he wants to be. I may not be the best parent in the world, but I can do this for Kate. She deserves happiness, she deserves love, and the boys deserve a man in their life who will be there for them, doing all the things that I should have done.*

He climbed into the driver's seat, started the car, and headed for his home in Santa Barbara.

Marcus sat on the back patio Saturday evening, watching the sky grow darker. He was not much of a drinker, but he had a bottle of eighteen-year-old scotch next to him. He had already drunk a third of the bottle. He hoped it would help deaden the pain that he couldn't stop feeling, but all it did was make him think about Katherine and miss her even more.

Marcus thought about the way she always took a deep breath and let it out slowly when she was nervous. He thought about the way she tilted her head and jiggled it when she felt victorious or triumphant. He thought about how her smile would warm his heart and how her eyes were like two pools that he just wanted to fall into. He found himself missing the little things that made her so wonderful.

And yet, with all the happy things he remembered about

her, and with his talents for writing and speaking, he couldn't pick up the phone or find the words to tell her how much he still loved her, missed her, and was sorry for how he acted.

The scotch didn't do anything to help that.

Finally, he grabbed the bottle and his glass, went back inside, put the glass in the sink and the bottle back in the lounge, and went into his office. Doing the one thing he always did when he felt devastated—immersing himself in his work—he channeled the pain into his writing, weaving how he felt into the storyline of his new novel.

Sunday morning, Greg asked the boys to come into the living room of his house. They had been fighting the whole weekend, and Greg knew that it was time for them to stop fighting and start listening.

"Boys, this has to stop. You're brothers. You're supposed to be looking out for each other, not fighting each other."

"It's Ben's fault," Jack said. "He made us come back to California when Mom and I wanted to stay in Tennessee. Now Mom's alone, she hurt Uncle Marc, and it's all because of Ben."

"Mom said I could choose whatever I wanted. I want to be here."

"Why?" Greg asked.

"My friends are here."

Greg looked confused. "What friends are those? I know you're in sports, but you can play sports anywhere. Are you talking about the kids in your neighborhood?"

Ben nodded.

"And what do you do with your friends?"

"We play video games, mostly," Ben answered.

"You don't go outside and play?" Greg asked.

Ben hesitated, thinking. "Not really. We just play video

games."

"Online games?"

Ben nodded.

"Did you play those games when you were in Tennessee?"

Ben nodded.

"With your friends from your neighborhood?"

Ben smiled and nodded.

"So, you can play video games with them anywhere in the world, right?"

Ben's mouth opened, but he said nothing.

"Let's come back to that," Greg suggested. "What else made you want to come back here?"

"This is where Mom's house is. It's where I live."

"It's not the only place you've lived, is it?" Greg asked.

"I don't remember, but Mom says we all used to live somewhere else when you and Mom were married, but then you moved here, and we moved to Mom's house."

"What did you think of Marc's house?"

Ben started listing all of the great things that Marc's house had, including the theatre, hiking trails, the stables down the road, the large bedrooms that he and Jack had, the cannons, Mariana…

"So, you enjoyed being there?" Greg asked.

Ben nodded.

"And if your mom moved there, then *that* would be her house, wouldn't it?"

Ben stared at Greg open-mouthed again.

"So, why else did you want to come back?" Greg asked.

"Because you're here," Ben responded.

"Well, let's talk about that. As it turns out, I'm not going to be here much longer. I'm moving to Atlanta, Georgia, which is about two hours from Chattanooga. The drive from where I'll be living to Marc's house is not much longer than the drive from here to your mom's house, and since I won't be traveling as much in my new job, I'd be able to come see you in Chattanooga several weekends a month. But I won't be back in California more than once or twice a year, so if you stay here, we won't see each other very much."

Ben turned to Jack, "You were right. I thought you were lying."

"He wasn't lying, Ben," Greg said. "Jack overheard something he wasn't supposed to hear. I was waiting until after you came back from Tennessee to tell you, because it'll change where I live in Georgia. If you stay here, I'll live closer to the office. If you move to Tennessee, I'll move north of the city so I can get up to see you quicker. It never occurred to me that you'd use me living here as a reason not to move to Tennessee. I should have said something sooner."

Ben stared at the floor for a while. "Mom's been crying a lot lately. I've never seen her do that before."

"She's very sad," Greg said.

"Because of you—" Jack began, but Greg held up his hand, and Jack sat back with his mouth shut.

"What did I do to make her sad?" Ben asked, confused.

"She's in love with Marc very much, but she didn't think she could stay with him if the both of you didn't agree. Jack did, you didn't, and she had to say goodbye to Marc. And now she's sad because she realizes what she had to leave behind, and she knows she hurt Marc very badly when she left him."

"And that's because of me?" Ben looked sad.

"Partly," Greg said.

Ben threw up his hands. "Why does Mom have to marry Marc when she has you?"

Greg chuckled. "Your mom and I are no longer married, Ben."

"But you could be," Ben insisted.

Greg shook his head. "No, we can't. Your mom and I used to love each other very much, but when she wanted to spend more time with you two, and less time on her acting career, I didn't want her to. I didn't see a reason to, but she did, and when that happened, we realized we couldn't be married anymore. We're still friends, but there's no love there. All our love is for the two of you. Because of my job, I've never been able to find someone else to marry, although I'd like to. Your mom's job made it hard for her, but then she met Marc, and I know that she loves Marc much more than she and I ever loved each other. In fact, the only people she loves more than Marc are the two of you, which is why she left Marc when you asked to come back to California. But she still loves him, even though she loves you more, and being without him is tearing her up inside. She doesn't want you to know this, but this has made her more sad than anything else in her life, including divorcing me, and she doesn't know how to handle it. So, she cries."

"And it's my fault?" Ben looked like he was going to cry.

"It's not a matter of fault," Greg said. "You made a choice; a choice that your mom allowed you to make. But your mom and I have been teaching you about choices, right? Choices have consequences. Your choice didn't just affect you. It's affecting Jack, your mom, Marc, and even me. And that's why your mom is so sad. She gave you a choice that involved other people without really explaining that to you before she let you choose. You didn't know that so many other people would be made happy or sad by your choice."

Tears ran down Ben's cheek.

"Tell me this, son. If you had known what your choice would cause, if you knew then what you know now, would you have made a different one?"

Ben wiped his eyes and nodded slowly.

"And would you be able to live with that choice, knowing that you weren't just making the choice for what you wanted?"

Ben looked uncomfortable. "I think so, I guess. I don't know."

Greg nodded. "Let me put it another way. If you hadn't made the choice in Tennessee, if you were making your choice for the first time right here, right now, what would your choice be?"

Ben shrugged.

"Okay," Greg said. "Think about it and tell me before you get home tonight. Think about yourself, Jack, your mom, me, Marc, your friends, what we've talked about... and make your choice. If it's the same choice, then it's the same choice. If it's a different choice, you need to let your mom know... quickly."

"Why?"

"So she can try to get Uncle Marc back," Jack said, unable to keep quiet any longer.

"Right," Greg agreed. "So she can try to get Marc back. It might be too late, but who knows. He might be willing to give her, to give all of you, a second chance."

CHAPTER 16

At the same time that Greg was talking to Ben and Jack, Marcus was flying to New York to meet his publisher before flying to London for the first of several signings in the British Isles.

When he landed in New York, his publisher and Olivia—who was handling the events in Britain and Canada—were there to meet him at baggage claim. As they walked to the international terminal, so Marcus and Olivia could catch their flight to London, they went over the itinerary for the next three weeks. Marcus was okay with the plans, and he handed over a flash drive containing the final draft manuscript for *The Spy Upstairs*.

His publisher accepted the drive and asked, "Is Katherine Delaney still on the list of people you want sent a pre-release review copy?"

Marcus nodded. *What's the harm. She was in the movie, and C.J. is getting a copy.*

His publisher left him when they reached the queue to check in for the flight to London.

Thirty minutes later, Marcus and Olivia were onboard their plane, waiting for takeoff.

Greg turned into Katherine's neighborhood. "Ben, it's time to make your choice. I need your answer."

"I don't know what I'm supposed to say," Ben lamented.

"What does your heart tell you?" Greg asked gently.

"That the right thing is what will make everyone happy."

"Even if it makes you unhappy?"

"Yes." Ben sounded grumpy.

"Can you live with that choice, knowing that it might take longer for you to feel good about it?"

Ben didn't answer. He just stared out the window.

"Ben?"

"I want Mom to be happy," Ben finally said.

"And can you be okay knowing that your mom is happy, even if it makes you sad?"

"I guess so."

"You can do better than that, son."

Ben squirmed in his seat. "I don't understand why this is so important."

"Do you trust me?" Greg asked.

"Of course I do, Dad."

"And if I tell you that making Mom happy and going with her to Tennessee is the best thing for you, will you believe me?"

"I suppose."

"Then trust me, even if it makes you sad right now. I promise that the sad won't last long, and you'll be happy once we're all out there."

"And if it's too late?" Ben asked.

"Then it's too late, and that's not your fault either."

Greg pulled up into Katherine's driveway. "Wait here for a moment, boys. I'll be right back."

The boys stayed in the car as Greg walked up to the house

and knocked on the front door. Katherine opened the door and immediately turned away. Greg stepped inside, caught Katherine's shoulder, and spun her around.

He looked at her face and said, "Ah, Kate. I shouldn't have left you alone this weekend."

Katherine looked terrible. It was painfully obvious that she had cried almost the entire weekend and had hardly slept.

"The boys are outside, and I think Ben wants to talk to you. Go get cleaned up, and I'll bring them in and send them to their rooms to unpack."

Katherine nodded and slowly walked upstairs.

Greg quickly straightened up the living room and threw away the piles of tissues on the floor before motioning for the boys to come inside.

"Go unpack and then come back down," he said.

The boys ran upstairs.

"I truly hope we're not too late," Greg said to himself.

The boys came back down a few minutes later, and Greg told them to sit and wait for their mother. He was about to leave, but he decided he needed to stay for this. He sat down on the couch, facing his sons.

Katherine came downstairs five minutes later. Greg was happy that she had cleaned herself up and didn't look as haggard as she had when he'd entered the house.

She gave each boy a kiss and sat next to Greg. "Your father said you have something you want to say."

Ben leaned forward, looked at Greg, and then looked at Katherine. "I think I did the wrong thing, Mom. I'm sorry."

Katherine looked confused. "What are you talking about, Ben?"

"I told you I wanted to come back to California. I should have told you I wanted to stay in Tennessee. I want you and Uncle Marc to get married and be happy."

Katherine looked at Ben, and then she looked at Greg. "Are

you behind this?"

Greg held her gaze. "And what if I am? You weren't doing anything to fix this mess, so I stepped in and… provided a bit of perspective."

"I didn't ask you to get involved," Katherine said, the anger evident in her voice.

"No, but I *am* involved. You don't think where you live affects me and my relationship with our sons? Well, it does, so I have every right to intervene. I *am* their father, after all."

Katherine didn't like fighting in front of the boys, but she had such a mixture of emotions hitting her all at the same time that she couldn't sort out whether she was happy, angry, grateful, insulted, or just confused.

Katherine looked back at Ben. "So, are you saying that you're changing your mind and want to go back to Tennessee?"

"Yes, Mom."

"And you want us to be a family with Marc at his home?"

"Yes, Mom."

"And you're okay with this?"

Ben nodded slowly.

Katherine looked at Jack. "And you're still okay with this?"

Jack smiled. "Yes, Mom."

Katherine then looked at Greg. "And I take it you're okay with this?"

"Nothing would make me happier," Greg said. "You deserve to be happy with the man of your dreams, Kate. And as long as I get to see the boys more often, and Marc already made it clear that I'd be welcome to come and visit, then everyone wins. What could be better than that?"

Katherine didn't know if she should slap him for interfering, so instead she hugged him and whispered, "Thank you, Greg."

"Anytime, Kate," he whispered back.

Katherine gestured for the boys to come for a group hug.

As they held on to each other, Ben asked, "It's not too late, is it?"

Katherine looked at him. "I don't know. But I'll tell you this. I'm gonna find out. I know Marc's out of the country for the next three weeks, so it might be hard to reach him, but I'll try."

When Marcus landed in London Monday morning, he saw that he had several missed calls on his cell phone—all from Katherine. He wasn't ready to speak to her, so he put the phone back in his pocket and followed Olivia to baggage claim.

He had his first book signing that afternoon, followed by a reception that night, and another book signing the next morning. All of the signings and receptions in London went well, and the normally reserved British fans seemed more exuberant than usual, making for an enjoyable stay in that glorious city.

Marcus and Olivia caught the train to York, and the signing there was well attended. The next morning, Marcus and Olivia took the train to Edinburgh, which was one of Marcus' favorite cities in the world. They were in Edinburgh for two days before heading for Glasgow. The first day was the signing, which was also well attended, and the second day was free. Marcus spent the day visiting his favorite places around the city.

The next morning, they caught the train to Glasgow for a quick event, and then they flew to Dublin for the last signing before heading for Toronto.

Marcus noted that he had at least ten if not fifteen missed calls from Katherine each day, but she never left a message, so he changed his voice mail greeting, hoping that it would induce Katherine to tell him why she was calling him so often.

Katherine tried to reach Marcus again, and she noticed that his voice mail greeting had changed.

"Hello, you've reached Marcus Buchanan, and I can't take your call. Leave a detailed message, and I'll call you back. If you don't leave a message, though, I won't call you back. Have a great day!"

"Um… Hi… Marc. It's… it's Kathy. Look, I made a terrible mistake, and I'm sorry. You were right. I never should have left the decision to the boys. Greg actually had to step in and help… Ben now sees things… more clearly. I was just about to tell Ben that I couldn't live without you and that he'd have to get over it, but whatever Greg said to Ben worked, because Ben changed his vote. We all want to be with you, be a family, and… live with you in Tennessee. If I've hurt you too much, if I ruined everything beyond repair, I understand. And I'm truly, truly sorry. But if you can find a way to give me… to give *us* a second chance, I promise I'll love you and cherish every day with you for the rest of my life. Please call me. Bye."

Katherine ended the call. *Please God, give me a second chance to make things right.*

The book-signing event in Toronto was wild. More people showed up for that event than any other on either tour for Marcus' latest book. The event began at ten that morning, and it didn't end until nine that night. Marcus signed thousands of books that day, and he was exhausted and happy by the time they reached the hotel that night.

He listened to Katherine's voice mail while he waited for room service to bring up his dinner. He wanted to call her back immediately. He looked at the clock and realized that it was only seven o'clock her time. He decided to wait until after he ate, so they wouldn't be interrupted. Plus, he needed to think about what he wanted to say.

Marcus was still deeply hurt from Katherine's decision to leave, and he was still feeling terrible about his own behavior. If he and Katherine were to have a future together, neither of the things that happened on that Friday after Thanksgiving could ever be repeated. She could never leave major decisions in the hands of the boys again—he and Katherine needed to make the decision on important things until the boys were old enough to make the right choices—and he could never let himself react so cruelly when something made him angry.

Room service brought up dinner, and he ate it quickly. After dinner, he was so exhausted from jetlag and the day's events that he fell asleep before he could call Katherine back.

Katherine stayed up until after midnight, waiting to see if Marcus would call. She was so nervous about how he'd react to her message and if he even wanted to speak to her again.

When she fell asleep on the couch, she didn't realize that her phone's battery was almost dead. And even if she had, the charger was in the other room, and she didn't want to be away from her phone for even a minute.

Marcus woke the next morning, still dressed and lying on top of the bed covers in his hotel room. He looked at the time and swore. *I was going to call Katherine last night.*

He had just enough time to shower, dress, and check out so he and Olivia could make it to the next signing on the tour. The schedule was insane for the next five days, with multiple smaller events each day, several evening receptions, and crazy logistics to get from one event to the next. It was the weekend before Marcus finally had time to call Katherine back.

He dialed Katherine's number. It went straight to voicemail without ringing. "Kathy? It's Marc. I got your message, and I agree that we need to talk. I wanted to call you… to apologize for my behavior, but I just couldn't find the words. I'm sorry. I'm also sorry that it has taken so long to call you back. The schedule here in Canada has been crazy, but that's no excuse. I should have called sooner. I do love you, and I do miss you. But some things need to be… we need to reach an agreement on a few things if there's to be any hope for us. I can't go through this again. I'll be in Vancouver on the twenty-first, and then I'll be back in Tennessee on the twenty-second. Just leave a message, and I'll call you back when I can. Bye."

Katherine's house phone rang. This surprised her since so few people even had that number. She looked at the caller-ID and saw that it was one of her actress girlfriends, Lindsay.

"Hi girl," she said when she answered the phone. "What are you doing calling this number?"

"You weren't answering your cell phone," Lindsay said, sounding relieved. "I've been calling and calling. I was beginning to think you offed yourself or something else equally stupid."

"My cell phone? I never heard it ring."

"Go check it," Lindsay said.

Katherine reached over and looked at her phone. It was off. She tried to turn it on, but a red bar flashed, letting her know that the battery was dead. "Damn! The battery died. I forgot to check it before I went to bed. Hold on while I plug it in."

She came back a minute later. "So, what were you calling

about?"

"I was trying to get you to come out with me last night, but that didn't work out. How have you been? I haven't talked to you since before Thanksgiving. How did things go in Tennessee?"

"That's a little up in the air at the moment," Katherine confided. "Marc and I didn't leave things in a good way, and he's out of the country, so we're having a hard time reaching each other—especially since my phone has been dead and I didn't even know it."

"I'm sorry to hear that, Kathy. Do you think you can patch things up?"

"I have no idea, but I hope so."

"Well, I'm just glad you're alive. You scared me. We need to get together before New Year's. Call me and let me know what's going on, okay?"

"I promise. Bye."

"Bye." Lindsay ended the call.

Katherine glared at her cell phone. *Stupid phone. Now, I have to wait at least an hour before it has enough power to start up. Stupid phone.*

Marcus checked his phone several times in the days after he left Katherine a voice message, and he was surprised that he hadn't heard from her.

He didn't realize that he had spent most of the day in an area that had no cell service, and when he reached his hotel that night, he was surprised when he heard a steady stream of notifications, letting him know that he had text messages and phone messages all arriving at the same time.

He checked his text messages first. Several were from Katherine.

"Hi, Marc. My phone died and I didn't know it. I got your message. Let's talk. Kathy"

"Marc, Haven't heard from you. Are you okay? Please call. Kathy"

"Marc, I left you a voice mail. Please check it and at least let me know you received it, okay? Kathy"

Marcus checked his voice mails. He had several from Frankie about the three-movie contracts, and two from Julia and his publisher about *The Spy Upstairs*.

He finally reached the message left by Katherine. "Hi, Marc. My phone died, so I didn't get your message until last night. I haven't been able to reach you by phone or text, so I'm leaving this message. I know I can't put you through what I did before I left Tennessee, and I want to put your mind at ease about a couple of things. First, I know why you acted the way you did, and I don't blame you for it. I probably deserved far worse, so thanks for being gentle on me, all things considered. Second, I swear that from now on, you and I will make all decisions about our... our family—the important ones anyway. Once the boys are old enough to make decisions for themselves, we'll let them, but no one but the two of us will make decisions for us. What happened after Thanksgiving will never happen again. I promise. I hope you'll give me... us a second chance, and the boys hope that, too. Please, call when you can. I love you!"

Marcus tried to call her back, but the reception was so terrible that he couldn't understand what she was saying. He finally hung up and sent her a text.

"I listened to your voice message, and it was music to my ears. Cell reception is lousy up here. I'll call you when I get to Vancouver this weekend. I know they have good cell service there. I love you."

With the cell service being so bad, Marcus opened his laptop and accessed his email app. He sent an email to Frankie, asking her to send him a detailed email about what she needed. Then he sent a lengthy email to his publisher and Julia, answering the questions they had about the manuscript for *The Spy Upstairs* and asking them to email any further questions until he got back to Tennessee.

As he scrolled down through the list of unread emails, he saw one from Katherine.

Dear Marc,

It's clear that we're having trouble reaching each other by phone, so I decided to try email in hopes that you'll receive this.

I sent you a text. If you didn't get it, here's what I said. I understand why you acted the way you did our last Friday together, and I don't blame you. After what I did, you had every right to be even madder and meaner, and I'm grateful that you went so easy on me. That's to your credit for being such a wonderful man.

I also make this promise to you. From now on, you and I will make all decisions regarding our future and our family. Once the boys are old enough to make decisions for themselves, we'll let them, but we'll never let them make decisions about us. There will never be a repeat of what happened at Thanksgiving ever again.

Please, please, please, give me a second chance so I can make things right between us. We both deserve happiness and love, and you're the only man I want in my life. The boys feel the same way. They want us to be a family, living in Tennessee. Please let me know that it's not too late.

In case we continue having trouble connecting with each other, I'm extending you an invitation to spend Christmas Eve and Christmas Day with the boys and me in California. Your tour is supposed to end in Vancouver on the twenty-first, and you could fly down here instead of flying all the way back to

Tennessee to be alone for Christmas.

We start opening gifts at five on Christmas Eve, and dinner is at seven. I hope you'll join us, but if you're not here by dinner, I guess I'll have my answer.

All my love,

Kathy

Marcus read and re-read the email. *The ring is sitting on my desk in my office. I've got to get it before the twenty-fourth.*

Marcus used the hotel phone to call Frankie. When she answered, he said, "Frankie, it's Marc. I can't talk long since I'm not using my cell phone, so don't ask any questions, okay? Good. If I can have a package overnighted to your office tomorrow morning, arriving the next day, can you meet me at LAX and give it to me? Awesome. And can you have my place in Marina Del Ray available for the twenty-first through new year's? Perfect. I promise to call you once I get cell reception again and explain everything. Oh, and I just sent you an email about the contracts. Let's review them when I arrive in L.A., okay? Thanks, Frankie!"

Marcus' next call was to Julia. "Hi, Julia, it's Marc. I'm calling from a landline, so I can't talk long. Can you change my flight reservation on the twenty-first? Instead of flying from Vancouver to Chattanooga, I want it changed so that I fly into LAX instead. Yes, email me the itinerary. No, I don't know when I'll be heading back to Tennessee, but I'll handle that myself. Thanks, Julia!"

Marcus looked at the time and figured what time it was in Chattanooga. Deciding to chance it, he called Mariana at home.

"Hello?" Mariana answered the phone.

"Mariana, it's Marc. Sorry to call so late, but do you have a minute to talk?"

"Of course, Mr. Marc. What can I do for you?"

"First, you can forgive me."

"For what?"

"It looks like I'm not going to be back by Christmas. I don't think I'll be back until the end of the year. I know your family and Grant's family always come over for Christmas, and I promise we'll all get together in January, but I'm going to have to miss Christmas this year.

"That's okay, Mr. Marc," Mariana said. "We'll just have another Christmas when you get home. What else can I do for you?"

"I need you call Grant for me when we get off this call. He needs to know about Christmas. I also need him to go to the house first thing in the morning. On my desk in the office, there's a small leather box with a clasp on the top. Inside is a ring. I need him to overnight that ring and box to Frankie in Los Angeles. It needs to be insured, and it needs to have every kind of tracking available on it. Do you have Frankie's address and phone number?"

"No, I don't."

Marcus gave Frankie's address and number to her, along with the amount of insurance to place on the package, and he had Mariana read it back. "That's perfect. Now, if you have any additional catering gigs you can take over the holidays, please do, and feel free to use the kitchen in the house."

"Thank you, Mr. Marc. There might be one or two jobs I can take on. So, you're going to Los Angeles for Christmas? Then I'll forgive you as long as you bring Miss Kathy and the boys back with you, okay?"

"Okay, Mariana. But make sure that ring gets to Frankie, or the whole trip will be a bust."

"I'll make sure it gets there, Mr. Marc. You just bring home Miss Kathy and the boys."

"Thanks, Mariana!"

Marcus ended the call. *Is there anything that I'm forgetting?*

He thought of someone else he needed to call.

A moment later, Greg answered the phone.

"Hi, Greg, it's Marc. Do you have a minute?"

"Of course. My God, man, Kate is pulling her hair out trying to get a hold of you."

"Cell reception absolutely sucks up here. She calls me when I can't receive messages, I call her back when her phone is dead… it's a mess."

"So, why call me?"

"First, to thank you. In one of her messages, she said that you talked to Ben. I really appreciate that."

"Not a problem," Greg said.

"Second, I got an email from her tonight, but before I respond, I need someone to know that I'm trying to make arrangements to be in L.A. for Christmas Eve and Christmas Day, but nothing's definite, yet. If I can't get hold of her to tell her myself, I want someone to know that I'm trying my best to be there. I don't want her to think that I'm blowing her off or that I don't want us to be together."

"I'll be there Christmas Eve, so if you don't make it, I'll make certain that she knows you're on your way and just got delayed."

"Thanks, Greg."

"Just remember to send her an email reply. She's driving everyone crazy right now, worried that you won't give her a second chance to make things right."

"I'll send it right away," Marcus promised.

"By the way, has that gig you mentioned fallen through yet?"

Marcus chuckled. "Unfortunately, no. I sign the contracts when I get to L.A., and it's a six-year commitment."

"Six *years*? Wow. Good for you. Bad for us. But don't worry, I'll still let Kate know that you're on your way."

They both laughed, and Marcus ended the call.

Knowing that he'd never be able to have a short

conversation with Katherine, he decided to just reply to her email until he could use his cell phone again.

Dear Kathy,

I've been having cell reception problems like you wouldn't believe. Sending the email was a great thing to do, since I can still access them on my computer.

I'd love to be with you and the boys for Christmas. I'm doing everything I can to change my travel plans so I can be there. If I'm late, or I don't make it until Christmas day or the day after, just know that I'm on my way, and I'll be there as soon as possible.

Love you with all my heart.

Marc

When Katherine woke up the next morning, she heard Jack shouting.

"What's wrong?" she asked when she entered his room.

Jack was on his computer, hitting every key he could think of. "I think I downloaded something I shouldn't have. The computer has gone crazy, and I can't stop it."

Katherine looked over his shoulder, and pop-ups were appearing everywhere, announcing which file or which program it had encrypted so Jack couldn't access it again.

Katherine pulled the plug out of the power strip, and the computer shut down.

"I didn't think of that," Jack said.

"Let's just hope it works." She plugged the computer back in, and it rebooted. At first, everything seemed normal, but then the pop-ups started again. She pulled the plug.

"Looks like we'll have to take it to the shop to see if it can be fixed."

Jack nodded. “Can I use your computer? I have one more page I have to print off before school.”

Katherine nodded. “Sure. Just don’t download anything.”

“Thanks, Mom!” Jack ran out of the room and downstairs to the den, where Katherine’s computer was set up.

A moment later, she heard Jack yell, “Mom!”

She went downstairs to see what was wrong, and her computer was doing the same thing that Jack’s had been doing.

“What did you do?” she asked, unplugging her computer.

“I just went to the webpage that my teacher gave us so I could print out the last page of this document.” He handed Katherine a sheet of paper with a web address on it.

Katherine looked at the web address, and she noticed that the file name wasn’t a document, it was another web page. “This isn’t a document, Jack. It’s another webpage. It must have a virus on it.”

“But the teacher gave it to us,” Jack protested.

Katherine handed the paper back to Jack. “And when you get to school, you show this paper to your teacher, and tell your teacher that the website has a virus that took out two of our computers this morning.”

“Okay, Mom,” Jack said glumly. He went back upstairs to get ready for school.

Katherine went to her room to get dressed, and then a thought hit her. *I never installed the email app on my phone. Almost everyone just texts me—even casting directors and my agent. My computer is the only way I access emails. I need to let my agent know to call me instead of emailing.* She started to call her agent, when she thought of something else. *What if Marcus tries to email me? I don’t even know how to install the app and set it up on my phone. What do I do now?*

CHAPTER 17

Julia emailed Marcus with his updated travel plans. There were no seats available on the twenty-first to Los Angeles from Vancouver. The earliest she could get him to L.A. was a flight arriving the afternoon of the twenty-third.

That still gives me time to meet with Frankie, sign the contracts, get the ring and make it to Kathy's house by five the next afternoon.

He emailed Julie and told her that those plans worked perfectly. Then he forwarded the email to Frankie to let her know when to pick him up at the airport so he could sign the contracts and get the ring from her.

He didn't see an email from Katherine, but he decided that she probably didn't think she needed to reply. He had accepted her invitation and already apologized in case he was late. What else needed to be said?

The computer repair shop declared that Katherine's and Jack's computers were non-repairable.

"It's the encryption," he told Katherine. "I could try to wipe the hard drive clean and install everything from scratch, but the computer would still never work again because the virus has encrypted all of the utilities I'd normally use to fix the problem. Plus, your personal files are encrypted, so I'd never be able to restore any of your data back to the way it was before the virus attacked."

"So, what do you recommend?" Katherine asked.

"Two new computers with better virus protection and firewalls," the computer tech responded. "And before you ask, no, I don't get commissions on sales. I'm just giving you your best option."

"Thank God for last minute Christmas sales," Katherine muttered to herself. "At least I know what I'm getting myself for Christmas this year."

An hour later, she walked out of the store with two new computers, loaded with the finest anti-virus software money could buy.

The last book-signing event in Vancouver was a great way to end the book tour. The crowd was huge and friendly. Once the event was over, Marcus wished Olivia a pleasant flight home and a Merry Christmas. Then he went back to his hotel to make certain that all of the arrangements were set for Los Angeles.

Marcus had an email from Grant confirming that the ring had been sent to Frankie, and the tracking information showed that it had been delivered. Marcus checked messages and received a confirmation from her that she had the package and would give it to him on the twenty-third. Frankie also confirmed that his place was ready and that the keys to his car were waiting for him in the apartment.

Marcus sent a quick text to Greg, letting him know that he'd be arriving in Los Angeles on the twenty-third. He tried to call Katherine, now that he had decent cell reception again, but the call went to voice mail. Marcus didn't leave a message.

Katherine and Jack were busy hooking up their new computers, installing software, and testing the features of these newer and more sophisticated machines. Ben, who didn't have his own computer yet, just watched.

Katherine had no idea that her cell phone battery had died again.

Katherine concentrated on getting Jack's computer working first, since he needed it for school. There was plenty of time to get hers up and running. She went to bed at the same time as the boys, exhausted from having to be both mom and computer expert.

Marcus' plane landed at five in the afternoon on the twenty-third. Frankie met him at baggage claim and escorted him to her personal car in the parking area.

"Everyone's renting limos for holiday parties," she explained when he asked why she didn't have a car service pick him up. "Nothing's available. And the traffic. Ugh! I've never seen so many cars around here before. I had just arrived when your plane landed… an hour late."

She handed Marcus the package. He opened it and double-checked the ring. It had suffered no damage that he could tell. He put the ring in his jacket's inner pocket.

When they got to the apartment, Frankie came upstairs with him so they could review the contracts together. "Dinner will be delivered in thirty minutes," she said.

They sat at the bar and went through the contracts section by section. It was pretty standard, and it contained all of the clauses that Marcus insisted upon.

"Do you see any red flags or parts that should concern me?" he asked.

Frankie shook her head. "Actually, no. They've worked with you before, so they know what you want in your contracts. It was all there already. The question is, are you okay with the compensation?"

"Are you kidding?" Marcus asked, grinning. "This is the most per film I've ever made for an original script, and there are three scripts total, not to mention the book rights. I could retire from this contract."

"But you won't, will you?" Frankie asked, sounding concerned.

Marcus shook his head. "No, but if these movies do well, we're upping my rates."

"That, I can guarantee you," Frankie said.

Dinner arrived, and they ate as Marcus told her what was happening the next day.

"So, you *will* be getting married?"

"It looks like," Marcus said. "I think so, anyway. We've worked out the points of contention, so there's nothing standing in our way."

"Church wedding?"

"Only if she wants one," Marcus replied. "Personally, I just want a justice of the peace at the courthouse to do it. She's been married before, I've been married before, so why make a big production out of it?"

"You're *such* a hopeless romantic," Frankie joked. "You ought to have it at the house. Imagine what the wedding photos will look like."

"With all the flowers in bloom?"

Frankie nodded.

"Not a bad idea, Frankie. We'll see what Kathy wants."

"*That's* the right answer, Marc!"

When they were done eating, Marcus tossed the delivery containers and put the utensils into the dishwasher.

Frankie put the signed contracts into a folder and headed for the door. "I'll email you copies of the signed contract after the holidays. Good luck tomorrow. Let me know how things go."

"I will Frankie. Thanks for everything."

Frankie kissed his cheek and left the apartment.

Katherine had been running non-stop, trying to get everything ready for Christmas. Between the grocery shopping, last-minute gift shopping, trying to find something for Marcus, and several meetings with her agent to discuss scripts that had been sent for Katherine to consider and auditions her agent was setting up for January and February, Katherine didn't have time to look at her phone to see if it needed to be charged until she got home.

"I can't believe my phone died again," Katherine exclaimed when she finally realized that the battery was dead. She plugged it in as soon as she got inside the house. Then she picked up the house phone to call technical support and find out why she couldn't access her network or most of the apps on her computer.

After spending three hours troubleshooting the computer, the support desk finally realized that the firewall was preventing the apps from installing correctly. The firewall had to be deactivated, all of the apps reinstalled, and the firewall reactivated before anything would work properly. Katherine was so frustrated that she shut down the computer as soon as the firewall was active again. She was too tired to test any of the apps.

Her cell phone was almost fully charged, so she turned it back on and waited for the notifications to let her know if she had any messages waiting.

After several minutes, she saw that she had a number of missed calls from Marcus, but he hadn't left any messages. She had one text from him, but it just confirmed that his cell reception was lousy and that he'd try again later.

She decided to call him. She had no idea he was already in Los Angeles. She thought he was back in Chattanooga.

The call went to voice mail, and she decided that she'd call him first thing in the morning. *He probably forgot to take the phone out of his briefcase. I'll have to help him remember to keep his phone close to him at all times.* Then she went to bed. It never occurred to her to check the email app on her computer.

Marcus was in the shower when Katherine called, and his cell phone was on the kitchen counter, so he never heard it ring. When he exited the shower, he was so tired from traveling, and so nervously excited about seeing Katherine and the boys the next day, that he went straight to bed.

The next morning, he did some quick shopping to pick up Christmas gifts for Katherine and the boys. He didn't consider the engagement ring a Christmas gift, since he had already given it to her once before. He found what he thought were perfect gifts, based on observing them all in Los Angeles and Chattanooga.

A few minutes before four in the afternoon, he put the gifts in his car, triple checked that the ring was in his pocket, and headed for Katherine's house in Woodland Hills. He didn't want to be late.

He didn't realize that he'd left his phone on the kitchen counter.

Greg arrived at Katherine's house at four-fifteen. The boys greeted him and pulled him inside.

"Mom's acting funny," Ben said.

"Yeah, she's being... you've got to see it yourself, Dad," Jack said.

Greg walked into the kitchen. He took one look at Katherine and understood what the boys meant. She was a nervous wreck, and it showed. Her eyes showed that she hadn't been crying, but she was stressed almost to the breaking point.

"What's going on with you?" he asked. "I thought you'd be happy today."

"Why should I be happy?" she asked. "I haven't heard from Marc in over a week. I don't even know where he is."

"You never received his email?" Greg asked.

"What email?"

"The one where he told you he's coming for Christmas."

Katherine stopped dead in her tracks. "He's WHAT? How do you know?"

"Because he called me when he couldn't get through to you. He wanted to make sure that someone you trusted knew that he was coming, but he was having trouble with the arrangements. When I talked to him, he didn't know if he'd be here today, tomorrow, or the next, but he said he'd be here. Then he sent me a text a couple of days ago letting me know that he was coming into town yesterday. If all went well, he's in Los Angeles right now."

Katherine's shoulders slumped and she visibly relaxed. "My computer died, and I haven't finished setting up the new one. I haven't checked emails in over a week. I still can't get Marc on the phone, even when my battery's fully charged."

She tried to call Marcus, but it went to voice mail. "He's not answering."

"I'm sure he's on his way. Just relax. He might be late, but he's coming. And didn't you tell me that he's notorious for forgetting his phone? That's probably why he's not answering."

Katherine smiled. "Thanks, Greg. Tell the boys to get ready for presents."

"Will do," Greg said.

Katherine double-checked what she was cooking for dinner. Satisfied that it would all be ready on time, she took off her apron and joined Greg and the boys in the living room to open their presents.

The pile-up on the 405 where it crossed the Ventura Freeway, or US 101, was the biggest back-up Marcus had ever seen. He had been stuck in traffic for over an hour, and it seemed like he was no closer to the US 101 exit than he was when he reached the back-up.

He could hear the sirens from the emergency vehicles racing toward the pile-up, but not even the radio had a clear picture of what had happened.

Marcus wanted to jump off the interstate and take the back way through Sherman Oaks, but he wasn't familiar enough with the area to chance it.

I should have taken the 27 through the Topanga State Park and come at Katherine's from over the mountain. Well, it's too late for that.

Marcus reached for his phone to tell her that he was stuck in traffic, but he couldn't find it. *Did I leave it at the apartment? That's just great! Oh well, she got my email, so she knows I coming. And Greg knows I'm here.*

As his car inched forward, his frustration grew.

All of the presents had been unwrapped, and the boys were picking up the trash from the wrapping paper so they could throw it away. When the boys took their toys and gifts up to their room, Katherine started putting the final touches on dinner.

Greg looked out the window, wondering where Marcus was.

"Maybe he changed his mind," Katherine said as she started putting the food on the table. "It's understandable, after what I did to him. Maybe he decided he can't trust me with his heart."

"Do you honestly believe that Kate? He loves you. And he certainly wouldn't tell *me* he's coming if he's not. I'm sure he's on his way. If his flight landed yesterday as planned, he'll be here. Why else would he be in L.A. at Christmas. He hates L.A., but he loves you."

"You're sweet to say that, but he's not here, and if he doesn't come, I only have myself to blame. Maybe I don't deserve a second chance."

"A second chance with Marc, or a second chance at love?"

"Both. Either one. Maybe you don't get second chances in this life."

"You don't believe that," Greg stated.

"And yet he's not here."

"He's COMING," Greg insisted.

"We'll see."

Greg just stared at her. "Were you this neurotic when we were married?"

"Who knows? We barely saw each other the last five years before the divorce. I could have been worse, and you would never have known."

"That was harsh," Greg said.

"I'm sorry. I didn't mean to be. I'm just…"

"I know," Greg said, helping her bring in the rest of the

food. "He's coming."

Marcus finally reached the off-ramp to the Venture Freeway. He was nearly two hours late getting to Katherine's house, and he was still at least twelve miles away. He drove as fast as he dared so he wouldn't miss dinner.

Katherine, Greg, and the boys sat at the dining room table, getting ready to start eating. Katherine looked sad, but at least she wasn't crying. She picked up her fork and was about to take a bite when she heard something outside. Turning, she saw the headlights of a car pulling into the driveway.

She looked at Greg wide-eyed, and he smiled and nodded. "Answer the door, Kate."

"Yeah, Mom. Answer the door," Jack said. Ben nodded.

Katherine stood and headed for the living room. The boys followed her to the edge of the living room so they could see what was happening.

Katherine heard a knock on the door, but she didn't see anyone through the peephole. She opened the door, and kneeling in front of her on one knee, holding her engagement ring in his outstretched arm, was Marcus.

"Am I too late?" he asked, looking intently up into her eyes.

She knelt in front of him and took his outstretched hand in hers. "Too late for presents, too late for dinner, or too late for a second chance at love?"

"All of the above," Marcus said.

Katherine smiled and took the ring from his hand. She put it back on her finger and said, "We've already exchanged presents… but you're right on time for everything else."

He stood and helped her up, then he put his arms around her as she wrapped her arms around his neck. "Sorry I'm late. Traffic."

"You're here. That's all that matters."

"I love you, Kathy, and I want to marry you."

"I love you, Marc, and I want to marry you and live with you in Chattanooga with the boys."

"Done," Marcus said.

"Done," Katherine said.

He leaned down and kissed her. The sensation of her lips was as strong as it was the first time they kissed, and in that instant, the rest of the world didn't exist.

The End

About the Author

Award-winning author and publisher William Speir was born in 1962 in Birmingham, Alabama. He attended the University of Alabama, and graduated from the University of Alabama at Birmingham in 1984. He spent over 25 years in corporate America, serving as a management consultant, leader, IT executive, and HR/Payroll executive for top tier consulting firms and Fortune 100 companies.

During William's corporate career, he published several articles on leadership and the human impact of organizational changes and technology changes.

His first experience with book publishing was with a series of ten textbooks he authored about field artillery in the 19th century. These textbooks were later consolidated into a single volume and re-published in 2015 as *Muzzle-Loading Artillery for Reenactors*.

In addition to his artillery manual, William has published 21 novels, including a 9-book action-adventure series (*The Knights of the Saltire Series*), five historical novels (*King's Ransom*, *The Saga of Asbjorn Thorleikson*, *Nicaea – The Rise of the Imperial Church*, *Arthur, King,* and *The Besieged Pharaoh*), one fantasy novel (*The Kingstone of Airmid*), one science fiction novel (*The Olympium of Bacchus 12*), two stand-alone action novels (*Shiko Unleashed* and *The Day of the Dead*), and two espionage/geo-political thrillers (*The Trinity Gambit* and *Codename: Mountbatten*). *Love's Second Chance* is William's first Adult Fiction/Contemporary Romance Novel.

William is a 5-time Royal Palm Literary Award winner: 2014 Second Place Unpublished Historical Fiction for *King's Ransom*, 2015 Second Place Unpublished Historical Fiction for *The Saga of Asbjorn Thorleikson*, 2017 Second Place Published Historical Fiction for *Arthur, King*, 2017 First Place Published Historical Fiction for *Nicaea – The Rise of the Imperial Church*, and 2017 First Place Published Science Fiction for *The Olympium of Bacchus 12*.

For more information about William Speir, please visit his website at WilliamSpeir.com.

Progressive Rising Phoenix Press is an independent publisher. We offer wholesale pricing and multiple binding options with no minimum purchases for schools, libraries, book clubs, and retail vendors. We offer substantial discounts on bulk orders and discounts on individual sales through our online store. Please visit our website at:

www.ProgressiveRisingPhoenix.com

If you enjoyed reading this book, please review it on Amazon, B & N, or Goodreads. Thank you in advance!

www.ingramcontent.com/pod-product-compliance
Lightning Source LLC
LaVergne TN
LVHW020708110826
845149LV00012B/2154